W9-CPW-275

Sweet Dates in Basra

ALSO BY JESSICA JIJI

Diamonds Take Forever

Sweet Dates
in Basra

Jessica Jiji

An Imprint of HarperCollins*Publishers*

This book is a work of fiction. The characters, incidents, and dialogue are drawn from the author's imagination and are not to be construed as real. Any resemblance to actual events or persons, living or dead, is entirely coincidental.

SWEET DATES IN BASRA. Copyright © 2010 by Jessica Jiji. All rights reserved. Printed in the United States of America. No part of this book may be used or reproduced in any manner whatsoever without written permission except in the case of brief quotations embodied in critical articles and reviews. For information address HarperCollins Publishers, 10 East 53rd Street, New York, NY 10022.

HarperCollins books may be purchased for educational, business, or sales promotional use. For information please write: Special Markets Department, HarperCollins Publishers, 10 East 53rd Street, New York, NY 10022.

FIRST HARPERLUXE EDITION

HarperLuxe™ is a trademark of HarperCollins Publishers

Library of Congress Cataloging-in-Publication Data is available upon request.

ISBN: 978-0-06-198017-6

10 11 12 13 14   ID/RRD   10 9 8 7 6 5 4 3 2 1

Dedicated to Daisaku Ikeda,

for many years of encouragement and inspiration.

Sweet Dates in Basra

PART ONE

Chapter I

Basra, early 1941

Omar slipped the note through a hole in the wall that separated his house from Shafiq's.

Or, as the boys liked to think of it, that joined them.

Smuggle her over to the market.

Shafiq knew this meant breaking the law, but he never could resist his best friend's plots.

The hole had been created one hot summer day shortly after Shafiq's family got running water and decided to send a pipe through to Omar's home so they could have it too. When the water started flowing, both families gathered in the yard for a drink. Shafiq would never forget that taste, deliciously metallic, the flavor of shared prosperity. Relished even more because they were all so tired from working in the afternoon heat.

Once the pipe was secure, no one bothered to fill the space around it, and the boys had been planning escapades through that narrow space ever since.

All manner of sellers, shoppers, fortune-tellers and their targets competed for a piece of the crowded market, redolent with the mingled scents of blood from the butcher's knife, mint from the farmer's crop and onions simmering in tin pans of white beans. Wicker bowls on the moist ground swayed to the erratic beat of so much movement, and it seemed as though the night-purple eggplants and sun-ripe tomatoes they held were ready to topple out at the feet of passing customers.

"It's always worked before," said Omar, who was the taller and sturdier of the two twelve-year-olds, a smile zipping across his face.

"That doesn't mean it will again." Despite the waver in his voice, Shafiq kept a firm grip on their product: a spotted white pigeon shrugging occasionally against the constraint.

"The best bird you will ever fly!" Omar started calling out to potential buyers. The ability to exaggerate wildly was really the only license required at this market. "Soars through the air like a plane!"

Shafiq blocked his face with the pigeon and muttered, "This is not worth three *fils*."

"This bird will bring good luck to all who touch it!" Omar bested his own slogans. "This bird can cure loneliness and regret!" Under his breath, he added, "Three *fils* buys a new Ping-Pong ball, which is a lot better than the crumpled paper you try to pass off as sports equipment."

Against his better instincts, Shafiq craved the prize. There was no substitute for the clicking bounce of a white orb careening back and forth across their rooftop court.

A woman approached and Omar's prominent smile overtook his face again. "Last chance for this magnificent pigeon!" he urged, but she switched course, apparently doubtful it could cure even her remorse.

"Each time we do this it gets more dangerous," Shafiq pointed out, watching a shady group of men in the distance with an abiding fear that they were eyeing him with equal suspicion.

Omar took a break from his community outreach to scold his best friend. "Hey, brother," he said. "She's going to do what she always does—fly home. And if we have a problem, we do the same."

"Sure," replied Shafiq, a sarcastic smile curled on his lips. "We'll just fly like a plane at top speed."

Omar could have taken offense, but instead he grew philosophical. "You need a running start if you ever want to take off," he observed. "If we're chased, just think of that as our running start."

That night the bird, whom they had dubbed "Beiti" because it meant "my home" and she was so good at returning there, escaped from her unsuspecting new owner and flew back to Shafiq as planned. The short-lived sale with its secret, self-activating expiration date had earned the boys a skittish Ping-Pong ball. It worked again the next week, and the next, until—

"YOU!"

If Shafiq had looked to the dramatic movies from Egypt, he could not have cast a more menacing-looking adversary. "GO!" he shouted to Omar as the man in black charged toward them, one hand on the curved dagger that hung from his worn leather belt.

Shafiq held on to his frightened bird only long enough to realize that she would easily make it home if he let her go. Then, in violation of the emergency escape plan, he raced after Omar. "We'll spread out to different cafés and hide behind the backgammon players," Omar had suggested, even adding a clever detail—they would put on hats to confuse any pursuers. But what had seemed like a sophisticated theory proved utterly useless under the sharp scrutiny of reality. Scared to get caught alone, Shafiq followed Omar, stumbling across vats of simmering beans and past vendors peddling screeching chickens and over boxes of watermelons wondering what made him think there would be a handy fedora to put on while they tore through the market looking for an escape.

"Thieves! Get them!"

Soon the twelve-year-olds, wishing fervently their legs had at least grown to adolescent proportion, reached the outskirts of the market, where the carpets were more threadbare and the vegetables more wilted.

"Robbers! Those two!" The shout came from much too close behind.

Omar maintained the lead, and Shafiq followed him out of the market with a sick panic, knowing that if the curved dagger didn't slice him to death now, his parents would finish the job when they heard he'd been selling Uncle Dahood's best homing pigeon over and over again for weeks.

The panic escalated to terror after he rounded a corner and realized he had lost sight of Omar. And then, as though his body had on its own volition decided to follow his deflating hope, Shafiq fell flat on his face.

"Here!" It was Omar, who had grabbed—or maybe tripped—his best friend to stop his rush ahead and steer him into a small alley.

"What?" Shafiq was panting so hard his whispered question was barely audible, but Omar understood and pointed up. "Look!"

There, on the back door of an unassuming house in a decent section of Old Basra six terrifying blocks from the market, was a mezuzah, the Jewish symbol of good luck. "Any of 'em your friends?"

Shafiq shook his head, but Omar was already banging the brass knocker on the door. A sharp-looking man in his thirties opened it to face the two breathless, guilt-ridden boys.

"Soufayr!" He used Shafiq's last name like the football coach at school, as if to say, *You're a man, so act it.* "Good that you brought a friend. Maybe one of you can solve the political crisis shaking this country—or at least my living room," he added, laughing at his own in-joke.

Their running start had not exactly led to takeoff, but it seemed as miraculous as a ten-ton plane floating in air that Shafiq and Omar had landed in the home of Salim Dellal, one of Basra's most gregarious lawyers, known for hosting ongoing salons that attracted all types of people on any given day to his buzzing parlor.

"Sure we can," offered Omar, winking at his friend.

For a second, Shafiq believed even that was possible.

The obvious strategy was to blend in quietly with the indifferent crowd of sophisticated men debating the politics of the day. Which was why, as soon as the boys entered the shaded living room, Omar had to open his big mouth.

"Our principal says the British are back to control Iraq's oil."

Shafiq glared at Omar with his mouth pinched in the universal sign for *Shut up!*

"Of course!" boomed a gray-haired man wearing a loose Western suit that might have fit before he'd shrunk with age.

"Imperialists," spat another guest.

Shafiq felt Omar's sharp elbow in his side.

The stakes were too high, the day too bright, Omar's confidence too infectious not to chime in. "Her Majesty wants to own everything in Iraq from the oil fields to my uncle Dahood's best pigeon," Shafiq declared, buoyed by his best friend's riotous sense of possibility.

"And my mother's secret recipe for stuffed grape leaves!" jeered Omar, setting off a wave of approving laughter across the room. The two boys exchanged a mischievous smile.

It was all so clear now. Just blame those blimey British.

After an hour of cocky banter, Omar whispered, "Time to break out of here?"

Shafiq, who had relaxed so much he'd forgotten about their knife-wielding pursuer, suddenly wanted the adventure to continue. "I'll scope out the front door," he offered gravely. Omar only nodded in response, trying for equal seriousness.

Shafiq left the room stealthily, as though the British might be spying on his movements in search of national security secrets—or at least a good stuffed grape leaf. By the time he reached the front door, he half hoped he would open it to see an angry mob of people who had paid three *fils* for Uncle Dahood's pigeon only to watch it fly away. But looking outside he was confronted by the familiar lull of a Basra afternoon—too much sunlight shimmering off the windows of the attached houses that lined both sides of the tranquil street.

The spell was broken, and Shafiq headed back to the living room with diminished flair. But passing the kitchen, he was confronted by a sight that triggered an adrenaline rush of genuine fear: the huge, black eyes of the most stunning young girl he had ever seen, her luminous face framed by cascading dark curls. And if that weren't terrifying enough, she was sobbing.

Shafiq was so struck by the sight, he couldn't move. "I . . ." he stammered with a weak smile, but as soon as he spoke he realized that he had nothing to say. "Are you all right?" he tried.

For some reason this upset the girl, who began fighting a fresh wave of tears. Shafiq was reminded of the old expression—how did it go?—*You applied mascara to make her more beautiful . . .*

The thought fled as he grappled with a doleful stare from the girl, who blinked fat tears from her spectacular eyes. "Go," she finally answered, in a honey-husky voice that made him ache even more.

Shafiq turned to leave, the full expression now ringing in his ears: *You applied mascara to make her more beautiful but ended up blinding her.*

Chapter II

Kathmiya rubbed the hot tears off of her face with a stained dish towel, but instead of soothing her sadness, its smell of moldy cooking oil only reminded her that she was stuck working as a maid.

At thirteen, with budding breasts and hormone-drenched emotions, she should have been ushered to the protection of a new home under the guard of a stern husband in the dewy marshlands north of Basra, where she had spent life since she remembered. Instead, she had been exiled to the city to earn wages as a live-in servant.

Tears blurred her vision, but Kathmiya could clearly picture the afternoon she had overheard her parents make the terrible decision to banish her to Basra.

Like all other reed homes in Iraq's storied marshes, hers sat on land that was scarcely solid, and seemed to ease off from earth to water with no clear separation between the elements. Her family's small canoe was so close to the woven walls of their reed home she could hear her mother's soft voice and her father's slurred one inside, as she rested her bare feet on the ribs at the boat's base.

Kathmiya liked to play a game of holding so still she might cause the least possible movement in the worn canoe, watching the ripples in the river and challenging herself to minimize them. This was the same way she tiptoed through life, trying not to leave an impression.

A hopeless attempt.

Anyone who laid eyes on Kathmiya was, like Shafiq, immediately mesmerized not only by her unusual beauty—the chiaroscuro effect of her glowing face and raven hair—but also by the range of emotions animating her features with such wrenching passion. A searching gleam in her oversized eyes seemed to accommodate both severe pain and vast wonder.

The boat remained still, Kathmiya easily staying as calm as the river until, at the sound of her father's voice, she flinched.

"Fatimah will marry soon," Ali declared.

A sour premonition gurgled in Kathmiya's gut, but she fought it by telling herself she'd be next.

"Yes, and then Kathmiya." Her mother, Jamila, read her thoughts.

"Kathmiya?" her father asked with disgust, as though his wife had just suggested that they marry off the neighborhood goat. "No."

NO? Among all of her dozens of cousins, not one had remained single.

Kathmiya watched a marbled duck lead four chicks in a zigzag path through the sun-faded reeds. Gliding so easily, in place in nature.

"How can you say that?" Jamila challenged. Kathmiya appreciated the defense, but what she really yearned for was a father who cared for her without any urging. "She's becoming a woman," her mother continued ominously, as though Kathmiya were catching cholera instead of entering adolescence.

"She can work. You like it so much."

Jamila was silent, so Ali taunted, "What?"

It was as if Kathmiya could hear her father glaring from under his dark eyebrows.

I can't go to work, she thought. *No single girl is sent to the city.* Her mother only left the marshes after she was married with a baby—and then only because their home had been washed away in a flood of water while Ali's sense of duty drowned in a river of alcohol.

"She is good, stable, devoted . . ." Jamila's voice was rising with mounting distress.

Maybe I'm too stupid and ugly, Kathmiya guessed with a young teen's utter blindness to her own charms.

"Ask your brother. His son has the first right to marry her, and I'm sure he will insist," Jamila pressed.

The mention of Uncle Haider gave Kathmiya a jolt of hope so palpable it registered in a strong ripple on the river. He was always warm where her father was cold. Tall where her father was slumped. Near, somehow, even comforting, when her father had always been irretrievably distant.

"You want me to ask my brother?" sneered Ali. "Kathmiya has to work for money." He swished out words between sips. "With her sister getting engaged, we need even more."

"But—" Jamila began.

"It's a double win," Ali interrupted with cruel glee. "We get Kathmiya's salary, and we don't have to feed her because she works as a sleep-in maid."

There was a long silence. The boat did not move. In the distance, a cooking fire sent gray puffs of smoke up to the sky, where they merged with the colorless expanse. Kathmiya waited.

"Yes," Jamila sighed with a resignation that was as familiar to the doomed beauty as the dried reeds that formed the walls in her home. "A double win."

During her first week, the only person who spoke to Kathmiya besides the strange boy who caught her crying was Salim Dellal's bossy mother, Odette, who just barked commands. She had already warned Kathmiya twice that she would have to sweep more often when the dust storms started.

Finally the weekend came, Kathmiya's chance to meet her mother at the port and go home for two days. She searched every woman wearing a flowing black cloak, hoping it was Jamila, but their walk or their height or their indifference proved her wrong.

"Are you ready?" a soothing voice asked from behind.

Kathmiya relaxed immediately, taking her time to turn around.

"My sweet," Jamila said tenderly.

"Don't leave me," Kathmiya blurted out, even though her mother had only just arrived. Grown now, nearly too old for irrational fears, she still carried the anxiety that she had endured since her father first branded her with his cold touch.

"What are you talking about?" Jamila asked, sounding surprised by the question. "I'm always with you."

"You are not," Kathmiya bit back, her child's hopefulness fighting against her teenaged skepticism.

Jamila crinkled her eyes. "Some mothers are with their daughters night and day, but they are not so close, because they never really talk. You and I will be different, *tamam?*" Okay? "Whatever is on your mind you can always tell me. You have to tell me."

Kathmiya just followed her mother onto the steaming ferry that would take them up the river toward home.

"I learned so much in this big city," Jamila was saying. "You are living with a rich family. You're going to taste the most delicious food—like flaky, sweet pastries—and even hear music on the radio!"

Kathmiya brooded.

"Look," Jamila pressed on. "If anything ever worries you—anything at all: your heart, your mind, your body, anything—you tell me right away. And I'll tell you. By sharing our sufferings, we can break them into little tiny pieces so they just scatter away."

"*Tamam,*" Kathmiya said. "And we'll share our happiness, too."

"Especially that," Jamila answered, but her smile was more nervous than convincing.

"I was terrified when I first saw the motorcars they drive," she added, changing the subject as she took a seat on one of the damp trunks that served as benches for the poorest passengers.

Smiling, Kathmiya confessed that she had been stumped at the sight of an icebox. "And their sinks!" she said. In the marshes, there was no machine that made water come out, only an abundance of rivers and rainfall and wetness.

"Well," Jamila said with a conspiratorial smile, "they need those things because they don't have what we have, right?"

Kathmiya smiled with pride. She had not been in the city long enough to realize that Marsh Arabs were vilified as backward in Basra.

When they switched from the noisy ferry to the placid canoe that would shuttle them home, Jamila gave Kathmiya a turquoise dress she had secretly retrieved after her own employer put it in the rag bin. In truth, the color was not flattering on Kathmiya, who looked better in the dark purple and henna shades that brought out her raven-haired beauty, but Jamila was smiling.

"You can wear it at Fatimah's wedding."

At the mention of her sister, Kathmiya looked down. *Maybe I'll be next,* she told herself. "Thanks," she mustered. But even she could see the color was all wrong.

Chapter III

Like all families in heat-drenched Basra, Shafiq's did not sit down together for breakfast or dinner, but lunch was a production. Children scampered home from school to escape the midday sun, fathers crowded into jitneys headed back from work and mothers put out dishes: sweet-and-sour eggplant, chicken and rice, lentils and yoghurt, okra doused in tomatoes, and grape leaves stuffed with secret ingredients.

The best part for Shafiq was mining the conversation for a laugh that would entertain Omar on the way back to school. As usual, though, his sisters had nothing to offer. The older one, Leah, was just bragging about being in the class play, and the younger, Marcelle, was going on about some new kind of fabric called nylon. As Omar would say, dull as daytime.

At least Shafiq's brother Naji brought the excitement of soccer to the languid lunch, recounting his latest match.

"You're third best in assisted goals, and that foul won't go in the record books because it was only a practice," recited Shafiq, who never tired of keeping even the most trivial of his favorite brother's soccer statistics. Ezra, the eldest, hardly played sports.

"You sure?" Naji teased. Even through his school shirt you could see the roped muscles that rippled when he reached for a scoop of yoghurt to pile on his orange lentils.

Ezra was more slender than Naji but no less kinetic. He waited until everyone was quiet before announcing dramatically, "The owner of the sewing notions store has a new baby boy."

"*Ma-sha Allah*," said their mother, Reema. A blessing from God.

But Ezra wasn't finished: "He's named the boy Hitler."

Shafiq burst out laughing. *Jackpot!* What a stupid thing to call an Iraqi boy! He was imagining the jokes Omar and he could make. *Who is your uncle—Churchill? Is your middle name Adolf? I bet your brother's name is Franco . . .*

"Don't you know what that means?" Ezra interrupted Shafiq's mirth with a perversely smug look of doom.

Reema glanced nervously at her husband, Roobain, for an answer, but Naji broke the tension with a laugh. "Let's hope this new baby is better than the other Hitler," he said.

Shafiq wanted to smile, but a memory was shoving at him like a bully. Two summers ago, in 1939. Family vacation. Swimming in the warm Tigris with his cousin and spying on party boats where belly dancers, jewels on flesh, swayed through crowds of men. Traveling up north to meet his Kurdish relatives. The girls wearing jingling coins that scored their pretty outfits with melody. And then ending the idyllic trip in Karada, a suburb of Baghdad, in a little rented cottage with wet branches outside its window to circulate cool air. Naji had discovered a stack of movie magazines from Egypt, and the other siblings were reading them when Shafiq went out to play with the son of the local barber. Thinking, *He's not like Omar he's more boring can't even throw a rock to hit a tree branch*, and then the kid looked at Shafiq and he said, "Hitler is coming to Iraq and he's going to kill all the Jews."

In that moment, Shafiq could not wait another second to get back to Basra to see Omar.

And in this moment, he knew he had no jokes to share.

But maybe—hopefully—Omar would.

Shafiq met his best friend outside of their nearly identical houses, both square-shaped and three stories high, with inner courtyards open to the sky and second-floor balconies facing the street.

"Hey, look, the new kid," Omar said. Shafiq already knew the routine and was ready with his lines.

"You!" Omar called, and the boy, around eleven years old, stopped. "Did you meet my brother?"

The boy squinted at Shafiq, with his soft curls of brown hair and coffee-and-cream skin, and Omar, with his dead-straight darker hair and deep olive skin.

"Just today, when our mother woke us up, she said she loves Omar the most," said Shafiq.

"She loves you the most!" Omar pretended to protest.

"Actually," said Shafiq, "do you know who she really loves the most?"

The boy studied one and then the other. Nothing about them looked like brothers, but they were so intimate he couldn't be sure.

"Who?" he wondered.

"Our brother," said Omar.

"No, it's our sister," Shafiq countered.

"BROTHER!" Omar shoved Shafiq.

"SISTER!" Shafiq punched back.

The boy wasn't sure what was true or—as Omar and Shafiq's shoving match escalated into a full-throttle wrestle—whether they were fighting for play or for real.

But Shafiq knew.

They really were brothers.

And as he sweated and tackled and poked and punched his best friend on the way to school, and received the same affectionate blows in return, Shafiq thought about how it had all started.

It was one of those when-you-were-a-little-boy stories he never tired of hearing, like about how they used to call him peanut because he looked like one all swaddled in his little blanket. Or about the way they used to put him in front of a metal trunk at his father's warehouse and watch him open and close its hinges with the precision of a railroad engineer. Or how Leah used to bring him to school, where all her pretty friends would coo at the cute little boy.

How he and Omar were christened brothers:

"The fever, the chills, it was the *jinn* in my body." Shafiq was used to hearing his mother blame every malady, from a tragic death to a missed bus, on the evil eye.

"One second I was putting you down to sleep on the swing and the next I fainted to the floor," she continued. Shafiq had endured malaria often enough to know the aches and cold sweats and blackouts. He imagined his mother thumping to the ground while her little boy floated on the swing that gently rocked him back and forth, swish, swish, creaking hinges on the A-frame, the living room swaying by, his content, six-month-old self unaware that its protector and guardian had just collapsed.

"You were such a part of me then," his mother explained years later. "Like a little piece that broke off from my body. All I cared about when I woke up was you. I was calling out your name even though you were barely half a year old and could never have answered. My throat was so sore. I don't know if anyone could even hear me. But then Leah came over, she put another wet towel on my head and she said, 'We brought him to Salwa.'"

Omar's mother, the neighbor.

"After I heard Salwa had you," his mother continued, "I could sleep. I didn't wake up for five days. The *jinn* was trying to kill me, trying to get both of us, but it couldn't."

His mother's milk had run dry, but Salwa, who was nursing her own little Omar, saved Shafiq's life.

When Leah first brought her Shafiq, Salwa famously told Omar, "Make some room for your brother."

Salwa never expected Shafiq's mother, without ever having heard those words, to mimic them when she picked him up after the fever broke. But as soon as Reema scooped up her glowing, sated baby, she said, "Shafiq, you have to leave a little milk for your brother."

So it was that they were and ever would be related.

Chapter IV

It wasn't new dresses, smooth clay pots, her own thatched roof, or even so much a husband she envied as it was the freedom to stay home in the marshes, Kathmiya thought as she watched her sister Fatimah prepare for the wedding.

Well, maybe she did want one dress. Fatimah's was made from delicate cotton and it swayed when she moved and had been dyed in so many red berries it glowed deep burgundy.

"Isn't it perfect?" the older girl asked.

"I've seen better in the city," Kathmiya answered. It had only been one week since she'd started work, but she had already figured out how to exaggerate her own sophistication.

"Right, in the stinky home you have to clean."

"It is ten times bigger than any home here." *Why are you so jealous?* Kathmiya wanted to shriek. *You are the one he always favored.* "Not that you would know. And I have my own bed with a big mattress and soft sheets."

"That reminds me," Fatimah sang. "Just because I'm moving out, you can't have my bed. I'll be around more than you ever will anyway."

Kathmiya hadn't even thought about the slightly larger mattress on the drier side of their simple, sweet, ten-times-smaller home, but in that moment, she had to have it.

Stepping outside, she found her mother pounding rice for the day's bread. "I want a dress like Fatimah's." Kathmiya pouted.

"You are lucky then," Jamila said in a singsong, soothing tone.

Kathmiya stared.

"Because you work, so you can buy one," her mother finished the thought.

"I'm saving for *Abuyah's* burial at Najaf," Kathmiya announced.

A pious declaration, but—how morbid!

Kathmiya knew it sounded twisted. It was twisted. Ali, named for the martyred son-in-law of the Blessed Prophet, wanted to be laid to rest near him in Najaf like any other Shi'a. By the sad calculus of Kathmiya's circumstances, if she stayed a maid long enough, she'd be able to bury her father there, and then maybe he would finally appreciate her.

The poor thirteen-year-old started crying at the thought.

"He's not dead," Jamila tried with exasperation.

"By the time he is, I'll be an old lady scrubbing floors." Kathmiya's tone curdled like old buffalo milk.

Jamila shook her head. "Come on, my sweet."

"Yeah, I'm so sweet I get to clean up someone else's stinky home." Fatimah was right. "Big lonely place where no one ever talks to me."

Jamila gasped as though she had been physically cut by her daughter's words and not just hurt in the loose, diffuse, emotional sense. She was living with a widow who barely even barked commands to the maid, enduring the deafening blows of quiet abuse daily—but she was thirty, not thirteen.

"Aren't there any friends there you could play with?"

Now Kathmiya sighed. "One."

"What's her name?" Jamila asked.

"I don't even know."

"Well, maybe you could find out."

"And it's not a 'her.'"

It took less than a second for Jamila to smack her daughter. No one was around to notice. Only Kathmiya felt the sting.

"I told you I don't even know his name," she said, and felt Jamila grab her hair and twist. Kathmiya screamed, exaggerating the pain to make her mother stop, but when Jamila did, Kathmiya felt lower than the wetlands.

"Don't," Jamila said.

"I won't," Kathmiya promised, staring at her furious mother and wondering what had corrupted them all, the way pure water turned cloudy when her father added it to his alcoholic drink.

Kathmiya didn't know what made her father care about his bottles of *arak* more than any person, but she was starting to understand that the most dangerous feeling anyone could indulge was longing. Not pure like hope, which left the future open, longing was the pain of hunger combined with the delusion that it could be sated. Maybe that's what made her father so thirsty. She couldn't understand doing anything as stupid as wasting life in the false cheer of inebriation, but she knew well enough how stupid a person could be when they thought their longing might be fulfilled.

That boy who had asked if she was okay was the only person in Basra to really look at Kathmiya, to see

beyond whether or not she could iron shirts. Her longing, she told herself, was not for the forbidden friendship that scared Jamila into violence but just for the
simple chance to have a conversation.

All she had managed when they'd met was a single
word and a stream of tears. Next time, it would be different. The awkward maid from the marshes—even if
she had never seen a movie, eaten at a table or switched
on a light in her life—would shimmer with poise.

He showed up again on a day when, as usual, the
house was crowded with the visitors who came at all
hours to argue about politics.

Kathmiya noticed him sitting on the arm of a couch
with his hands on his skinny thighs, looking around,
maybe for a better seat. But actually no, he was staring at the room's arched doorway; he was searching
for her.

She bit her lower lip and watched as he caught her
eye. She had prepared for a scare, but the warmth that
lit his face melted her fright and she smiled back.

Just that. Nothing else.

A week later she was in the courtyard sweeping
below a wooden cage where the family kept a singing
bird—gray, black and white, not as colorful as the wild
birds of the marshes, or as free, but its little melody
reminded her of home.

There were sparrows, too, nesting in the vine-laced trellis that stood at the back of a plot of blooming plants and scarlet-dotted pomegranate trees.

When he stepped into the courtyard, she remembered with shame her mother's pleading, but it wasn't enough to stop her from aching for a short conversation. The flames of hell were too far underground to reheat Jamila's warning.

The boy was dribbling a soccer ball, showing off. He smiled and gently passed the ball to her. Although she was barefoot, she managed to stop it awkwardly with her instep.

"It's easy," he said, demonstrating how to punt. When she kicked it in the air and it sailed toward him, Kathmiya felt so happy it was dizzying.

"You're a natural!" he shouted, enthusiasm making him sparkle like the burnt-brown patterns that the sun printed on his hair.

Her cheeks flushed and she relished the feeling.

Their short game was interrupted when his older brother appeared. "We're leaving," said the teen, who kicked the ball straight up and caught it in one fluid move.

The younger boy didn't say good-bye, but his eyes did, sweetly enough that Kathmiya felt reassured, until, in a smack that hurt more than her mother's hand against her face, Odette shouted from the entrance, "I TOLD YOU TO SWEEP THE MESS UNDER THE BIRDCAGE!"

Then she turned to the younger boy and said sternly, "Go—Allah is with you, Shafiq."

Shafiq. Just when she had learned his name, Kathmiya had no choice but to hope he would leave forever, so he would never again see her dressed down for anything as wretched as being a kid trying to have fun.

Chapter V

"Did you do anything special for fun when you were growing up?" Shafiq asked his father in search of distractions. Omar looked ready to try anything new.

"Fun? I had to work," came the answer.

Feeling sheepish for seeking adventures, the boys were ready to drop the subject when Roobain quietly added, "But there was this one time"—he told them something too fantastic to be true—"when we flew a kite that had lit candles on it."

"How?" Shafiq asked.

"You put the candles in paper lanterns and hang them on the kite string," Roobain said.

"But doesn't the wind blow them out?"

"Not if you are good," Roobain said.

"Which we are," Omar declared.

The boys aimed higher than just recreating the fabled kite; they were going to outdo the original. In Roobain's day, the candles were wrapped in hurricane lamps of brown paper. But through begging, borrowing and perhaps using just a bit of—well—money taken from people who thought they were buying a pigeon when they were really just renting, Omar and Shafiq managed to procure spectacular shades of paper: magenta, sienna, chocolate, rose, orange, jade and violet.

It was easy enough to get a kite in the air for a boy in Basra, which had nothing but sky: up it went. And then, with Omar holding the soaring kite steady, Shafiq carefully began tying the rainbow of hurricane lanterns to the kite string. Each was attached to a three-foot string of its own, hanging straight while the kite flew up at an angle.

As the kite reached higher, tiny flames flickered against the black sky in Technicolor like in a movie from America. Omar's brother Anwar and all of Shafiq's siblings had joined them on the roof to watch the show.

"You did it!" Naji held Shafiq and Omar's hands up like champions while the kite hovered above.

"Impressive," Ezra allowed as the wind twisted it up farther.

"I wish I was up there . . ." Leah said wistfully. One candle flickered out but the rest held on.

"It's like a glittering necklace," cooed Marcelle. She was right—like jewels on a chain.

Sure, the delicate suspension collapsed under the forces of nature. The wind blew out the candles as it went down. By the time it was recovered, the magical kite was just a tangled pile of paper, string and wax.

And no, it hadn't ignited an impressive fire in the palm farm below, as Omar and Shafiq might have mischievously hoped, but the drama was enough to send them the following day to Omar's father in search of another idea.

Omar's living room was just like Shafiq's, with deep couches and woven rugs from Iran and a sweet sense of security that they had both enjoyed since Salwa breastfed them there a dozen years before. Only the Koranic verses on the walls made it different from Shafiq's home, but the fact that the family was Muslim just reminded him of the Maiden's Hair pastries that Salwa made special for Ramadan. She always brought over platefuls to his house. "It's the least I can do—we eat more of Reema's Purim cookies than all the synagogues in Old Basra," she would joke, referring to how Shafiq's mother sent over dozens of the date-and-cheese pastries she baked during the Jewish holiday. The only exegesis gleaned by the boys was, well, religious diversity is good for dessert.

When they asked Omar's father what he had done for amusement as a child, he looked out the window, as though picturing the kite for inspiration.

"I'll let you see something very precious," he said, reaching up to a vaunted place on the mantel.

The two boys were singularly unimpressed when he retrieved a package wrapped in a brown paper sack. "From Beirut," he declared.

Whatever. Lebanon wasn't far enough to make what looked flat and square comparable to a kite on fire.

"Nice," said Shafiq politely when Hajji Abdullah gingerly brought the two books out of the bag.

"What are they?" Omar was impatient.

"Well," his father began, "you will have to tell me."

Okay, fine, they were used to reading for the older generation. As Roobain said, in his day boys had to work; school was never in the equation. Omar's father had managed to start a paper goods business, but the store had burned to the ground years before, along with its entire inventory. Ever since then he'd been a school custodian, on the outside of the classroom looking in.

"Khalil Gibran," Omar read the author's name.

"I hear you can travel far by reading," the old man said in a gravelly voice that seemed even more muffled by his coarse moustache.

Yeah, yeah. Shafiq had been to the Kurdish north and to bustling Baghdad and he doubted any book would be as vivid. Omar looked skeptical too.

Trying to save his friend from embarrassment, Shafiq read the title of one of the books. "*A Tear and a Smile*." Both boys were nearly as illiterate as their fathers when it came to the second book, which was all in English.

Now that was pretty interesting. It could say anything. It might be from Beirut, but it had a US-of-A sheen.

Opening *A Tear and a Smile*, Shafiq discovered enticing chapter names: Love, Poetry, Beauty and Peace.

"Omar, listen," he said, reading a passage at random:

One hour devoted to the pursuit of beauty and love is worth a full century of glory given by the frightened weak to the strong.

"My turn!" Omar nearly grabbed the book. Too nearly. His father took it back.

"Another time," Hajji Abdullah commanded, wrapping both editions and putting them back on the shelf.

Then, as if he had been too harsh in taking back the prize, he offered a gentle explanation. "It was a gift from Sayed Mustapha."

The school principal, and the most principled man that either boy had ever met. Teachers came and went, but there was only one person who could enter a room and instantly command the full attention of a squirming class of twelve-year-olds.

"Who originated the first codified legal system known to man?" Sayed Mustapha once asked the middle-schoolers.

"King Hammurabi." Everyone knew the ancient Babylonian ruler.

"There is a near-perfect copy of the Code of Hammurabi still in existence—a treasure, an Iraqi treasure," the principal said.

"Of course it's an Iraqi treasure!" Shafiq whispered to Omar.

"Yeah—who else's? The Canadians?" They giggled.

"You don't know where the Code of Hammurabi is because you have never seen it," Sayed Mustapha said in a soft but firm voice that made the boys feel like he was revealing secret and even subversive information. "Because it sits, today, in a museum in Paris." The last word he spat out in disgust.

They stole our laws, Shafiq thought, *but they still don't know how to follow them.*

"Despicable," Sayed Mustapha instructed, "but that's our world." Shafiq felt exhilarated by this information, but grew confused when the principal added, "The only answer is for each of you to be a *rafiq* to each other."

Rafiq? There were boys named *Rafiq*. But he was using the word to mean "comrade." Shafiq's father had warned him darkly about Communists. "The police will beat you," Roobain had told his son. "Maybe even to death."

Still, hearing that the book came from their fight-the-imperialists principal, the boys took some interest. So when Hajji Abdullah, who had been taking longer and longer naps that started earlier and earlier in the day, fell asleep one afternoon, they explored its pages.

> *I am the lover's eyes, and the spirit's wine, and the heart's nourishment.*
> *I am a rose.*
> *My heart opens at dawn and the virgin kisses me and places me upon her breast.*

It was impossible to read more without giggling. Not because it was funny, just that it was so embarrassing. The boys convulsed with laughter.

Shafiq wanted to tell Omar about the maid from Salim's house and her amazingly large, dark eyes. But all he could croak out was, "Ever see a really pretty girl?"

It wasn't the first time he and Omar had broached the subject since their voices had changed, but for the first time there was a definite answer. "Are you kidding? I know where there's a whole bunch of beautiful women."

Soon they were plotting to sneak into the Port of Basra Club with their friend Iskender.

"I'll break in even if none of you come along," Omar declared.

"I'm not missing this," Shafiq said with totally false bravado. He would get in a tank of trouble if they got caught. And it still wasn't clear how they would sneak into the Port of Basra Club and swim with all of those European beauties without being apprehended, imprisoned and possibly killed.

Although most of the troops the boys saw in the streets were from far-flung parts of the empire, the white Brits from the United Kingdom had also managed to set up a life for themselves in the "Venice of the East." That was Europe's name for Basra, insulting to residents, who were sure it was much more beautiful than the Italian city, which would be hard-pressed to earn a "Basra of the West" rating from them.

For days, the boys practiced short phrases in English hoping to sound casual. "We shall meet Fouad at the café today," Iskender said in English, trying to come off like a sophisticated gentleman.

"Fouad?" Omar laughed at his friend's hopeless attempt to sound British. "Do you think they have a Lord in Parliament named Fouad?"

"Yeah, we need English names," Shafiq said.

"Winston!" Iskender suggested.

"Are you a donkey or what?" Omar asked.

"A donkey who never left the backyard." Shafiq laughed. "They'll know in two seconds that we're just a bunch of Iraqis who have only ever heard of the big prime minister." He wanted to be the first to think of a good English name, but Iskender beat him. "Fred," he christened Omar. "We are going to meet Fred Astaire at the café," he stammered in horrendous English that sounded like it was trapped at the back of his throat, unable to flee.

The image of the great American performer turning up on one of the wooden benches where their fathers smoked hookah pipes sent the boys into new gales of laughter. It was about as likely as the three of them swimming in a British pool.

Flipping through their soft-cover, poorly bound English textbooks, they hunted for names and bits of more realistic dialogue. "John" worked well because the sounds were familiar. "Henry" was another story.

"Henrrrrry," Shafiq tried. Even these native boys had heard enough BBC to know he sounded all wrong.

"I know!" Omar brightened like he had just discovered Aladdin's magic lamp. "What about *Al-Masseeh*?" It was the Arabic word for Jesus.

Muhammad was such a common name in their crowd it seemed only natural that the Christian prophet would be as popular in the West.

Luckily, Iskender, a Christian, had gone to a Catholic elementary school. "They say 'Christopher,'" he remembered.

"Christ," Omar repeated.

"Christopher," Iskender corrected.

"Christ-o-fer," Shafiq tried.

"Just call me Chris," said Iskender.

And so it was that Chris/Iskender, John/Shafiq and Hen (short for Henry)/Omar put on their best-pressed shorts to visit the British swimming pool located in the fancy neighborhood of Margeel. The area was full of foreigners, and not the Iranian or Indian or Lebanese kind. Just lots of pink people from Europe.

The three boys were middle-class enough to wear Western-style clothes, unlike the poorer Iraqis who sometimes went out in pajama-like robes. But even dressed in button-down shirts and slacks, the boys didn't look as crisp as real Westerners, whose mass-produced clothes managed to fit them better than the Iraqi hand-tailored versions.

Worse, their darker skin could easily give them away, but the small gang fought this impediment with practiced phrases in "casual" English, like "I am cross the road to the chemist's for buy the packet of biscuits."

Any confidence that this would disguise them evaporated when real British people came into view. The men were so intimidating the boys hardly dared to look at the women.

And that was the whole point of the adventure!

They managed to move through the gate silently, but once they sat down at the side of the pool, their enthusiasm unleashed their tongues and they tried their see-Spot-run English. "I am look," Iskender began. Omar and Shafiq squinted at him, trying to catch the meaning.

"Yes?" One of just two words Shafiq felt confident saying in English. He was ready to shout the other if anyone asked whether he was looking for trouble.

"I am look—you look too?" Iskender tilted his head toward a plump woman wearing a swimsuit skirt shorter than any dress they had ever seen. Shafiq stared at the striped wonder, his eyes lingering across her breasts before noticing a matching scarf on her head. She was grotesque but he was fascinated.

"I think look very . . ." Omar never ran out of things to say in Arabic, but his insistent verbosity met its match in English.

Maybe it was for the best that they had an excuse not to talk. Even in their own language their tongues would have been tied by the strange mix of arousal, disgust and bottomless curiosity gripping them.

But what a feeling, to be inside the British club!

Shafiq was elated to trespass on premises owned by the United Kingdom, that country which had caused so much trouble in his homeland.

Like two years before, in 1939, when the king of Iraq was assassinated. Sure, the government said King Ghazi had died in a car accident, but every self-respecting Iraqi knew it was a British plot. Looking down at the ripples on the surface of the pool, Shafiq remembered the exhilaration of marching through the streets and chanting:

"ARAB YOUTH BEAT ON YOUR CHEST,
WE AVENGE OR WE REVOLT!"

He was with Omar and the other students from the public school, but he felt a sweet sense of harmony when he saw that the giant procession filling the streets included kids from the Jewish school draped in black, all mourning in outrage with the rest of the country. Walking over a bridge he saw an array of heads below like the different stars in the Iraqi flag—the Muslims wearing the *kaffiya*, the Kurds with loose headscarfs, the older generation sporting the Turkish fez, and modern men looking smart in fedoras.

Some in the crowd wore the *sidara*, a narrow-brimmed hat invented by Iraq's first king, Feisal, to unite the country. It was impossible to tell the religion or ethnicity of a man wearing a *sidara*, since the hat was a purely national symbol. He had no use for fashion but suddenly wanted one for himself. And for Omar, too, of course.

The principal, Sayed Mustapha, explained the king's death at school. "The British are back, trying to make Iraq their property!" he railed. "First they drew the maps. Then they 'liberated' us—but only as long as Iraq was willing to lease out its oil fields for a pittance."

Shafiq had seen the tall oil rigs pictured on Iraqi stamps. He felt a rush of energy when Sayed Mustapha told the students to unite against the imperialists.

"Do you know who will do this?" he interrogated the class.

"Us." Shafiq knew.

"That's right," said the principal. "The Arab youth."

A splash of water shook Shafiq from the memory and he watched with a terrible sense of foreboding as Omar slid into the shallow end of the blue pool. Iskender was next. Shafiq sensed some movement in the distance and instinct told him they were definitely going to be caught any second now.

Any second now and it would be over. He might as well take the plunge.

Warm water washed over his body. He couldn't swim by any measure but felt a certitude that comes with impending capture.

"Hey, you!"

Of course.

Commands were coming at them from all sides in English, and the boys, as if by prior arrangement, hoisted themselves up on the side of the pool and began walking, then skipping, then dashing to the gate, breaking into a rush forward like the racehorses whose owners prodded them with hot pepper to make them run faster.

The English people shouted a few more unintelligible threats but let the terrified boys get their own wet bodies out of there. They ran and ran and, even realizing they weren't being followed, kept running until they collapsed on a muddy street corner too poor and too Iraqi to attract any British attention, wanted or otherwise.

"Son of a whore," Omar said.

"Son of a whore," Shafiq repeated. It felt so good to curse the imperialists. Kicked out of the pool, when the British should have been kicked out of the whole country!

Chapter VI

After she had been scolded by her employer in front of Shafiq, Kathmiya engaged in one tiny act of protest: she stole a moment of rest and a glimpse at a different life by putting down her dank rag and picking up a fresh magazine.

Its lurid photos of belly dancers and actresses captured her impressionable imagination, even if the letters were just a jumbled blur. But halfway through, her sweet escape was marred by one glance at a full-page photo.

In the movie ad, the bride wore a flowing dress that sparkled with a thousand hand-sewn beads. Her groom was tall and striking in a brocade suit, his moustache stylishly thin. It all would have been pleasant enough except for the girl in the background: bedraggled and poor, she had only a broom to lean on for support. Kathmiya just knew she was the bride's poor cousin.

Or maybe her sister.

A burning guilt told Kathmiya she never should have taken a break from scraping the bitter remnants of Turkish coffee from the depths of her employer's cups.

Work was her only absolution, and the entire place sparkled when she left that weekend for home.

"They got a very good bride-price for me," Fatimah bragged, pivoting toward her sister with a merry aggressiveness.

"Will *Abuyah* buy a buffalo?" Kathmiya asked spitefully. It was already obvious from the crate of *arak* bottles in back of the hut that Ali hadn't invested the bride-price wisely.

"We don't need an animal," Fatimah replied smartly, "now that I am getting married and you're not a burden on the rest of us anymore."

Kathmiya sought refuge from the hurt in an old memory. Very faded, but cherished like a favorite blanket, she called up the time that Uncle Haider had said Ali should be feeding her more meat. Such a nothing little comment but it had sustained her over the years. Except that as always, her uncle played the role her father should have.

That evening, Kathmiya watched Fatimah grandly march into their home for her last night on that precious bed she had sworn Kathmiya would never inherit.

Taking in the waist of the turquoise dress she'd be wearing the next day, Kathmiya tried to tell herself that life in Basra wasn't so bad. But each silent attempt at encouragement just reminded her how badly she needed cheering. *Don't be sad*, she thought, but that only made her feel worse. Soon she couldn't see the needle because her eyes were too wet.

Basra was a strange prison of brick walls and artificial light. People either stared or ignored her, except for Shafiq, but her fleeting moment of fun with him taught her never to be caught like that again, up where her employer could knock her down. The only safe position was flat on the ground, where she couldn't be pushed any further.

She could escape the fortress in Basra if only she could marry in the marshes.

Preparing to face the ceremony the next day, she felt her breath turn to sobs as confusion about her father metastasized into resentment. Ali loved Fatimah with a natural affection that manifested itself in ways large, like finding her a husband, and small, like holding her hand as she waded through the marshes to refill their water pitcher.

Ali never held Kathmiya's hand. The walls in the marshes might be soft reeds where Basra had hard bricks, but the barrier between her and her father was more impenetrable than either.

The day of the wedding, Fatimah's fine hair was combed neatly and then twisted into two spirals that crossed in front of her neck and draped back over her shoulders. Although she had spent most of her young life patting buffalo dung into flat discs, she easily rose to the role of bride, stepping regally into an elegant stretch canoe surrounded by the trappings of marriage: new cushions, woven bedding and clay pots.

Following in a plain canoe wearing someone else's cast-off dress, Kathmiya still attracted more looks than the bride-to-be. The banks of the river were lined with her relatives and other tribespeople, probably just watching out of curiosity, but Kathmiya felt like they were staring at the odd younger sister who had been banished to Basra.

Entering the home of the local sheikh who was hosting the feast, Kathmiya was astounded by its magnificence. Standing over fifteen feet high at the apex, with stout poles down the spine and a carpet of woven reed mats on the floor, the building was as magnificent as any she had ever seen, including those in Basra.

Square and diamond shapes cut out of the walls acted like stained-glass windows, reflecting nature's colors instead of painted ones.

A sheep had been slaughtered in honor of the bride and groom. Meat dishes, along with a great spread of fish, rice breads and even juices, were laid out on clean mats. The women crowded inside while the men, who had already raided the food, danced on the dry ground outside as drummers pounded out rhythms to keep the party going.

Kathmiya had promised herself not to think about her own wedding until it was closer at hand; she didn't want to scare away her good fortune. But she couldn't help but hope that she would be next.

"Will my ceremony be as nice?" she whispered to her mother.

"What?" Jamila had not heard the soft appeal over the sounds of the party. Or maybe she just didn't have an answer.

Her mother's blank response punctured Kathmiya's hopes, and she was immediately sorry she'd asked. So she concentrated hard. Maybe if she could just be happy for Fatimah, could really celebrate her sister, she would be able to enjoy the same fortune.

Kathmiya's attempt to be cheerful didn't hold for long, though. The more she took in the sight of the lavish wedding, the more obvious it was that Ali didn't care about her. *We get Kathmiya's salary, and we don't have to feed her because she works as a sleep-in maid.* As if they could barely afford a meal for her, when Fatimah was having the biggest wedding in memory.

The singing rang in Kathmiya's ears, the stomping of the dancing men beat at her heart, and for the first time ever she missed her lonely life in the city, where at least she was accepted, if only as the maid.

She watched the rowdy men waving daggers and sticks over their heads as they shuffled and jumped on the dusty ground of the *sheikh*'s luxuriously dry compound. Kathmiya wanted to like her father, but confronted with the sight of Ali weaving through the crowd, she felt only an empty contempt.

Then she saw Uncle Haider through the gaps in the woven reeds that made the walls. He was leaning down to speak to someone, looking both earnest and commanding. Fun even. She wished—not with rebellious anger or even guilt, but only with longing because she needed someone kind—that her father had been more like his brother.

A chant rose up from the crowd. "Now, NOW!"

The bridegroom was ready for his wife. Jamila grabbed a flushed Fatimah by the arm.

"Can I come?" Kathmiya asked.

"No!" Jamila refused.

"Why not?" Fatimah said generously, or maybe just imperiously, strutting ahead.

Kathmiya whispered to her mother, "It may be my only chance to see . . ."

It had been a bluff, the terrible statement. Of course Kathmiya expected to marry someday. But Jamila just looked horrified, as though to ask, *How do you know?*

Her black eyes at once accusing and scared, Kathmiya responded with a penetrating stare: *What do you mean, how do I know?*

Jamila broke the silent exchange. "Of course you'll be married someday." They were hurrying toward the shelter where the bride and groom would spend the next week sequestered from the rest of the tribe.

"Come along and see." Jamila was suddenly, even contritely, gentle. Kathmiya tried to believe she'd been invited so she could be prepared for her own wedding night, and not because it might be her only opportunity to witness one.

In the bedroom of the new couple, she watched as the groom's mother helped Jamila remove Fatimah's fresh underpants and hold her down while her husband wrapped his index finger in a white cloth. She was not the only witness; there were six other female relatives in the room, including a woman with a blunt knife in one hand and a live chicken in the other.

"What are they for?" Kathmiya asked, fascinated. The squawking bird, the chaos of all those people, none of it seemed to suit the solemnity of the moment.

"You'll see," Jamila said.

"But . . . a chicken?" Kathmiya persisted. Nothing was ever explained. Not this time either. Jamila stayed quiet.

Fatimah was relishing her reign as queen of the moment, and didn't flinch when her husband poked his finger between her legs and then pulled it back to show blood on the small rag.

"Fine," said his mother, examining the pink spots.

"But just to be sure," Jamila added, with a nod to the knife-wielding woman.

Kathmiya had killed her share of chickens by snapping their necks, but she recoiled when the woman took a razor to the bird's flesh.

When the husband dipped his finger in the warm blood, Kathmiya understood. Of course. Fatimah was a perfect virgin but this would underscore the proof. The cloth was good and drenched in poultry blood when her husband ran outside to show the crowd.

The sound of cheers rose up. Fatimah glowed. Kathmiya tried to feel happy for her sister, not sorry for herself.

"A woman's purity is her most cherished possession," Jamila said quietly, nodding at the dead bird. "We care so much, we gladly kill for it."

"Kill chickens, or girls too?" Kathmiya asked saucily. She already knew they gladly killed both.

Jamila didn't tolerate the insolence. She picked up the bloodstained knife and wiped it on Kathmiya's wrist, grazing her flesh with the sharp end. "If you lose your virginity, you will never marry, because you will be dead."

Kathmiya was impudent enough to shrug off the dramatic gesture. But she would never be so stupid as to give up her virtue only to be slaughtered like a helpless bird.

Chapter VII

With their older brothers both on the same soccer team, Omar and Shafiq went to watch a game against the boys from Amara.

White lines had been painted on the field, with the goals clearly marked and closely guarded. When the action began, the boys cheered and yelled and grinned and wrestled each other with rambunctious glee. Omar's brother Anwar was quick with a pass, stepping lightly on the ball and then kicking it in an unexpected direction, while Shafiq's brother Naji seemed to be all over the field.

As the game drew to a close tied at one all, the sweating players moved more aggressively, each hoping to capture victory. Naji loudly shouted while he kicked, a move Shafiq knew from watching him in the yard was intended to distract and unsettle the defense. "*Yellah! Imshee! Yellah!*" he said as he weaved between players and approached the goal, his body so lean his white tank top caught the air around him like a sail. "*Yellah!*" he shouted, setting up a pass that would have led to the final score.

Suddenly, a man in a suit stepped onto the field, thrust his chest toward Naji and shouted, "*Ya Heskel,* calm down! Just calm down, little Heskel."

The other players fell silent.

The ball was taken out of play.

And Shafiq felt as though he'd been kicked in the gut.

Ya Heskel. The worst kind of certain foreboding told Shafiq that the man in the suit—a coach from the opposing team—had not mistaken Naji for their cousin Heskel. Shafiq was filled with dread, especially when he realized that the insult—equivalent to the slur, "Hey, you Jew!"—had been excreted from the mouth of the authority figure.

Shafiq watched the rest of the game in a daze, and when it ended in a frustrating tie, the lack of satisfaction all around matched his pensive mood. Slowly he turned to find Anwar facing him. Naji was in a corner toweling off his sweaty body as Omar's brother crouched down so that he was eye level with his neighbor.

"You . . . okay?" he asked. The teen was tender but cautious.

"Oh, yeah," Shafiq shrugged.

Anwar punched him lightly on the shoulder. "Some people are stupid," he sneered in the direction of the coach. "Next time we'll shellac them."

Shafiq, smiling at the expression, understood that Anwar was not talking only about the match. As he realized this, a vague memory was coaxed from his mind. Just old enough to go to school in a homemade jumper with a white shirt underneath, playing gingerly in the yard one afternoon, and seeing a pudgy bully push a small Jewish boy. Shafiq cowered at the scene, looking down and feeling his cheeks go red and fearing that his loud heartbeat—that his fear itself—would be palpable to those around him. But the taunt did not hang in the air for long. "Give me your hand!" shouted Sayed Mustapha, who had rushed over, grabbed the bully by the collar and forced him to present his knuckles.

Shafiq strained to remember more as he walked home in the comforting company of his brother and their friends. Yes, now he recalled the principal's words: "This pain is nothing," he had told the child as he smacked the back of his hand with a ruler, "compared to the suffering you will experience if you do not learn to respect your fellow countrymen."

Shafiq had buried the memory again by the next week when he sat with Omar listening to their mothers gossip while they ate feta-and-date sandwiches in the yard.

"I know a crooked marriage broker," Omar's mother, Salwa, said.

"Really?" Shafiq's mother, Reema, wanted details.

The boys were resoundingly unimpressed. "Can she match the king of England with a *Midaan* girl?" Omar asked with typical sass.

Shafiq laughed loudly—too loudly in trying to cover his affection for the sometimes-tearful, onetime-soccer-ball-punting, always-captivating Marsh Arab maid.

"Don't you boys have anything else to do?" asked Salwa, shooing them.

Not really, but off they went. It was a short bike ride over to Shafiq's father's warehouse in the commercial district on the port, where at the very least they stood a chance of finding his Kurdish business partner, a grown man with the heart of a twelve-year-old.

They were so focused on the route they hardly stopped to notice a distant wail, but something in the sound rattled Shafiq. He felt an anxiety that reminded him of the war spreading across the world, the headlines that made him recoil: "Germany Organizes Afrika Corps" or "Somaliland Port In Flames" or "Yugoslavia Joins The Axis."

Pumping his legs on the bike, Shafiq thought about how his family's afternoon lunches had gone from banter about his cousin Heskel and his aunt Yvette to arguments over Adolf Hitler and Benito Mussolini.

The worst was talk about the Nazi Erwin Rommel, nicknamed "Desert Fox." That *nom de guerre* just hit too close to the arid Middle East.

Then came reports of fighting in Tobruk. The Nazis were gaining ground among the Arabs. This frightening advance was confirmed when Shafiq saw, in the magazine *Akhbar El-Youm*, a picture of the Libyan port city. It foreshadowed a Basra he never wanted to experience: tranquil palm trees shading menacing Italian soldiers.

How far can a submarine go? Shafiq kept reminding himself that Basra was on the Persian Gulf, not the Mediterranean, but that was small comfort with the war moving closer . . .

The eerie cry was still seeping into his nerves when he and Omar approached the port, pedaling through the roads clogged with donkeys carting goods and men loaded with merchandise that was trafficked in and out of the warehouse.

As usual, Roobain sat outside the large entrance in one of two beat-up wicker chairs that comprised his informal office.

"Hey, Baba!" called Shafiq as he kicked down the bike rest. "Where's Sayed Barazani?"

Roobain nodded toward the door.

The boys rushed into the wide warehouse, where their noses filled with the strong scent of spices coughed up in dust clouds from large burlap bags on the wide, open floor. Mingling with the aroma of coriander and cumin were the smooth, perfumed smells of European soaps stored by the crate. Sacks of wheat, rice, nuts and dried fruits jostled for space against barrels of olives and tins of oil.

Shafiq and Omar weaved through the haphazardly stacked goods until they found Sayed Barazani. Roobain said his partner, who had started as a stock boy, had a character as sturdy as his build. Neither he nor Sayed Barazani were ever educated, but both had the wisdom to value honesty. "A trustworthy man is the best investment," Shafiq's father used to say. He rewarded his staff in accordance with this philosophy, never growing rich but never suffering a fall precipitated by greed.

"So, are you ready for a challenge?" Sayed Barazani asked the boys, gaps showing where a few teeth had been lost.

There was no need to answer that question. Omar and Shafiq shoved each other with excitement as they followed Sayed Barazani toward the giant balance used to weigh all the varied objects that came in through the warehouse. Bigger than any man, it towered over the center of the floor like an arbiter of might and right.

"Let's bet—who weighs more, the two of you put together or me?"

"Us." "We do!" Omar and Shafiq tripped over each other answering.

"I have to go deal with a delivery, but you guys clear off the scale and I'll be right back to beat you," he ordered with a wink.

The moment Sayed Barazani disappeared, Shafiq felt a shift in his sense of security, as though that disturbing wail were echoing still. But he shook it off and joined Omar, who had already started moving the square iron weights off of the four-foot platforms on either side of the balance.

"Jump on!" Sayed Barazani urged when he got back. They did, Omar reaching up and pressing on Shafiq's shoulders as the plate they stood on fell slowly. The two huddled close, trying to increase their weight.

"Jump," Omar suggested.

But no matter how hard the boys tried to tip their side of the scale, when Sayed Barazani stepped on it fell in his direction, pulling down their hopes of winning the challenge.

"But," Omar laughed as their side floated up, "we're bigger than you!"

"Yeah!" Shafiq protested. "Get us down from here!"

"I can't!" Sayed Barazani said with a dramatic wave of his arm that suddenly sent an old rusty wrench flying out of his sleeve.

Shafiq and Omar wasted no time climbing down to grab it.

Sayed Barazani aped a guilty face. "Okay," he confessed. "So I added a little weight." From his pockets, he retrieved bags of almonds and pistachios, which he handed to the boys. And then he pulled a long copper pipe from the back of his shirt.

"I guess you get to keep all this, since I cheated." He laughed, showing the gaps in his smile.

"Really?" Shafiq couldn't wait to get his hands on the smooth pipe. It was junk to most people, but to these boys, what a score.

"Wow!" said Omar, aiming the wrench like a gun.

"Guess I couldn't fool you." Sayed Barazani grinned.

Shafiq held the pipe like a rifle. It reminded him of the sticks they used to march with in boy scouts, chanting nationalistic slogans about Iraq.

By the time they were wending their way out of the crowded warehouse, both boys felt richer than kings.

The distant moan was long forgotten.

But the anxiety it inspired returned again as they crossed the small estuary that marked the edge of their neighborhood. Dark drops were trailing in the dirt: oil, wine . . . or blood.

And then a shout in the distance.

"My finger was corrupt, so I cut it off!"

The boys dismounted their bikes and started walking stealthily forward along the dusty street. With a stab of dread, Shafiq saw a man who had literally sliced his own finger entirely off of his hand, which was soaked in blood that dripped past his sleeve and down his shirt.

"I cut out the bad—so send me to jail!" came the soul-shattering cry. "At least I have HONOR!"

The last word boxed at Shafiq's ears. "Do you think . . . ?" he asked Omar. Honor plus blood equaled more than just an amputated finger, that much they knew.

"*Allah yistir,*" Omar replied.

God forbid, indeed.

The boys stopped at a café, blending into the crowd. Shafiq put the copper pipe down at his feet, and Omar also kept the wrench close. They strained to glean what it all meant.

As the murmurs grew louder, the story came together.

"The reason he went right past here was so everyone would see."

"He wants witnesses."

"Then, straight to the police."

"Shouting about his rotten finger."

"And had he cut it off?"

"Didn't you see? Completely severed the pinky. Waved his bleeding hand in the air to prove it."

"The law is on his side."

A pause.

Long pause.

Too long.

But finally someone asked: "And the daughter?"

"Dead."

Horror twisted through Shafiq.

And swelled grotesquely when he heard another man declare, "It was the honorable thing to do."

Shafiq tried hard to picture the man's daughter, who was his neighbor. He struggled to call up an image of her, as though that would make her exist just a bit longer, but the more he attempted to remember her, the more the sight of the man's bloody stump obscured the memory of the girl he had killed. It seemed somehow more unjust that she had been so indistinct, as though her anonymity should have saved her.

"Well." The silence was broken with a simple explanation: "He had to protect the family's reputation."

"Of course."

Shafiq wanted to be twice his real age so he could ask a question, but he was too young to rightfully even listen. Still, he couldn't resist whispering to Omar, "What did she do?"

Omar shrugged. The man sitting next to him, though, curved a hand around his belly.

That evening, lying in bed on the rooftop, Shafiq tried again to remember the dead girl, but it was impossible to conjure an image of her; she had never left the house unveiled or alone.

But she had had a secret lover!

And now she was dead. Killed.

He looked up at the stars—which glittered as they always had despite the dramatic day—and soothed his spinning mind by connecting the sparkling celestial bodies into shapes and inventing stories to go with them, in awe of Allah's great designs. He thought about the murdered king, and the bloody British trying to steal Iraq's riches. He imagined there were peaceful places in the world untouched by war and prayed Basra would stay safe. He remembered the barber's son and bullies past and present, and said a prayer for the girl who had been killed on his block by her own father. And he thought about his principal, Sayed Mustapha, who had said it was up to them: the Arab youth.

Love of country was a much safer choice than love of women; that much was clear.

Shafiq fell asleep resolved to serve Iraq.

Chapter VIII

Fatimah was already in her new home, leaving Kathmiya one night alone before she would have to go back to Basra.

One night to plan an escape. "When can I stop working?" she asked her mother.

"In good time."

"Is that what *Abuyah* says?" Kathmiya felt her anger growing and wanted to hone its sharp edge.

"He does care for you, he really does," Jamila said with sweet affection.

But she was answering a question that hadn't been asked. "Maybe Uncle Haider can speak to him," Kathmiya blurted. Somehow she knew this would provoke her mother.

It did. Jamila went from tender to annoyed. "Leave him out of this," she hissed. "And leave it alone, will you?"

Kathmiya's only possible rebellion—and it was pitifully slim—was to take over Fatimah's comfortable bed that night.

But as though her sister had planted spite there, Kathmiya couldn't sleep. The bed, constructed from wood and mud, seemed to accommodate more than the fat reed mattress she slept on. As Kathmiya tossed and turned she wondered whether she had been in the city too long and had lost the knack of falling asleep in the marshes; suddenly the melodies that used to lull her into unconsciousness were grating: the sounds of the wind in the reeds, the flap of a bird's wings, the buzz of life all chafed at her ears.

Listening to the rhythm of her parents' breathing, she thought of moving back to her own bed, but it seemed like a retreat. Instead, she lifted the mattress to rearrange it.

And found underneath three very strange objects.

Kathmiya could barely see them in the blackness of the night. One was a book, flat and smooth. The other was paper money, like a *dinar*. And the last was some kind of glass bottle. She was curious but suddenly sleepy, as though a spell had been broken.

When she woke the next morning as the sun streamed through the worn patches in their walls, Kathmiya had rested so thoroughly she almost didn't remember the discovery.

She studied the book, which had a bright red barn on the cover and strange letters that even she could tell were not Arabic. And she examined the glass bottle, which had a rubber tip that looked obscene, as though it were trying to imitate a part of the body.

She tucked the *dinar* in her pocket and then confronted her mother.

"Where did you get those?" Jamila was obviously startled by the cache and not at all ready to answer for it.

"Just found them. Yours?" Kathmiya studied her mother's face.

Jamila was staring at the book, nodding thoughtfully. After a pause, she said, "It was for you. You can have it now if you want."

"Mine?" An irrational sense of hope washed over Kathmiya, as though this little worn children's book might unlock her whole future.

"Some people I worked for ages ago gave it to you."

Kathmiya gripped the book tightly, forgetting the bottle in her other hand. "Not Fatimah?"

"They never met her, my sweet. But they used to read this to you," Jamila said. "You were too young to leave at home, and they were kind enough to let me bring you to work."

That terrible feeling of being different: Kathmiya had always thought it was her fault; somehow she must have hurt her father, that's how it seemed. But now this obscure little gift held out the promise of a different story. A glamorous one, involving foreign strangers who doted on her as a little girl.

"Where are they now?" Kathmiya looked over her shoulder. Fatimah would likely show up any second to ruin the moment.

"Well, I don't work for them anymore, do I?" Jamila's tone was curt. Kathmiya could feel her mother purposely trying to dampen any hope.

"So . . . why . . . did you leave?"

Jamila was looking in the distance. Kathmiya ground her teeth trying to calm her normally trip-wire temper, knowing she shouldn't ruin this moment with an outburst.

But when Jamila emerged from her thoughts, she had reconsidered. "Give me that." Kathmiya instinctively protected the book but it was the bottle her mother lunged for. Jamila unscrewed the rubber top and threw it off to the side. Then, as if deciding that the smooth bottle was not worth keeping, she crashed it against a rock, sending shards of glass into the river. The river! Where they drank, fished, lived.

Kathmiya was incensed, feeling as though she had lost a piece of the puzzle she'd only begun to realize was hers to assemble. "That was mine too, wasn't it? From the people you worked for? The ones who liked me?" she demanded.

"You ask too many questions," Jamila scolded.

Instead of sparking the usual anger, this just made Kathmiya sad. She stared with her round eyes.

Maybe that's what touched Jamila, opened her up for one more brief second, just long enough to say, "No. The people who liked you left only the book."

Kathmiya had been planning to show her mother the *dinar*. But after she saw what happened to the bottle, she kept it hidden inside her loose-fitting dress.

And anyway, it wasn't a *dinar* at all.

Something close, but very different.

She could make out the letters. And although she couldn't hope to read them, she tried:

ACIREMA FO SETATS DETINU EHT

They were just shapes on a page, but Kathmiya tucked the mysterious note in her new book. It was a portent of something, she just didn't know what.

By the time she returned to Basra, Kathmiya felt aglow with a new sense of possibility. It was as though a colorful past brightened her future.

Even work that day had its benefits. She started paying attention to the living room chatter, trying to locate herself in the world, determined to eventually figure out the meaning of those little foreign gifts.

Either life had always been dramatic while she hadn't been paying attention, or her decision to sit up and listen came at a time of special turmoil, but the house was buzzing with talk of the end of the monarchy.

The royal family was out, someone named Rashid Al-Gailani was in.

Kathmiya took longer than usual collecting the dishes full of olive pits and pistachio shells, always keeping an eye out for Salim's mother, Odette, who never mixed with the men but seemed to have a sixth sense that told her when her maid stole a moment to think.

"So now Iraq has officially joined Hitler."

The room, where conversation always decorated the atmosphere like wallpaper, was quiet.

Kathmiya concentrated intently, trying to make sense of the sudden shift. But she was rewarded only with a brisk, "Move it along now."

It was Odette, ordering her back to the kitchen. Kathmiya was obedient enough to leave the room, but defiant enough to double back and sneak outside to steal a breath of fresh air.

Across town, Shafiq heard about the coup that same afternoon, as he watched his mother sauté freshly chopped lamb's meat with onions, turmeric and coarse black pepper.

"Rashid Ali al-Gailani has deposed the monarchy," Ezra announced darkly.

"Churchill won't let Iraq fall," Roobain said. Reema stirred the pan and the fat crackled.

"Only the British can get Iraq away from the Germans, but what do they care about this little country? The Luftwaffe is bombing the United Kingdom," Ezra pointed out.

As Reema turned off the kerosene flame and started spooning the meat onto their plates, Shafiq tried to ignore all the talk.

"They care about the oil," Naji said.

"In a way this is better. Now the British will have to return," said Roobain as Shafiq tasted the steaming food.

"That," said Ezra, "is our only hope."

Lunch should have been good, but now it was ruined.

Hope for the British to return?

After a lifelong diet of hate-the-British-imperialists, Shafiq was stunned.

What hope could there be for Iraq if it had come to this?

He left the house too restless even for antics with Omar. Shafiq didn't quite know what he needed.

But then again, he did.

Jumping on his bike, he headed over to Salim Dellal's house.

He told himself he was going to ask questions about the political situation. Salim was always railing against the British. The only ones he mistrusted more than the British were the Zionists. Salim was Jewish all right, proud as any rabbi, but strictly as an Iraqi nationalist— not for any other cause. Constantly talked up the Jewish officials in Iraq's government, like Senator Daniel, who said all Jews should be loyal only to Iraq, and Sassoon Heskel, the country's first finance minister, who, Salim would always point out, refused to have anything to do with Zionism.

But the closer Shafiq got to the house, the more he started to dread the conversation he knew he would hear inside.

"Zionism." "British." "Hitler." Sharp edges everywhere.

He reached through his mind for the memory of that march against the king's death, when all of Iraq—Jews, Christians, Armenians, Turks, Muslims—united in anger against the British.

But before he could feel better, the heartening image mixed in his mind with the memory of another public march. During the holy period of *Ashura*, Shi'a worshippers took to the streets to reenact the Battle of Karbala, when their Blessed Prophet's grandson, Husayn, was killed in fighting against the caliph's military. Wailing, tearing at their bare chests and mortifying their own flesh, the mourners expressed their determination never to forget that tragic day.

It was a ceremony of remembrance. Shafiq's family had its Passover seder, where they retold the story of the Jews' exodus from Egypt. But, frightened by the mournful cries that filled the air, he couldn't appreciate the similarity. All he saw was a deep fissure between his home life and that of the majority of his neighbors, who were almost all Shi'a.

The anxiety disappeared when he caught sight of the maid outside of Salim's home, sitting with her arms around her knees and weaving bits of palm leaves together. She looked happy, even a little rebellious, and all the more pretty.

If he could sneak into the Port of Basra Club, Shafiq told himself, he could think of something to say. "Hello," he tried. It should have been easy, just a greeting, but even that was a challenge to pronounce.

"Hello!" She sounded happy.

"I'm Shafiq."

"I know."

Now he was out of words. But she continued. "Kathmiya," she said.

"Hello, Kathmiya." It was better than all the verses of the world's greatest poets. "Do you want to ride my bike?" he asked.

"I think I'll fall!" She laughed.

The specter of Hitler was fading. The British occupation of Iraq was so remote it felt like it dated from a century ago. And he had forgotten Zionism as completely as an amnesiac.

"I can catch you." Shafiq blushed at his own words. But he blustered on. "Or I'll give you a ride!"

Kathmiya was unsteady but unafraid as she sat on the seat of the boy's bike, with its one gear, hand brakes and small kerosene lamp at the front. Shafiq stood in front pedaling. Both of them felt an unaccountable joy, relishing the warmth of the sun, the easy melody of the birds and the budding companionship, which was unfamiliar but serendipitous, like a horizon coming into view.

He pedaled forward, aware of the weight she added but full of the energy needed to pull it. They rode slowly in a loop, passing the nearby houses, singing birds, feathery tamarisk bushes and fruit trees over and over.

The world was at war, whole continents were being ravaged, and attack planes were flying directly toward the southern part of Iraq. But in that moment, tucked away in a quiet corner of Basra, these two felt nothing but peace.

Chapter IX

Just as Kathmiya started understanding the world around her, it shattered.

Within days of the news about Hitler, all of the living room's regulars had evacuated, leaving only Salim to pull Kathmiya away from the window when the British warplanes started scraping against the sky.

But not before she saw one of them through the shutters. She watched three bombs that were so far in the distance they looked like grapefruits dropping down.

The quiet of the house was suddenly too loud. Kathmiya wanted to bury herself in the folds of her mother's layered clothes, but she didn't even know where Jamila worked.

In her small room, squinting against the light that streamed in through the battened shutters, she tried to find solace in anger against her parents.

How could you leave me here alone like this, in a house full of strangers who use me like a dry broom?

But the war could be in the marshes too, for all she knew. This conflict was bigger than her mean father, her overwhelmed mother—more encompassing than Basra and even Iraq.

Her dresser had a broken leg that made it list to one side, so that the clay vase where she kept the *dinars* she was saving for her father's funeral in Najaf, a tiny mausoleum-to-be, leaned precariously.

She crumpled—her body on the bed, her face in a frown—listening to the silence that had replaced the random, improvised song from the street, which she had never before appreciated.

Slowly, she realized that more than her heart was pained. A quiet burning rocked her abdomen. A sign she was a woman. A sign that time was running out.

Her future was as bleak as the broken pavement on the cold city streets. But what could she do?

Draw on her last source of hope.

She felt childish looking at the book, but that was the point. For one short second she was glad to be alone with her thoughts.

Kathmiya studied the drawings of a yellow-haired girl at a farm. She liked the character's round face but was startled by her blue eyes. The color was dangerously unlucky—anyone who had ever been warned by the old men of the marshes would know that. Kathmiya could almost hear them ordering her to black over the irises.

But she had no pen, no ink and no will to change the image. With so much about her life shrouded in mystery, she didn't want to deface this one clue.

"My father is the sheikh," she whispered to the page, endowing the girl with a sweet, soft voice. The sheikh loved this daughter the most, even though she was the youngest. He would never dream of making her work. And he promised she would marry someday.

Jamila had once told her a story about a girl whose father was a king in a faraway land. She had ended it by pretending Kathmiya was the princess, saying, "And so you have a blessed life."

But that was a long time ago. And now she could only think, *Blessed with what? Servitude?*

Trying to think of a way out, Kathmiya's imagination was too impoverished to hope for a wonderful husband. Any man would do.

If only she could learn to ride a bike. It seemed that utterly simple. And that completely impossible.

Shafiq wanted to crawl back in his mind to the moment when he was biking with his new, pretty friend, but there was no escaping the war now.

First came the ludicrous change in tone on Radio Baghdad, with news announcers reversing their coverage of the Allies from craven fawning to sharp derision. Armies that had for so long been "charging bravely toward certain victory" were suddenly mocked for "retreating like cowards destined for defeat."

The dissonance between the two accounts was nothing compared with the clash between the government's confident embrace of Germany and the fear that throttled Shafiq's home. Whichever news account was true, his once-fused identity—Iraqi and Jew—was cleaving apart.

When Ezra observed that the Nazis hated the Arabs by saying, "Hitler says they're all monkeys," Shafiq was left to wonder why it wasn't "Hitler says we're all monkeys."

Okay, and then he admitted to himself the simple explanation: it was already obvious that the Jews were reviled.

"The British are fighting for our oil." Ezra's cynicism bit hard. "But not for us. Because they think we're monkeys, too."

It was "we" again, but Shafiq got no relief. *We, the hated people of the Middle East.*

Only the Jews were cheering the British. Or so Shafiq thought, until he heard more news from his cousin Yusef. "The Assyrians joined Her Majesty's Indian soldiers to win back Habbaniya," he said.

Although the rest of Shafiq's family looked comforted, he was more distressed than before. Having another minority on their side wouldn't bring the country back together. He had been taught at school that the Assyrians tried to rebel against the Iraqi government in 1933 and had to be "put down."

A quiet term for a gruesome massacre.

Everything was starting to shred. It wasn't inconsistencies in his history lessons that kept Shafiq up during the night; it was the fact that there was no one left to trust.

The British—their great hope—scared the Pro-Axis regime out of Baghdad. In just days, Iraq was brought back to the side of the Allies.

But Shafiq never got the chance to exhale, because right after—moments it seemed—the collective Iraqi wrath about re-occupation was unleashed.

Against the Jews.

Chapter X

The United Kingdom: tight, disciplined, orderly. *Civilized.*

Shafiq would have thought the *civilized* British with all of their *sophisticated* machinations and *superiority* to the backward colonies could at the very least take over a country and siphon off its oil without too much *fuss.*

But no sooner had the hack news announcers on Baghdad Radio relearned the script that put the Allies on top than the looting began.

The family was in the living room—chatting about the news, Shafiq rolling his eyes and working up comfortable scorn against the occupiers—when a commotion drew them all to the window.

"That's from the silversmith, Ben Yaqob," said Reema, watching a gang of men carrying ornate plates and cups.

Leah added nervously, "Yossef Menashe's fabric store." It was another group, arms heavy with bolts of fabric.

And Ezra announced what everyone had just realized: "Belboul's electrical supplies. All the Jewish shops are being looted. And only them."

Shafiq was hypnotized by the spectacle for a terrible moment, which unfolded in a painful slowing of seconds into minutes. The image was imprinted on his mind: the fine silk stuffed under men's arms, the stacks of beveled silver platters piled on their heads, the brand new wires and sockets bulging from their pockets.

Roobain broke the nightmarish reverie with a hand tugging at Shafiq's shirt. "Move. NOW!"

Everyone in the family rushed away from the window as though the British warplanes were aiming bombs right at it.

If only, Shafiq thought. If only it were the hated colonialists, instead of beloved fellow Iraqis, on the attack.

"Hurry! Double-bolt the front door, but quietly!" Roobain shouted in a raspy whisper.

The house darkened, but the scene was still too bright for Shafiq, burning itself into his unwilling memory.

"What is going on?" Marcelle asked plaintively. "Are they coming here next?"

"No, my dearest," Roobain said, struggling to sound gentle, commanding and certain at once.

Shafiq wasn't fooled. His father was scared. Suddenly, Roobain looked very old, with his untucked shirt and sagging collar.

Not fit for a fight.

"They were taking carpets," Leah murmured. "Some houses are full of carpets—"

Involuntarily everyone looked down at the wine red and river black woven pattern swirling beneath their feet.

Shafiq felt an empty sickness, all stomachache with no nausea to expel it.

Marcelle backed away, like she couldn't stand to be on that tempting carpet, and knocked a ceramic vase that shattered on the floor, its white artificial roses flat as bodies on a battlefield.

Everyone jumped, and when Shafiq looked again he saw Naji protecting their mother, his broad arms wrapped over her slumped shoulders.

Outside, the looters stole and ran with no chanting or fanfare. Inside, the quiet beating of hearts rang like a ticking bomb, with each lost second stripping away their protection from encroaching danger.

Naji asked what everyone was wondering. "What should we do?"

"We have to leave!" Ezra said, his eyes narrowed. Shafiq was grateful that his brothers were both strong. "Crawl over the roof maybe, to the Abd El Hamid's."

To Omar's place—of course! Shafiq felt a rush of relief. The safe haven where he had been nursed to survival at six months and could return again for a second miracle at twelve years.

But Ezra wasn't finished with his plan. "And then we run."

No, Shafiq thought. *Bad idea.*

"I say we hide at the Abd El Hamids," Naji said. "Stay there, among friends."

"It's better than sitting here like chickens at the butcher shop," Shafiq said.

When everyone agreed, Shafiq felt just a bit safer. It was, after all, a short distance between his rooftop and Omar's. He had crossed that path more than any other.

Marcelle was the last one to step out onto the hot, tarred surface of the roof.

"Look!" Ezra leaned over the small wall shielding them from the street below.

"Let's go!" Shafiq urged. With the action in the streets, now was the time to climb over to Omar's home unnoticed.

But they were all inexorably drawn by the scene: mixed among the looters like raisins in a bunch of grapes were the shrinking figures of refugees trying to find shelter from the mobs.

"It's Abraham Zabyloon and his children," said Ezra.

"Plus the whole Mehlab family," Naji observed.

"They're running here!" Reema said with rising panic. "It makes no sense!"

"Safety in numbers," Ezra pointed out. "We have a big house. Jews from the neighborhood are coming together here."

"They need our help," Naji said.

"Yes," declared Roobain. "So we stay."

Shafiq should have been even more terrified, but his well-honed fear was drowned out by an irrepressible pride. The whole world could go to pieces and his father would still keep faith with the Arab way. Roobain had always shown them how hospitality coursed through Iraqi blood. Now he proved that emergencies only increased its flow.

Shafiq felt pumped . . .

"Look, there are at least six men among them," Ezra pointed out. "In case we have to fight."

. . . and jolted by adrenaline.

The first two bedraggled families were followed by a steady stream of shell-shocked cousins, distant relatives and friends. Roobain treated them all like kin, throwing open the door to his home long enough to take them in and then shutting it tight against the unknown dangers beyond.

Shafiq felt the hair on the back of his neck prickle.

"They can't sell a dead body," somebody said.

I'm safe because my corpse isn't worth anything, he thought.

That first night Shafiq still had a bed, but within twenty-four hours every spot in the house was taken, and he slept with a rolled-up towel for a pillow on the interior balcony. He could smell the fresh air from the inner courtyard it looked out on, that large, square, open space at the heart of the house, and hear voices from the rooms that bordered it.

Trying to relax his back on the brick floor, staring at the ceiling, wishing he could see the night sky and shut his ears to the buzz of people everywhere, Shafiq felt his mind cramp up.

The riots hadn't stopped. Some families were talking about moving to India. Shafiq wanted to wrap his fears in the Iraqi flag, but he wasn't sure what it stood for anymore. He tried humming one of the patriotic tunes sung every morning at school assembly:

Hey, Europe!
Don't brag.
Don't think your progress can last.
Prepare for nights of destruction,
You will drown in your tears.

Shafiq could almost feel how he used to exult to the rhythmical beat of the song as he pushed gales of sound from his lungs, imagining that the warning might reach the British Isles and strike fear in the hearts of colonizers there.

Never, never, never did he imagine the destruction would blow back.

Chapter XI

The streets were quiet, but inside the house where Kathmiya worked Salim was raging against the British while Odette blamed the Muslims for the madness that kept them all trapped.

"The Union Jack is a symbol of hate!" Salim sounded unhinged.

She was clever enough to outsmart Odette, to snap back at her sister Fatimah, even to strike up a friendship with Shafiq, but this new turmoil was beyond Kathmiya's capacity to manage.

Disparate bits of information hovered like mosquitoes around her and she could only hope she was immune to whatever malaria they carried.

Better yet, she wanted to take her red book, her strange *dinar* from the Western world, and the small vase where she had been stashing money for her father's funeral, and disappear in the placid world of the marshes.

At least she hoped they were still placid . . .

We Midaan are tough. We can move in ways the British would never understand. We will always survive.

Kathmiya told herself this but she didn't feel too sure because so much had changed—in her life and in the world.

Odette was insisting they leave but Salim refused. "This is my house, in my country!" he shouted. The pitch in his voice seemed to match the urgency of the pounding in the streets. "This is my homeland."

"Salim!" breathed Odette in exasperation. "You can't just send your old parents into the streets to get killed."

The accusation muted her son's nationalistic fervor.

"Of course you are not going alone," Salim conceded. "I'll help you flee to the Soufayrs' because they have a big place in a Muslim neighborhood. But don't expect me to stay there too, hiding like a coward."

Kathmiya wouldn't be sorry to see Odette leave, but at the same time she wished the ground would stop shifting.

"You're coming," the matron ordered Kathmiya. "Gather all of the food from the kitchen and pack a full set of linens and towels."

Kathmiya pressed against the wry smile trying to curl around her lips. Good old Odette, always there with a command.

Salim unplugged his most prized possession: the elegant wooden radio he listened to obsessively. "They'll need it more than me," he said. "I'm not the one living in ignorance, blaming the Iraqis when the imperialists staged these riots."

As soon as they went outside, Kathmiya noticed the absence of any other women on the narrow streets. She drew her shawl tighter.

Next to stores that had been looted sat cafés in perfect condition, bustling with festive customers garlanded with spoils taken from the ransacked businesses: bundles of light fixtures, stacks of carpets, bags of coffee beans and the necks of silver decanters in tight, sweaty grips.

"Hey there, Hamad," Salim called to a café worker. "I'm going to beat you at backgammon when you get off this afternoon!"

"You weight the dice, that's why!" Hamad replied with a teasing smile.

"I have to 'cause you're such a lucky fella," Salim said with a quick wave.

His mother was scowling, but for Salim it was another chance to teach his brand of solidarity. "See," he told her pointedly. "We are all Iraqis: Jews, Christians, Muslims—even the *Midaan*."

Even? Kathmiya stared at the patchwork of shattered storefronts, suddenly overcome with a longing for the marshes, where there were no businesses to ransack, just waters and animals and home.

Fatimah was safely married in her tribe, and all Kathmiya could shelter under was the phantom shadow of a book whose heroine had unlucky blue eyes.

She resolved to throw away the false little amulet as soon as possible.

They arrived at a large brick house with elegant balconies looking out on the street. It appeared ordinary on the outside, but when the door opened briefly and they were sucked in, Kathmiya was startled to see scores of disheveled and desperate people: old men mumbling prayers, young mothers trying to soothe sobbing children, women everywhere hoping to restore order by manically folding, dusting, sweeping and scolding.

Salim cut through the din. "I refuse to run and hide!" he announced.

The folding, scolding and even praying stopped so that only the crying children could be heard hiccupping their little wails out while he went on.

"We should invite all of our Muslim neighbors in for tea," he suggested.

"Are you crazy?" scoffed an old man.

"How many of you are Iraqis?" Salim asked.

I am, Kathmiya thought, *but this is not my home. Not my problem.*

"All of you—that's who!" Salim charged ahead. "You're Iraqis, and your best friends are Muslims."

Kathmiya looked down, wishing she could escape but knowing that would be impossible. The streets were forbidding: no women, no children, no fun. Hope was just incongruous, even unseemly.

Shafiq was a few feet away. Only she didn't see him.

"It's the imperialists who have you all terrified and pathetic," Salim was saying.

"Hey," protested the old man, "the British aren't looting and rioting. That would be your Muslim friends."

Salim steamed. "How narrow is your mind? You don't wonder why the colonialists unlocked all the Jewish stores? And then went to the most uneducated people and invited them in?"

"Oh, please!" shouted an outspoken great-grandmother. Kathmiya stared. She had never known a woman to contradict a man. It was something.

She'd like to see her mother stand up to her father for once . . .

"Oh, yes!" Salim boomed. "The British have it all figured out—they've been doing this for centuries. Find a scapegoat; here it's the Jews."

"He has a point . . ." someone murmured.

"The Jews—you!" Salim continued. "Then these fancy, special Europeans rile the mobs. 'Take whatever you like and get drunk on a massive looting spree. Just ignore us while we reoccupy your country.' Iraq should know by now how imperialists work. If they want to stop the violence they can. They brought enough bombs and bullets. But they chose hate instead."

"The British are our only hope." A bearded man dressed in somber browns bristled.

Kathmiya's legs felt weak. She looked around to see whether anyone would notice if she slipped into a squat. Her eyes traveled the crowd.

There he was. Shafiq. Staring right at her. The only bright face in a room of dark expressions. Like a planet alone in a cloudy night sky. She smiled.

He did too.

But the show wasn't over.

"The British are selling you to the highest bidder," Salim thundered. "They want you to see the Muslims as your enemy. They want the country to be fractured. So much easier to exploit us that way."

A hush gripped the room, nods here and there. The argument was holding the audience. Shafiq was holding Kathmiya with his gaze.

"But if we unite—Jews, Christians, Shi'a and Sunni—we can take back our country." Salim stomped his foot.

Now he had gone too far. Nods turned to quiet "tsks" of disapproval.

Kathmiya looked down, too shy to keep her eyes on Shafiq.

But she thought, *Maybe it is okay to hope. Or at least, it is not so wrong to want friendship, even if the world falls apart around us.*

"Then Iraqis must unite with the Lebanese, the Egyptians, the Persians and rescue the whole region from the yoke of the imperialists," Salim concluded, setting down the radio and hugging his mother before turning to leave.

"Allah be with you," a few voices muttered.

Kathmiya followed him out, but not before stealing a last glance at Shafiq, who curled his hand softly in a wave good-bye.

The small gesture gave Kathmiya strength while she walked behind Salim through the ravaged streets.

By the time they got back to the empty house, she was prepared to act.

Teeth clenched in resolution, she went to her room and retrieved her small treasure. Approaching the garbage can in the backyard, she was ready to get rid of the book and its friendly, curly drawings. "Good-bye, little girl," she said, flipping through the pages. The character was inert, but when she saw its blue eyes, she felt as though it had feelings that she wasn't entitled to hurt. Closing the book and holding it to her chest, she thought: *What did you ever do to me? Just because you're different . . .*

Kathmiya was out of place too, but she didn't know why. All she understood, with images of broken glass and scattered debris swirling in her mind, was how dangerous that was.

Chapter XII

After Kathmiya slipped out of his front door, Shafiq felt like he had sent a kite up into the sky only to watch it spin out of reach.

The brief glimpse of her was the one cause for hope in the days that followed the riots.

Shafiq might have experienced a blossoming of love but instead he felt like a poisonous scarlet flower was blooming in his chest. Montages flitted across his eyelids when he closed them: the open wound of the honor killer, the menace of school-age bullies, the gray headlines about the triumph of Nazism, invisible but floating closer like deadly gas—all these were just seeds of a new fear so palpable it seemed to be flowering inside him.

And the tranquil moments in between—when he realized that most girls were not killed by their fathers, that his school was filled with more friends than foes, that the war in Europe remained far off—these were mocked by the uncertainty that governed his days of effective house arrest.

"We gotta be ready to fight back," urged a teen who was constructing makeshift weapons, studding round bars with heavy metal bolts.

Shafiq was comforted by the belligerence only until the older men started stoking his doubts.

"We've lived in peace for so many years because we don't fight," insisted one man with a long gray beard that seemed to testify to his ability to survive. "Jews don't make trouble or invite trouble. That's not our way."

"Yes—trying to fight will be the death of us," warned another gravely.

But eventually they stopped sounding the alarm and turned inward instead, facing their traditional *tallit* shawls and reciting the *Shema* prayer. Shafiq understood the word from the Arabic, *ism'a*, to hear. "Hear, Israel, the Lord is our God, the Lord is One," they mumbled.

The sound of the prayer competed with the banging of the men making weapons. Both disturbed Shafiq in equal measure.

Reema stretched food in every way she knew how, exhausting the bags of rice in the underground storage room, opening the last bottle of homemade wine, emptying jars of pickled vegetables and baking bread until the flour ran out. But even Shafiq could see there was no keeping up with the appetites of a crowd of some three dozen anxious and restless people.

And no cash left to replenish the stocks.

Until that moment, money meant little more than trinkets to Shafiq. He preferred the feel of a scalloped ten-*fils* coin over a bill worth ten times as much. And he never realized that his father kept the family's savings in a safe at his warehouse. The place held only one great treasure as far as Shafiq was concerned: Sayed Barazani with his endless supply of treats.

"I have to go to the warehouse," Shafiq's father told his family. They were all crowded in a small washroom, the girls huddled on an overturned basin while Ezra paced and Naji sat close to their mother, one strong hand on her smaller one.

"The place is called 'Roobain's Warehouse,'" Leah said gently. She was reminding her father of what all the children felt acutely: anyone could tell it was a Jewish business. And if they didn't figure that out from the name, they probably remembered Roobain himself, always conducting transactions in front of the building in his two-chair, no-phone, no-fan, just-have-a-seat-and-join-me-for-Turkish-coffee "office."

"So?" Roobain asked.

Naji had closed his hand over Reema's, but Shafiq just wanted to crawl into her lap. More than the primitive comfort it offered, he craved the innocence of the past.

Just days ago, it seemed, he was playing stickball in the streets like any normal Iraqi twelve-year-old. And now, suddenly, he was a prisoner in his own home.

"You can't go," Reema pleaded.

"People here are hungry," Roobain countered firmly. "Besides, I have to check on the workers."

Shafiq saw Ezra look over at Naji and understood they were thinking, *You don't even know if there's any warehouse left for them to work in.*

"It's too soon! We can get by with what we have," Reema insisted.

"Are you going to cook the empty rice sacks?" Roobain snapped.

"Maybe some of these people can help," Naji said earnestly. "In a collective effort," he added. Ezra shot Naji a look, but Shafiq couldn't understand why. The visitors were already joining in the cooking and cleaning, living less like guests and more like family.

Shafiq's father would never, ever consider imposing on them for money. Convincing him would be like trying to make Salim leave Iraq. "Don't mention any of this to them," he warned sternly. "I'm going to the warehouse."

"But," Reema stammered, "what if something happens? What if . . ." Her eyes were wet and Shafiq was startled. *Mothers don't cry. The streets of Basra are safe. And I'm an Iraqi patriot.*

Nothing was right.

"You can't go; your accent," Ezra pointed out.

Yes, Roobain sounded more Jewish than a torah. The children had enough schooling to shed the dialect in mixed company, but their parents had never even learned to read, much less speak without an accent.

"I'll do it," said Naji, casual and brave.

"And I'll go with you," offered Ezra, formal and dutiful.

"No!" Reema said, gripping Naji's hand so hard his brown skin turned white.

"Don't worry, Nana, I'll be fine," he said with such a lilt in his voice, Shafiq almost believed his middle brother could cruise through the violent streets and turn all the thorns into flowers.

"You stay here with them," Naji said to Ezra. "I'll be okay. I have friends out there, just like Salim."

"Friends?" Ezra pressed.

"Comrades," Naji answered cryptically. That word again: *rafiq*.

Ezra turned to his parents. "You cannot let him go," he pleaded. "I'll go and I'll be better off . . . because I don't have 'comrades' out there."

Shafiq didn't want to let Ezra walk out the door and face the warehouse alone. "I'm going too," he said, trying to sound as firm as his brother.

"Not Shafiq," Naji protested, ever protective.

"Why not?" Ezra asked bluntly. "He deserves to see the world as it is."

"Yeah, why not?" Shafiq repeated, avoiding Naji's eyes.

"It is better if there are two," said Roobain, nodding sadly. Shafiq straightened up and stood tall. But when his father added, "Naji stays here," all his bravado evaporated.

The trip to Ashar was eerie, as the two brothers wobbled with fear navigating streets that Shafiq had only known as life's ordinary backdrop. Suddenly, Basra seemed different, though what he perceived to be most striking was not the terrible material damage—shops destroyed, with nothing left but their broken facades, small booths ransacked and emptied—but the severe change in his brother, who witnessed this all with a frown that looked etched into his face.

"They will pay for this," Ezra pledged to himself. Shafiq had never heard anyone in his family talk like that. There had never been a "they" that the tribe wanted to take on. He feared his brother's fury more than the mob attacks.

The young men passed the silversmith's store, where a section for *Kaddish* cups and menorahs was upended and emptied.

"They can destroy the objects, but the faith—never," Ezra pledged to himself. Then he added to Shafiq, "Walk confidently, like we own the street. Fear has a strong smell, and you'd better not stink."

Approaching the warehouse with hidden trepidation, Shafiq wondered how he would tell his father the news in case of the worst. Ezra craned his neck to see ahead, and Shafiq watched his older brother's eyes grow wide. He was afraid to look, but turning toward the *Khan Roobain* he saw it standing, as ever, in perfect condition.

"Sayed Barazani," Ezra said, rushing toward his father's business partner.

The Kurdish manager was guarding the warehouse along with his son and four other men. The double doors, normally open, were shut.

As Ezra and Shafiq drowned Sayed Barazani in hugs, he immediately asked, "How is the family?" This question was common, posed daily or even hourly, often repeated several times within one conversation, but never with so much urgency as now.

"*Alhamdu lil-lah, Alhamdu lil-lah*, thanks Allah. Fine, fine, everybody is fine," Shafiq and Ezra clamored together.

Looking at his older brother, Shafiq could not find a trace of the frown that a moment before had seemed permanent. Ezra's face glowed with gratitude toward Sayed Barazani and the other good men who worked for their father, as though whatever wound his spirit had suffered from the calamity was healed by the sight of them.

"Roobain?" Sayed Barazani asked. "Your mother? The children?"

Ezra was happy to report that they were well. "But stuck at the house," he added. "And my Baba was worried . . ." His normally sure voice wavered. The *khan* looked untouched, but of course the inside could have been pillaged.

"No problems here," Sayed Barazani said like a sergeant to a general. He then spoke in Kurdish to one of the porters, who nodded and backed away.

"Thank you for all that you have done for my family," Ezra said. "We'll never forget that you saved our warehouse."

"Thank you for protecting us," Shafiq put in. *Thank you for being here to welcome us*, he thought. *Thank you for being a friend to the Jews, and for cleansing the anger from my older brother.*

Just then, the porter called out to Sayed Barazani in Kurdish. In the distance, a crowd could be seen approaching the warehouse.

"Go," Barazani said urgently, and before the boys could change their expressions of gratitude, they were being pushed through the creaking doors, prisoners again in their own land.

But Shafiq felt uplifted enough by the scene at the warehouse that he could muster the courage to leave alone. "I'll run home to let them know it's safe," he said to Ezra. "You stay here and get the cash."

Ezra nodded. Sayed Barazani took off the headscarf he was wearing and wrapped it around Shafiq. "*Allah wa-yak*," he said, turning to go back outside to confront the mob. *God protects you.*

"Sayed Barazani," Shafiq said quickly, "*Allah y khaleek.* And to your sons," he could not help but add. "*Allah y khaleek.*" He kept repeating the phrase over and over, gratitude flooding his pores. "*Allah y khaleek. Allah y khaleek. Allah y khaleek. Allah y khaleek.*"

"*Ala al-ain wu ala al-raas*," the older man replied, smiling. It was an expression that meant literally, "At the eyes and at the head," but really signified, "I was glad to be helpful. I would do it again and again. It is my honor."

There were shouts outside. As Shafiq dashed toward the back door, he heard Ezra climbing the steps in the unnaturally quiet warehouse.

On the way out, Shafiq grabbed three tins of olive oil, as though he were looting the place. A Jewish boy dressed as his Kurdish protector pretending to rob his own father's warehouse. Life had never been so absurd.

Running through the streets, Shafiq felt safe behind the disguise. For a moment, he imagined he really was a looter on the dominant side, free from having to pretend. He liked the feeling of security, but was ashamed that the smugness was not really his to own.

Then, when he got home and saw Omar's older brother standing in the doorway, he knew his friends were his security.

"Shafiq!" Anwar rushed over to embrace him. Shafiq's parents also appeared at the door.

"Where's Ezra?" Roobain asked.

"Everything's fine. He'll be back soon." Shafiq was bursting with confidence: in his happy news, in the brotherhood of his friends, in his father's partner.

Roobain only nodded, as though there had never been any doubt.

Anwar handed the family a basket that overflowed with fresh feta cheese, eggs, vegetables, bread and the quince jam they all cooked in summertime. "From my mother," he said.

Reema could barely carry the bulging package, but she managed to gather it in her arms. And she could hardly express her thanks, but she tried. "Thank you, and may God protect you."

Shafiq wanted to ask about Omar, but Anwar was busy dressing Naji in traditional Arab clothes, securing a white bandana around his head with black bands while he stepped into a *dishdasha*. The two of them would be able to escort Ezra back safely.

Shafiq suddenly remembered the headscarf. "Here," he said. "It's Sayed Barazani's. Please give it back to him with my thanks."

My thanks, and thanks, and thanks, and thanks. And my prayers to Allah: May Sayed Barazani be protected always.

When the boys returned with Ezra, he told them what he saw. "They were like a militia," he said, eyes aglow with evident admiration for the tough Kurds. "I watched from the roof—they stood in a line. It was like: 'You Do Not Touch This Place.' The looters couldn't penetrate."

The whole family was immensely relieved and, like Shafiq, uplifted by the loyalty of the Kurds.

But when only Shafiq and Naji could hear, Ezra added, "I was up there on the roof dreaming that I could spit bullets and kill all the looters."

"You're sick," Naji said flatly.

Shafiq didn't know what disturbed him more— Ezra's rant or the growing fissure between his two brothers.

Concern rested over Shafiq like a film that afternoon. Until he saw the note inside the hole in the garden wall.

Hope surged. The curled paper could only be from Omar. He took it out of the uneven cavity with so much tenderness it might have been a wounded bird.

Hey Shafiq,

Omar wrote in his typically messy handwriting.

Well I always wanted free time off from school but not like this! Too bad we never learned those

Bedouin tricks like how to smuggle ourselves onto trains and live in the desert and stuff . . . remind me once this is over we have to practice!

Anyway, I read this quote in "A Tear and a Smile" that I thought was great so here it is.

"You are my brother and I love you. I love you worshipping in your church, kneeling in your temple, and praying in your mosque. You and I and all are children of one religion, for the varied paths of religion are but the fingers of the loving hand of the Supreme Being, extended to all, offering completeness of spirit to all, anxious to receive all."

Your brother,
Omar

After a lurching tide of emotions—from fear to flight to fight—Shafiq was now overcome by one which drowned out all the others: affection.

I love you worshipping in your church, kneeling in your temple, and praying in your mosque. Shafiq read this phrase until he had it memorized. It seemed so simple, obvious, clear and sound. He looked up at the sky, wide and serene.

Back in the garden, a note was pushed to the neighbors through the hole near the water pipe:

My brother Omar,

*The Bedouins have no trick we can't learn. We
could probably steal the knives off their belts before
they realized we were there.*

> *Your brother,*
> *Shafiq*

P.S. Thank you for the perfect verse.

Chapter XIII

Basra was tear-stained, but Baghdad was blood-splattered.

"Men, yes, but also women, little children, babies even, all killed," cousin Yusef was saying to the ragged crowd still stuffed inside Shafiq's home, their clothing grimy from days of continuous wear. The looting had largely run its course and a local businessman set up a militia to enforce calm.

These families had thought they were beaten down to their last reserve of strength—until they heard about the orgy of violence in the capital. Now they were terrified, not for themselves but for this friend or that cousin or this aunt who might be dead.

"Dragged out of cars, slaughtered in their homes, stabbed with knives, beaten, raped." Yusef knew everyone wanted information.

"Who was killed?"

"The Simhas?"

"What about the Jews in Government? They couldn't stop it?"

"Is my family okay? The Shamouns . . . what did you hear?"

"My daughter's there! My little one!"

Yusef held his hands out, palms down, to quiet the questions. "We are trying to figure this out. Right now we only know one thing for sure. This is an enormous tragedy and we may all have to leave the country."

It seemed incomprehensible, but suddenly the crowded masses in Shafiq's house who had already left their own homes were talking about going all the way to India—and never coming back.

Not everyone was ready to leave. "We've been here since Adam," protested one father.

"And we've always lived peacefully," said another, but he sounded doubtful.

"This is our home," echoed a third.

Shafiq was thinking: *India?*

"You cannot imagine the devastation," said Yusef. "Worse than anything in our history here."

But after he delivered the most gruesome news, he shared another side of the story. "So many were saved by our Muslim brothers. One young girl, she was separated from her parents and started running from the mob. They tried to attack"—the listeners gasped in revulsion—"but she was rescued by a man who pretended he was going to take her away himself. 'This one is mine,' he shouted, and he wrapped his coat around her little body. But the second they were alone, he took her in his arms, apologized with tears in his eyes for the fright she suffered, and rushed her back to her family. Now she's safe."

In the days that followed, as the news trickled in from Baghdad, it repeated the same pattern. There were atrocities: old men killed for nothing, young children brutalized, women murdered. And then there were reports that were as unbearably touching as the poetry of Khalil Gibran: the Muslims, and Christians too, who risked their own lives to stand guard in front of Jewish homes.

Shafiq had seen it in the Kurds at his father's warehouse. These were people of faith, but it didn't divide them, just made them stand for what was right.

His cousins in Baghdad had escaped the worst—but only barely. Yusef said the family hid in a small room on the roof when their house was attacked.

Shafiq thought of his own roof, a place for freedom: to watch birds soar, to look at sparkling stars, to eat the bread his mother baked in a conical oven she kept there. It was impossible to imagine his cousins huddling in a storage corner, hearing their house being ransacked and escaping death only because they were not discovered.

"Everyone was so scared that little Ghazi would cry, but he could feel the fear and was silent as death." Yusef looked down and spoke softly. "Just three years old, but he could tell it was too dangerous to make a sound."

Ghazi. The youngest of Shafiq's cousins, named after the king of Iraq.

A kind of numbing shock washed over Shafiq. His hopes were briefly raised when Salim came by that afternoon. But Salim didn't bring Kathmiya, only more jarring political lectures.

"Where were the occupiers when our brothers in Baghdad were being slaughtered?" Salim demanded. "My friend is an English translator and he told me they purposely played coy, refusing to enter the city until the worst damage was done."

This time, no one contradicted him. The displaced were too dispirited to care if the riots had been an intentional British tactic, but they were hardened enough to believe the occupiers had failed to subdue or rescue those they now controlled.

Salim pointed to the radio. "You can listen to the BBC all you want, but you won't hear them confessing to their complicity in murder."

Shafiq was sick of the grim politics. He just wanted to go outside. The closest he came was to peer through the shutters and steal a glance at the distant street.

The sentiments of Jews around Shafiq had definitely shifted. There was a fear like none he had seen before, even as members of the community started venturing out into the streets as calm slowly returned. Some, whose businesses were looted, carried a deep wound, speaking of how hurt they were by the devastation. Others were openly outraged, talking about appealing to the British for justice. And still others were simply planning to leave. "Escape," was the word they used.

There was a hushed silence among all of them when the announcement crackled across the airwaves . . . "Nazi Germany has dropped bombs on Zhitomir, Kiev, Sevastopol, Kaunas," the newscaster boomed from London.

"Hitler has invaded the Soviet Union!"

People were too frightened to cheer—just listening to the BBC could draw jail time—but their silent jubilance spread like a ripple crossing the Shat Al-Arab river.

"It is over," Shafiq heard adults rejoicing around him.

"Hitler's really gone too far this time. He'll never win now."

"It's a disaster for Germany," Ezra said.

Maybe so, but Shafiq knew that didn't mean it was the end.

Weeks went by before calm finally returned enough for Shafiq to climb over the roof and down into Omar's house. There he was welcomed with endearingly familiar grandiose schemes.

Within seconds, the two were plotting to follow the Bedouins up and down Iraq's railways to learn how they rob people and survive on nothing but their audacious crimes.

"What if they try to steal from us?" Shafiq asked.

"I have it all figured out." Omar lit up. "We promise to lead them to some rich people we say we're going to rob. Then just before we get to there, we jump off the train and run like we're being chased by killers."

"What do you mean, 'like'? We really will be running for our lives," Shafiq pointed out.

Omar just grinned.

The conversation rocked back and forth as casually as a porch swing until they headed out through Omar's living room, where Shafiq saw Hajji Abdullah sprawled on the couch, his frail legs tangled in a damp, crumpled sheet.

"Is your dad okay?" Shafiq whispered. For a moment he worried that he had forced an issue on Omar, who had been so considerate in ignoring the monumental disruptions in Shafiq's life.

But Omar just shrugged. "My mom's worried."

Shafiq felt a pang. "Are you?"

"Too weak to clean the floors at the school, probably can't keep his job much longer," Omar said soberly.

Hajji Abdullah stirred.

"Maybe we could read to him?"

"Maybe later," Omar replied. "After we come home with millions of *dinars*," he joked.

Shafiq pictured them rushing in, arms draped with stolen treasure. He wanted to thank Omar for the note, which had been worth more than gold, but they were laughing too hard, and there was no time to interrupt that.

Chapter XIV

It was another quiet morning in Salim's house when he announced that his parents were moving back home. "The Jews can come out of hiding now," he told Kathmiya since he had no one else to speak to. "Not because of any help from the British lackeys, but from Salih Bosh Aayan—"

"Bosh who?" she asked.

"Bosh Aayan—don't you know him?" Salim asked absently, as though he were speaking to a fellow attorney instead of a Marsh girl. "Controls half the businesses in this town. And now he's got his own militia. His forces are Iraqi, like they should be. So everyone can just calm down and go back to their own homes."

"Do . . . do you want me to come along and help pack?" she asked, following Salim to the door.

There were hardly any people in Shafiq's house this time, and at first Kathmiya resented being brought along without the chance to see him. But soon he appeared, looking at her with a warmth that felt like home.

"If we can drive out the imperialists, we can prove that Iraq is perfectly capable of running its own affairs," Salim was saying to his parents. Reema had brought tea. Their banter would continue for at least a few minutes.

By silent agreement, Shafiq and Kathmiya met in the kitchen, the natural retreat for a maid.

But he didn't want to stay there. "Come," he said. "I have something to show you."

Up on the roof, he opened the door to the aviary that Uncle Dahood had helped him build before the riots. The enclosed area used to be filled with junk, but now had woven metal strips over its small window and an open doorway. It was a sanctuary for birds, but more than that, it was an escape for Shafiq.

He found the tumbler—one of his most impressive pigeons. Among thirty or forty, only one could fly up in the sky and then start doing somersaults in the air.

"Watch this," he said, releasing the bird.

Sure enough, the pigeon flew up higher than the nearest rooftops and then starting rolling like a professional diver, tumbling on his way down with a joy and vivaciousness that delighted Kathmiya.

"How did you teach him that?" she asked.

"He's always been that way," Shafiq replied. "They each have personalities—I could tell you all about them."

"Personalities?" Kathmiya felt giddy. She understood; of course pigeons had personalities. In the marshes, she had known stubborn buffaloes, playful goats and fearless herons who grabbed their dinner right out of the water.

"See that couple?" he pointed to two pigeons, the male pure white and the female white with a light gray chest, walking near a stack of folded mattresses. "They always keep to themselves. I have a few like that. They're pretty snobbish, but very dignified!"

Kathmiya's laugh was like a shower of petals scattering.

"They hardly have any offspring—maybe one in their whole lives," he added.

"No sisters or brothers?" she asked.

"No, but you don't always want a big sister if you're a pigeon," Shafiq said.

Kathmiya felt a thought scratching at her mind. "Why?"

"The eggs hatch at different times, about two days apart. And the parents always favor the one that hatches first."

Kathmiya frowned and the spring shower was replaced by a wintry quiet.

She was thinking: *Do humans also favor the older one? Is that why I can't marry?*

But then she remembered that she was the only girl around, younger or older, who had been sent off to work before even getting married.

Shafiq began shooing his pigeons up in the air. He found a white towel he used to urge them to go higher, and as he waved it they did, flying ever upward but never far.

"*Njum njum,*" he said, using a verb from the noun *nejma*, or star. *Reach for the stars*, he was saying.

She watched the soaring birds aiming for the heavens, and wished that she, too, could be so free.

"I'd better go," she said.

"But let's meet again?" he asked sweetly.

Kathmiya's breath caught in her throat.

But she managed to exhale: "Yes."

Shafiq was humming with happiness that night. They were back to sleeping on the roof, and he pulled the covers over his head, grateful for the blackness that let him imagine seeing Kathmiya again.

... Watching the world with her from the rooftop ... guiding her hands on a kite string ... riding
her on his bike down the sparkling river walk ...

His unconscious started taking over and now
Kathmiya looked like one of his Kurdish cousins, with
flared sleeves and coins threading through her colorful dress, gently ringing like a melody ...

Lulled into sleep, Shafiq did not hear his brothers
approaching, until Naji's voice shattered the tranquility. "Did you see Odette's maid? She's gorgeous!"

Naji had invaded Shafiq's private thoughts.

"What?" Ezra asked.

"*Yaba yaba*," Naji said, a kind of Arabic version of
"Oh, boy!" Then he added: "What a piece. I've seen
some pretty fine girls, but no one as beautiful as her."

Shafiq wanted to explode in anger. Ezra did it for
him.

"Are you insane?" he rasped, voice tight as a wire.
"Don't you know anything? She's a *Midaan*. Her family
will kill you, Naji, do you hear me? They will come
here and kill you!"

Naji was silent, so Ezra drove the point home. "If
anyone defiles the honor of a young girl, it is their
duty—their sacred duty, Naji—to slice him into pieces.
Don't even think of going near the girl."

"I guess so. Yeah. All right. I was just saying ... never
mind."

Shafiq's immediate reaction was: As long as Naji stays away, I can be the one, I can approach her and I don't care if they come and kill me.

Until Ezra added, "*Kha-tigh Allah*, Naji,"—for God's sakes— "if not for you, think of the poor girl. They would murder her too, in a heartbeat."

PART TWO

Chapter XV

January 1945
Still in Basra

Like the swirled designs on the rugs she beat, Kathmiya's life moved in repetitious circles: the trip downriver to work, the brick floors she scrubbed, the weekend respite in the marshes and then back downriver. Give up, endure, hope, despair.

Shafiq would have been one shining spot on the pattern—purely decorative, but at least cheering—if he hadn't disappeared right after their time on the rooftop. Just after saying he'd like to see her again.

Kathmiya had gone to Basra at thirteen furious at the injustice of having to work. Four years on, she was more developed, more exquisite and more despondent than before. No marsh girl ever married so late . . . well, maybe one or two widows to their dead husband's brother, but not a first wedding, with the spangled promise it held.

Kathmiya felt like she was turning into that dry broom she used to push dust around Odette's floor.

Back home, Fatimah had two daughters and the smug security of a normal life. Seeing the little ones only reinforced Kathmiya's loneliness.

So when Odette ordered Kathmiya to polish the silver flatware for Salim's engagement party, she felt like the world was taunting her with a front-row view of elusive success.

She wanted to run away, but her money was stored in the vase that awaited her father's death, and if she broke it open she would violate a religious promise. Besides, how far could she go on a couple of *fils*? To Baghdad, or Ankara, or Paris? Even if she could travel, she'd never escape her class.

There was nothing to do but roast the lamb, bake the chicken in mountains of rice dyed orange with turmeric, burn the eggplant black and crush its smoky flesh with garlic.

"Clean the carpets," said Odette.

And that.

"Now!"

With pleasure.

Slam! She hit her father for making her work. *Bam!* She struck her mother for leaving her single. *Wham!* She didn't want to admit it, but the last blow was for that boy who never came back when he said he would.

Sometimes she wondered if she had just dreamed the bike ride and the pigeons. Other times, she thought maybe there had been a bad fight. Maybe Shafiq had suffered a grievous injury. Or maybe he had just forgotten all about the maid.

Salim's fiancée wore a harsh yellow dress, lemon to the butter Kathmiya would have picked. She decided the round-faced girl looked mean, and resolved not to be friends with her. As if the sophisticated bride would ever talk to the *Midaan* maid anyway.

It was easy to disdain Salim's fiancée, who looked closed tight. Her own engagement and she couldn't even manage a smile. Kathmiya took pleasure in the girl's impoverishment, thinking, *She may be rich, but she can't even enjoy a party in her honor.* Not even polite, staring frozen at her new family. Or maybe she was just too dumb to come up with anything to say.

Kathmiya kept trying on these unkind interpretations but none fit. Obviously, the bride-to-be was just terrified. The girl stood like a stone statue in front of Salim's father, as though she were facing her future. Watching her, Kathmiya realized the girl thought she was getting engaged to the father, not his son.

"For you," said the balding man, who had tufts of gray around his temples, draping a polished necklace over the girl's head. Salim was on the couch watching his father warm his fiancée to the family. Except that she was ice cold. But her parents tried to break the awkward silence with forced cheers of "Congratulations!"

"And these," added the old man, his blue-veined hand clawing around her wrist to slip on four faceted gold bangles.

Kathmiya had been prepared to hate the bride for her fortune, but the girl was too sorry a sight, holding back tears on her engagement day.

For so long, Kathmiya had dreamed that someone—anyone—would take her as a bride so she could leave the alienating city. But now she amended her prayer: *not an old man with liver spots.*

Pitying the bride, she slid behind Salim and gently nudged an ugly but intricate lamp on the table next to him until it crashed to the floor.

All eyes were on her, Odette's oozing fury. But Kathmiya ignored her you-stupid-maid glare, caught the bride's eye, and tilted her chin toward Salim. A smile spread across the girl's wide face. A smile of wonderment and realization.

"Thank you!" the girl said to her future father-in-law, genuinely grateful now that she realized she wouldn't have to marry him.

Kathmiya stooped down, sweeping the shards of glass into a magazine.

"Now meet my son, Salim Dellal!"

When Kathmiya stood up, she noticed that the groom was looking more at the magazine's cover photo of some official-looking men than his new bride. "Iraq joined the Arab League," Salim mumbled approvingly. Then, almost as an afterthought, he turned to the bride. "Did you sew that yourself?" he asked blandly, pointing to the girl's embroidered cuffs.

She blushed with pride. "Yes."

"Nice," he answered, but Kathmiya knew he would rather be shucking pistachios and talking politics than preparing to enter into holy matrimony.

He handed his finacée an apple. "Peel this for me," he ordered laconically.

The girl took the apple in one hand and, with a knife in the other, quickly separated the skin from the flesh and handed it back. When Salim took a bite, all the women in the room started ululating.

Except Kathmiya. She was collecting the browning peel.

We are having the Night of Henna," Odette told her a few days later. "The girl must be tattooed with flower petals."

"Why?" she asked, not being sassy but really wondering.

"To show her love for my son!" Odette seemed amused by Kathmiya's ignorance. "You know what happens to henna leaves when they are ground up?" she asked, almost as if testing her maid.

"They become paste."

"Well of course, but what I mean is the leaves turn from green to red. Think about it."

Kathmiya reflected on this strange symbolism, and could only figure it must represent a transition to womanhood.

If only she could participate and learn. As a guest, married, with a child in her arms instead of dirty dishes.

When the evening came, she was busy with chores, but still managed to watch the artists using the brick-colored henna paste to dot symmetrical tattoos on the bride's hands and arms.

"Kathmiya," Odette summoned her over to the couple. "You'll be moving in with Salim and his wife after they get married."

Instinctively, Kathmiya looked down, but the round-faced bride reached out and handed her a small mesh bag of sugar-coated almonds. "Please, have some."

So my life as a maid will get better, she thought. But she was still young enough to hope, and that made it worse. Because life as a maid was no life at all.

Kathmiya was up in her room after the guests left and the girl's family came to retrieve their inked-up bride.

She had seen and done enough. There was no reason to go back out. Except a sudden, calm certainty that she would be happy if she did.

Happy. Not a sentiment she experienced often.

Feeling strangely compelled, she walked to the balcony, looking down at the garden below. There, looking back up at her, was Shafiq, not twelve and bony like in her memory, but fifteen and strong, with wavy brown hair that hung softly around his face.

The look in his eyes was as clear as if he'd shouted from the rooftops: *You are stunning, more beautiful than before, and how is that even possible?* With a woman's sharp instinct, she understood that he was fighting the desire to stare at her.

It was a losing battle.

She saw in his eyes that long-forgotten warmth, but also a pained regret, and she knew, just knew, that it hadn't been his decision to stay away from her. Or that if it was his decision, it hadn't been because of her. And it hadn't been easy.

Chapter XVI

The crowd of family members ambled down the dusty street toward their home, but Shafiq stayed back, wanting, in the darkness of the calm night, to savor the memory of those black eyes. Leah was marrying Salim, and all of a sudden the captivating maid was back in his thoughts.

He had never forgotten Kathmiya's instep kicking the stitched soccer ball, the way her hair poked out from her scarf and skimmed his face while they rode the bike, the plan he'd made to see her again.

But then he'd overheard Ezra's warning. It was enough that one girl had been killed. He didn't want to be responsible for another bloody stump and dead daughter. So he'd contrived to stay away.

Adolescent longings intensified all of his feelings, but Shafiq's memories of Kathmiya had faded so much that he figured she once held him in thrall only because they met during the tranquility before the invasion, the riots against the Jews, and the mounting fear as Hitler continued his march across North Africa.

When Shafiq heard the marriage broker had picked Salim Dellal for his sister Leah, he experienced a rising hope—but he pushed it down. *You were just dreaming,* the teenager told his younger self.

But when he saw her . . . it was an oasis, not a mirage.

Shafiq suffered a fifteen-year-old's natural inflammation of desire, and he knew he should go nowhere near a young servant girl, no matter how pretty she was or how much he had sentimentalized their sweet, early encounters.

The family had turned a corner out of sight, but no matter, Shafiq knew the way home.

He strolled casually past an ornate mosque, stopping to look up the tall, narrow minaret. Fighting was distant in Europe. The war had left Iraq almost as quickly as it had come. But the North Africa battles were too close to home.

Shafiq felt a presence behind him. A stray dog. Time to leave. He started forward and the dog loped after him, cautious but still menacing.

"Hey!" Shafiq turned and shouted at the animal, which had a dull brown coat with pink patches of raw flesh along its back. It flinched and turned.

There had been moments of triumph along the way. Shafiq would never forget the jubilation four years before, when Hitler had invaded the Soviet Union. The cries of "They will finish him!" The predictions of an end to the Nazis.

Shafiq resumed his walk, still feeling the dog's lurking presence.

A year after the Nazis entered the Soviet Union, cousin Yusef interpreted more official reports crackling across the BBC. "The British are stalling the German advance towards Alexandria," he'd explained.

Two years had passed since then, but Shafiq could still feel the relief that traveled the room.

That dog, still there.

The euphoria had evaporated as soon as Yusef added, "But Rommel didn't retreat."

Shafiq shouted at the dog. "*Yallah! Imshee!*" He was telling it to move along, but in a threatening tone: *I'll hurt you if you don't.*

Then came the announcement, back in 1943, that Germany had lost the battle of Al-Alamein deep in Egypt. The Jews cheered, "Allah is with us!" But their relief was whispered behind shuttered windows.

That turning point helped eased the tension that lived in Shafiq's constricted chest, but the Germans were still fighting hard now, nearly two years later. No way to exhale yet.

The dog was panting. Probably rabid. Shafiq lunged for a sharp rock and hurled it near the animal, which bolted out of sight. But he couldn't be sure it was gone.

If the Night of Henna was a chance for women to rule, the real party, held just before the wedding, brought the men back on top. Sucking on different tentacles of brass waterpipes, blowing out blue smoke, arguing and laughing and besting each other with ever-more bountiful wishes for the bride and groom.

The whole cast of characters from Shafiq's life was there: his cousins and friends, his father's business partners, and Salim's fellow attorneys, along with the rest of the eclectic mix of opinionated men who constantly streamed in and out of that living room.

Plus one other person whom no one knew very well but everyone would grow to hold in higher esteem than any Emir by the time the night was through: Shant Bargadian, the Armenian caterer who introduced them all for the first time to that revolution in new cuisine: Jell-O.

Omar and Shafiq led the charge in passing out the dancing blobs of clear, sweet, bright-colored dessert: red, yellow, blue and green, like no food they had ever seen, much less tasted. "For you!" Shafiq said with a flourish, handing a plate to his old uncle Dahood, who shook his mystified head much less kinetically than the vibrating dessert.

"For you!" Omar said to Odette, and then he whispered to Shafiq, "It matches her belly."

With the way it melted with no effort, spread tangy sweetness, held its shape but bent with the elements, Jell-O was more than a food, it was an inspiration. Shafiq had never eaten anything as green as the Iraqi flag, and, buoyed by the magic he ingested, he carefully scooped out a tricolor spread onto a gold-rimmed dish and brought it to the kitchen.

"Hello, Kathmiya," he said. The maid was as shockingly beautiful as when he was younger, but now everything was amplified by the awakening of adolescence.

"You're back," she said simply. *She remembers me too*, he thought, soaring.

He tried to think of an explanation. He even looked to the dish of yellow, red and blue Jell-O for ideas. In the end, he just went with, "It was my brother who told me to stay away."

She should understand that, if her men were poised to kill them both.

"Oh," was all she said. Outside the drumming fortune-teller started performing, beating out rhythms and singing good wishes for tips.

"But . . ." Shafiq waited for Kathmiya to interrupt, to break the awkwardness of the moment, to let him off the hook. When she didn't, he tried explaining, "Now I'm the age he was when he told me that, and, you know, I—"

In the distance, they could hear the fortune-teller shout over the drumbeat, "May the bride and groom have children right away!"

"It's okay." It wasn't quite clear if she was forgiving him or saying that everything would be all right, but either was enough. He passed her the plate of Jell-O and she laughed.

A laugh that suddenly overpowered all the fascination of a rubbery treat.

"It tastes like giggles," he said.

The fortune-teller must have gotten a tip, because now a different chant echoed from the main room: "May you be wealthier than the richest sheikh!"

She swallowed some and laughed more. "It tastes like silly."

"Like laughing and you can't stop," he agreed. *Like talking to a girl and you don't want to stop.*

"May you have as many grandchildren as the seeds of a pomegranate," the performer said as the pounding beat worked up the crowd.

"This one tastes like watermelons," she slipped the red around her mouth.

"That one tastes like yellow rays of sun," he said.

"Shh!" She suddenly held up her palm to quiet Shafiq.

"And," the fortune-teller boomed, "may all of your children get married someday!"

"What?" he asked.

"Here she comes," Kathmiya mouthed. "Go."

"Sorry," he whispered softly.

"No!" she said, starting to sort dishes in the sink.

"May your sons find the most beautiful wives—"

Beat, beat, beat.

"I mean," he said earnestly, "Sorry for not coming back last time but I'd really like to—"

"—who will give them the most magnificent sons!"

Odette stomped in. Shafiq sidled out. Smiling.

"I'm in trouble," he whispered to Omar the next day at the formal wedding. A letdown from the party, it was held in a rented reception hall with no food, just prayers and ceremony and a chance to say good-bye to Leah before she moved in with Salim.

"Don't tell me—it's a dame," Omar guessed with swagger. No fifteen-year-old Iraqi boy could honestly boast of girl problems, but they had seen enough American movies at the *Cinemat Al-Basra* to talk like lovelorn cowboys.

"Yep," said Shafiq. The best part of having Omar as a friend was elevating all confusion into play. "Nothin' but trouble."

"Ain't they all," Omar drawled, palm where his belt buckle would be if he were an American frontiersman instead of a Sunni boy from Basra.

Their laughter was silenced by a sharp look from one of Shafiq's aunts as the rabbi intoned prayers in Hebrew. Soon it was time to break the ceremonial glass. Salim held the tumbler in his hand, wound his arm behind his shoulder, and smashed it against the wall.

The teens had mostly outgrown the street sports that used to occupy all of their younger days, but when Omar caught his eye, Shafiq knew both were thinking of starting a glass-throwing contest right then and there.

"Me too," said Omar.

"You what?"

"Dame problems," Omar confessed.

But Shafiq only laughed. What "dame problems" could Omar have? "You should be so lucky."

Chapter XVII

While the guests watched the vows at the wedding, Kathmiya was fluffing pillows and sweeping floors and wiping windows in the new couple's two-story home just blocks down from where she used to work.

The wedding suite was crisp with unscuffed Persian carpets, billowy sheer curtains, bright silk flowers and the most stunning apricot-and-cream satin bedspread Kathmiya had ever seen.

It was Odette who made the bed, with four old ladies watching intently when she started with a stark white sheet.

Seeing the look in the eyes of the older ladies, Kathmiya remembered the chicken that had been sacrificed in her sister's honeymoon suite, and knew they'd all be gathered around Leah, hoping that she would bleed freely, at least until the marriage was sanctified.

That night, Kathmiya watched from a distance when Leah came. Instead of acting regal like Fatimah, she just looked terrified.

It wouldn't be so hard as all that, Kathmiya thought. Fatimah had survived the ceremony. Not so bad, because your mother is there, and your sisters, and those old tribeswomen who sit like judges in court to make sure you are a virgin . . . a sisterhood to protect you through the process . . .

But instead, the bride and groom went alone into the bedroom.

How totally barbaric, Kathmiya thought with a shudder.

When the door shut behind them, all the women sat just outside with the grim determination of people who knew that the sacred must be upheld above the humane.

There was nothing to look at except a closed door, but Kathmiya was transfixed. Finally, it swung open and the women went inside. When they came back out they were holding up the sheet and pointing to the watery red streaks that made it go from pristine to priceless, at least for Leah and her family.

You should have brought a chicken, Kathmiya thought when she saw the lackluster stain.

Back in her new bed that night, she finally let her thoughts go to rooms in her mind that had been boarded up for so long . . .

. . . *My wedding will be in the marshes at the Sheikh's tent but much bigger than Fatimah's and I won't have an old husband I'll have someone young and handsome he doesn't have to be rich but we'll have enough that I never have to work again at least not in Basra I can weave carpets like a regular girl I can blend in with everyone else and no one will remember that I got married so late and no one will mind that I was sent away when I was young and everyone will treat me like absolutely nothing special and I can finally just live with simple blessings that take up all my time so I never have any reason to come back here for anything at all.*

She closed her eyes. First night in a new home.

But she still couldn't sleep. There was another room with its door wide open and a bright light shining through, and if she didn't go in she'd never put it out and it would keep her up all night.

. . . *Shafiq he never forgot me he always wanted to be my friend his brother said no of course just like my mother slapped me on the ferry but we can spend a little time while I'm stuck here waiting for someone to find a husband for me and we can eat Jell-O and ride bikes and best of all have a secret friendship that no one else knows about so even though I'm just the pointless maid with no life of my own I really do have a life and a reason to smile that no one else knows about but him and me.*

She tried to turn off that light but it only grew brighter. She could hardly sleep because she was wondering: will he or won't he? Would it be like last time, no contact for three years, or was this a new chance for true companionship? Everything she owned was paltry: a few coarse outfits, shoes for the city, a vase with savings waiting to be spent after her father's demise, a strange *dinar* she could not decode, and a book that was equally inscrutable. Anything clandestine, anything undisclosed or furtive or surreptitious or private would give Kathmiya a certain measure of power, she felt sure.

Her mind went black and she slept like she was tucked under an apricot-and-cream-colored satin bedspread.

Chapter XVIII

Getting ready to bike over to Leah and Salim's house, Shafiq felt as scattered as a deck of cards thrown from the roof.

He had never much bothered about his appearance, but now he started wondering, which side does my part look better on? He tried combing it on one side and then the other but couldn't tell which he preferred.

He knew he should ask Omar for advice, but felt too impatient. So he tried to imagine what his easygoing friend would say.

Just be funny and free. Don't worry about the part in your hair. And remember, it doesn't really matter how you look if you say the right thing.

Racing over to Leah and Salim's, Shafiq expected the couple would be too busy to pay attention to him.

And knowing that Odette was no longer around to embarrass Kathmiya, he hoped for a few minutes alone with her.

That bubble burst quickly. The room was filled with as many people as used to crowd around Salim back at his parents' place, only this time the living room was smaller and as soon as Shafiq sat down, he realized he was trapped. Leah sat quietly by her husband pretending to laugh at the jokes and decry the outrages but really, Shafiq knew, understanding less than half of what was going on.

"When the camps in Poland were liberated in January," said one of the lawyers, "oh, what they found . . ."

Leah looked unsure of whether to cheer or frown, but Shafiq noticed that no one was watching her anyway.

"Dead Jews," said another guest. Now Leah looked disturbed in earnest.

"Poles were killed too," Salim said.

Shafiq shifted restlessly. He wanted to see Kathmiya, not review the horrors of war.

"All this madness has to end."

"And what about Iraq?"

Shafiq lost track of the conversation as soon as Kathmiya entered. He stared at her until she looked back at him.

Smile. Wow. Like a sunrise.

When she passed close to clear the olive pits off a dish, he leaned in and whispered, "I wish I could write you a note."

She turned and looked straight at him. "Write?" she asked, puzzled and dismayed.

Shafiq realized, dismayed, that he should have consulted Omar before speaking to Kathmiya. Because that was absolutely the wrong thing to say.

Chapter XIX

Kathmiya was fascinated by letters. She stared at the books in Salim's study. Her eyes traveled across the newspapers he read in the morning. And she felt utterly defeated when she noticed that Leah casually wrote notes to herself, even using numbers.

Was everyone part of this world except her?

It became an obsession: *Who has this natural fortune that skipped me in life?* If Kathmiya saw a beggar in the market, she felt less alone. When she watched Leah's sister Marcelle flipping through a magazine, she was reminded of the utter waste—that so many people knew how to decipher words and didn't even realize how lucky they were.

Sometimes it seemed like the more tuned out she was by writing, the more she tuned in to people's moods.

Which was not always good. Just months after the wedding, Leah was giving Kathmiya a headache without making a single demand. No words, just her attitude. Lying around. Breathing hard. Wiping her brow. And brooding like she was the one who had no education, no home and nothing to look forward to in a too-open future.

Kathmiya tried to ignore Leah's quivering lower lip, her dramatic lethargy, her red-rimmed eyes. But at the same time, the two-years-younger bride brought out her maid's exasperated sympathy.

"Try some lemonade?" she asked, but Leah just waved her away.

"Maybe," Kathmiya scolded more than suggested, "you should really go to your family."

"Please come with me," Leah begged quietly.

Fine, thought Kathmiya. She was ready to see Shafiq, and demand that he unlock the meaning of all the letters flying around the world.

Despite whimpering that Kathmiya should come along, when Leah got to her mother's house she shot her maid the "please-leave-us-alone-now" look. Kathmiya might not be able to read, but she was an expert at understanding those silent commands, and retreated to the kitchen, her usual waiting room.

She knew Shafiq would show up, but when he did, she was surprised by how touched she felt by those warm, coffee-colored eyes. No one in the world seemed to want so badly to please her, and she rewarded his doting with a smile.

"Remember the pigeons I showed you?" he asked.

Kathmiya's mood lifted with each step up to the roof. Shafiq had disappeared for a few years, but now he was back to showing her his favorite birds. It was so pathetically small, it was nothing like an engagement or even a visit to the matchmaker, but it restored a little bit of her damaged dignity.

"They pick one mate for life," he said, pointing to the couples that followed each other in circles around the busy rooftop, with its folded mattresses stacked on one side and baskets of bedding on the other.

"How do they get together?" she wondered.

"I just pay the marriage broker and she works it right out," he joked. Kathmiya forced a laugh, but she was thinking, *Even birds find their mate but not me.*

"Some males, though," he continued, "want to get with all the chicks." He pointed to a pigeon chasing any female close to him, showing off by puffing his feathers, spreading his tail, turning in circles and cooing constantly.

Kathmiya wondered what this did to the balance of nature, but how could she ask about that? "I'd better go back down," she said. In truth, she knew she shouldn't disturb Leah unless she was called, but the feeling of being with Shafiq was so dizzying she actually started to worry it would send her off the roof.

He looked disappointed, but this only pleased her. "Next time," she added coyly, "you can show me your notes."

For a second, he looked as stabbed as she'd been when he'd mentioned writing messages. *Good*, she thought. *Now we're even.*

Once downstairs, Kathmiya spied on Leah and her mother by pretending to wipe the table with one of the balled-up rags that lived in her pockets.

Reema was too focused on her wilting daughter to notice the maid. "My sweet," she was saying, "please tell me."

"She keeps asking me for a grandson," Leah complained. Kathmiya had heard Odette hammering at the subject like the coppersmith banging on his pots— incessant and enervating. "Not a daughter, mind you, a son!" she would say.

"*In-sha Allah* you'll have one," said Reema.

Leave it to God, thought Kathmiya. *I should too.*

"But I'm not getting pregnant," Leah whined. "My sister-in-law felt my belly and she said there's nothing there."

To be married but barren—oh. Kathmiya almost felt sorry for Leah.

"Shh . . ." Reema patted her daughter's hand.

"It's worse than that," Leah screeched. "I'm sick, really sick. Can't stand the smell of fish. Can barely eat. Run out of breath climbing one flight of stairs."

Kathmiya recognized every one of the symptoms. Fatimah never shut up about them when she was pregnant. But the mother didn't get it. "Fever?" Reema asked.

No maid had a right to pipe up and join in, but this was just too ridiculous. "How does your sister-in-law know you're not . . . ?" Kathmiya prompted.

Leah started wailing, determined to be miserable, wallowing so much she barely noticed she was talking about her life to a servant. "She has four kids, that's how."

"Your mother has five," Kathmiya said under her breath, worried that she was being too forward.

But Reema nodded. And then she looked at her daughter sideways and asked, "The blood every month, is it—?"

This sent Leah rolling through a fresh wave of sobs. "How can I make it come out?"

Now Reema was beaming. Kathmiya said it first. "You're pregnant."

But Leah only got more anxious. "I'm not!"

Reema hugged her daughter, who stayed stiff as an ironing board.

"The smell of dinner . . . should I turn off the stove?" Kathmiya asked, trying to drop another hint and hoping it would land on Leah's thick head.

She got a desperate stare in response.

"My sister couldn't stand when my mother cooked spicy stew when she was, you know, a few months along. I think it gets better after a while."

"I even hated the smell of Persian lilacs," Reema put in. "But she's right, it gets better."

Leah finally smiled, shy but thrilled, and put her hand on her abdomen. It was like the letters of the alphabet—something Kathmiya could see but not get.

Chapter XX

More than his school exams on chemistry and the Koran, more than the drama of Leah's pregnancy, more than the armies crisscrossing the world, Shafiq was obsessed with one all-consuming thought: how to teach Kathmiya her letters.

He didn't have books from back when he went to elementary school dressed in hand-made jumpers. And anyway, he didn't want to insult Kathmiya with materials made for little kids. So he brought her a map of the world he'd saved from a magazine.

"That's India," he pointed, watching her face as she pored over the shapes of countries. "This is Iraq," he added. "The best country, of course."

Shafiq's patriotism had taken a beating during the riots, but his childhood had been dipped in so many nationalist anthems he could hardly separate the optimism of youth from his love of country.

"Iraq." He pointed. "And India." Kathmiya looked so determined and fetching. The sun was streaming in through the bare windows in the second-floor room of Leah and Salim's house, where the two teens crouched together on mottled brown floor cushions.

"But, how do you read?" she entreated.

Shafiq looked down at his hands. He didn't want to condescend, but there was only one place to begin. "*Alef, ba, ta, tha, jim, ha, kha* . . ." He was singing the alphabet like a six-year old.

"*Alef, ba, tha, ta* . . . you're going too fast!" she complained delightedly.

So he started again, three letters at a time, until she knew it better than how to scrape blackened rice off an iron pot.

They sang together boisterously, like sailors at a drinking fest, swaying back and forth to the little baby tune. Shafiq hoped she would stay stuck on that lesson for, oh, about a year and take another year to learn which letters matched the sounds and another to write words, so that by the time she was ready to read a sentence he'd be old enough to write a note that said . . .

"Hey there." It was Naji, looking at Kathmiya while he pretended to talk to Shafiq. "I brought you these."

He held out two bright oranges. To Shafiq they looked like grenades. His emotions started crashing: Naji, his favorite brother, handsome and charming and all the more infuriating for it. *Son of a whore, get out!* Shafiq thought, instantly depressed for insulting his brother and their mother at once.

Kathmiya reached out her hand, and just like every ball that Naji touched, the orange obeyed him and dropped gracefully into her palm. Shafiq could barely mutter "I'm not hungry" before looking back down at the map. *Do they have these problems in India?* he wondered. *'Cause I think I'm gonna move there.*

If nothing else, school had taught Shafiq enough *Alef, Ba* to impress Kathmiya. But he had to wonder what else it was good for when Ezra, the most studious one in the family, ran straight to the gates of law school only to watch them slam in his face.

"Oh, yeah!" Omar came rushing in to Shafiq's living room. "Anwar made it!"

"Fantastic!" Shafiq had expected that.

"So when's Ezra going up to the capital?" Omar asked.

"Ah, we're stuck with him in Basra."

"Yeah, sure." Omar didn't even consider that Ezra had been rejected. "We're gonna visit our brothers in Baghdad and go to the horse races, right?"

"Right, but—" Shafiq couldn't think of a line, much less explain. Omar, also his "brother," could con a market full of shoppers but he wouldn't be able to wrestle this one to the ground. Shafiq would have a long list of ways to describe Omar before he ever got to Sunni, and that went both ways. No doubt Omar didn't think of Ezra any more as a Jew than Shafiq's family saw him as a Muslim. As stupid as it sounded, it was also wonderful: Omar plain forgot that Ezra was different. "He got rejected," Shafiq finally said.

Omar looked confused for a moment, but then quickly recovered with a fresh idea. "Hey, now he can go to the American University of Beirut!"

"Sure." Shafiq went along.

"No, really—I hear they have lots of parties, and don't forget, the school is coed!"

"*Yaba, yaba*—that's better than horse races." Shafiq laughed, but he knew it would be harder for Ezra to see the possibilities.

"They took three Jews out of the whole Basra province," Ezra railed to his brothers that evening as the bright blue sky faded to pale lavender. "I probably came in fourth."

They were stretching under a mulberry tree in front of the house.

"There's always American University in Beirut," Shafiq tried. "You know, they accept girls, too."

"Oh, yeah!" cheered Naji.

"But how can I leave you all? Baba's not so young," said Ezra stoically.

"Baba's healthier than any of us," Naji pointed out. Shafiq thought of Omar's father in that dark living room with his frail legs looking like onionskins that would break if you touched them.

"I still have to be here to recite the *Kaddish* in case anything happens." Ezra pouted.

"He's not dying,"

"You go, Naji. Next year you go to University in Beirut," Ezra said. "I mean, if you don't manage to be one of the top three Jews in the southern part of this whole stupid country."

"I'm not running in that race. We're not any of us going to make it as lawyers or doctors," Naji said. "But who needs prestige and money when you can have fun?"

Ezra sneered. "I'll be having fun working as an Iraq Railways clerk for the rest of my life, is that what you're trying to say?"

Shafiq knew Ezra had reasons for being angry, but that frown . . . it reminded him of when they walked through the streets together during the riots. Etched on, with set eyes to match.

"See, that's your problem, you don't think big. But I have an idea," Naji said. A breeze rustled the tree's leaves and cooled them all. "We open the first cinema house in Old Basra. Show the latest movies from Egypt, even from America. People won't have to go all the way to Ashar to see them anymore."

"I can't even get accepted to law school and you think I can be a movie mogul?"

"Since you can't think for yourself, yes," Naji countered. "Let them all do law and deal with small-time criminals smuggling carpets from Iran. You and me, we'll be working with Egyptian belly dancers and American blondes."

"Fantastic!" Shafiq was all for the idea.

"And how are we supposed to pay for this?" asked Ezra.

"Our father can help." Naji stood up to shake off the extra energy that his own idea inspired. "He'll give us the money to get started."

"You still haven't even finished high school."

"I have one year left but after that I'm free. Meanwhile, you take a job—any job, at the train station, whatever—but just until I get out. Then we'll rent a place and order the films and screen them, and, well, charge admission of course."

Ezra still looked skeptical, but Naji was beaming. "I have a name for the place. Can you guess?" he challenged.

"Uh . . . the Town Movie House?" Ezra tried.

"How plain can you be?" Naji rolled his eyes. "Lucky you have me as a partner. Picture this," he said, flashing his hands across the air as if to frame a marquee: "The Roxy!"

Ezra laughed. "You don't need to go to Baghdad. You are already halfway to Hollywood."

"Wanna come with me then?"

"It'll never lead to law school," said Ezra, reluctant. "But I guess why not," he added, a rare, faint smile capturing his mouth.

"Oh, yeah!" said Naji, jumping up, grabbing a tree branch above with both hands, and doing a set of pull-ups in celebration.

Watching Naji's brown muscles flex in the sun, Shafiq almost forgave him. Stupid perfect Naji, charming everyone in sight. He shouldn't screen movies—he should star in them.

Shafiq always made sure to be alone with Kathmiya for her writing lessons. He pointed to words and mouthed sounds and put his hand over hers to guide the pen in the right sloping direction.

Her perspective was so fresh, like the smell of morning in summertime, that he experienced a startling appreciation for the Arabic language. How could he never have noticed the amazing way that letters changed their shape depending on what they were next to? That words changed their sounds just to rhyme? That they had different singular, plural and dual nouns, as well as masculine, feminine and neutral genders?

Kathmiya's extra-deliberate calligraphy showed him how magical it was.

Each time he went, he was spellbound, sneaking up to the second-floor room, feeling the sun warm their backs, dreaming of a kiss. It was almost more than he could take, but still not nearly enough.

Chapter XXI

L eah was swelling up. The only thing bigger than her belly was her outsized anxiety over the sex of the child.

"Odette insists on a boy," she reminded Kathmiya when they were alone in the hallway.

"Tell her she'll be lucky for any healthy grandchild," Kathmiya grumbled. Didn't Leah see that her "problems" were an embarrassment of riches? She would be ecstatic to have her own little sweet-smelling, soft-to-the-touch, warm and dependent girl. The dream was as vivid and as unattainable as the moon in the sky.

It was bad enough to have no husband or home, but caring for Leah was just one more reminder of how excluded Kathmiya was.

"**Don't leave** me," Leah begged when the midwives arrived. The three women dressed all in black presented a stark tableau. The only garnish of color came from the few branches of some green herb one held in a clutched fist.

Kathmiya wondered what the dried weeds were for. They didn't feed Leah the branches or burn them like incense, they just stuck them in a bowl for her to look at, as if that would relieve the pain she was screaming through.

It fell to Kathmiya to swab cool towels at Leah's temples while the midwives circled each other manically, waiting for something to happen.

Each time Leah convulsed with contractions, the old women told her to look at the branches. Or they yelled one incessant command.

"Push!" shouted the brusque women, holding Leah down by her wrists and ankles. "PUSH! PUSH! PUSH!"

As the hours dragged on and the blood drained from Leah's face, it seemed that death stalked the room as much as birth. All Kathmiya could do was slide out the sheets Leah had wet and bloodied and soiled and replace them with fresh ones.

Leah's face was swollen to three times its normal size, her wrists and ankles were badly bruised by the

midwives' manual shackles, and she looked dangerously spent. Finally, the oldest attendant, a severe
woman with her face pinched like a dried fig, went into
the kitchen and returned with a knife.

"We have no choice," she hissed. "We have to cut
you." The other midwife gestured for Leah to look at
the withered branches.

What was the use? To see a bit of nature before she
was murdered?

Kathmiya couldn't let it happen. She rushed to
Leah's side and started shouting at her. "Leah, they
have a knife, please, please try one more time. It's a
butcher knife they want to use to get the baby out . . ."
Kathmiya was shaking and sweating. That hatchet was
for chopping meat, not opening a woman's body. The
midwife was wiping it on her sleeve.

"Leah, they are going to cut you if he doesn't come
out now!"

Suddenly, Leah screamed like the fear had broken
her daze. "NOOOO!" she cried, tears, blood and per-
spiration streaming from her battered body.

The midwives were startled back to their poses,
holding down her straining limbs and ordering her
to push. "Your beautiful boy, your baby, he's coming
out!" shouted one, and Kathmiya could see the crown
of the head, slick and dark.

There, in the middle of this swirling storm of excrement and blood, a new person. Life.

"PUSH! PUSH! PUSH!" they urged, but their hoarse croaking was wasted because the baby was slipping out on his own. "God is great," they cried, and Kathmiya looked down to catch a glimpse of the newborn boy.

But beheld instead a tiny baby girl.

The midwives had left behind one last item from their arsenal: a small, triangular fabric decorated with shells. Kathmiya had never seen the amulet before, but she knew the type: designed to ward off the evil eye. That malicious force was everywhere—in the marshes, in the Jewish tribes, in Iraq and beyond. Everyone had a charm to fight off the *jinn*.

"If he were a boy, who would have gotten a dowry at marriage instead of costing one, they would have cheered, 'May he be a sign of seven,' " Leah said while she nursed her baby through a trance of pain and joy.

"Seven?" Kathmiya handed Leah a glass of water. She had also brought a little amulet, the same one her parents had given each of Fatimah's children. With colored threads woven around two sticks at perpendicular angles, it looked like a kite made of string.

" 'Seven' for seven more boys. Instead, all they could say was, 'May she be followed by sons.' "

"Really?" Kathmiya wasn't paying much attention; she was wondering how to tell Leah about her gift.

"Well, there is another expression," Leah said, flopping back on the sweaty pillow. "But even Odette wouldn't have said that to me."

"What?"

" 'Thank God for the health of the mother.' It's supposed to give you hope that you can get a boy next time but they couldn't—"

"Hey," Kathmiya interrupted. With Leah looking as though she had barely survived a stampede of buffalo, "Thank God for the health of the mother" would have been more of a wish than an affirmation. "I brought you this," she said. "It's supposed to keep away the evil eye."

Leah's eyes were only half open, but she rested Kathmiya's amulet on her newborn's tiny shirt next to the other charm.

"Thanks," she said, lolling off.

Kathmiya got up and dumped out the pointless herbs. Even though the branches had done nothing to alleviate Leah's pain, she couldn't help but hope the good luck pieces would keep the *jinn* away.

Leah's sadness evaporated. Or maybe it just got washed out, like all the blood and dirt on her sheets, by Kathmiya. In her best moments, Kathmiya behaved toward Leah like the nice big sister Fatimah had never been to her. At her worst, she was bound up in a ball of anger.

When she met her mother at the port that week in Basra, she was ready for a fight.

"My sweet," Jamila said. But the cloying term just made Kathmiya squirm.

"I'm too old for pet names," she complained.

"You'll always be sweet to me, my little one," Jamila said wistfully.

"Oh, I'm so special, that's why you look out for me, right?" Kathmiya narrowed her large eyes so much her face almost looked ugly.

Jamila just huffed.

The docked boat was swaying in the river near where they stood. "Why should I even go back home?" Kathmiya was too bright and loud, irrationally blind to the people around them.

Jamila grabbed her daughter by the shoulder and pinched. "I risked my life for you," she growled. "You don't even know."

It sounded too dramatic to be true, but with the sounds of Leah's agonized screams still ringing in her ears, Kathmiya softened.

"I just want what everyone else has," she said quietly, following her mother up the small path to the long deck, slick with water.

They sat, as usual, at the back, watching the modern city fade from sight as the houses became more sparse, the palm trees more dense.

"Please," said Kathmiya, trying to extract a promise. "He hates me, he always has."

"Who?" Jamila asked without a trace of irony.

"You KNOW!" Kathmiya exploded. "You're married to him!"

Jamila just pressed her fingers against her eyes.

Kathmiya seethed quietly as the sturdy brick buildings gave way to small farms in the distance.

Finally, when the sky turned a purplish gray, Jamila spoke. "Don't blame yourself, my sweet."

"Then it's your fault," Kathmiya shot back bitterly.

"Do you think I want you to work?" Jamila's voice flared. "Do you think I care whether you save money for Ali's funeral?"

"Stop," Kathmiya said, trying to hide in piety. "That's sacred."

"Of course I want you married," Jamila murmured. "Of course I have been trying. Ali has his reasons, trust me—"

"Will you at least speak to him?" Kathmiya just wanted to change her circumstances, not unravel her past and her mother in the process.

"When the time is right."

Tonight, Kathmiya decided. *And if she won't, then I will.*

In their straw hut, she almost lost her nerve. But there was Fatimah, preening to cover up the fact that she was fascinated by Kathmiya's life in Basra. "How can you stand the city?" she asked.

"You'd understand," Kathmiya said, "if you'd ever been there."

She waited until Fatimah and her children left and then poured her father a good cloudy glass of *arak* and water.

"So," she said once he'd smiled that here's-my-best-friend look he got when he saw his drink. "Don't you think it's time to arrange a marriage for me?"

Jamila was across the room or she would have pinched Kathmiya's shoulder black and blue.

"Marry? You?"

No, the sheikh's *daughter*, thought Kathmiya. All she said was, "Yes."

"You sound like your mother," Ali grumbled. Kathmiya looked over at Jamila. " 'She's getting older,' " he went on in a nagging mock-wife voice. " 'Time to go to Haider.' "

Uncle Haider. Kathmiya couldn't help it—she smiled.

Jamila joined in, "We should see your brother. Haider has first rights for his son to marry Kathmiya."

"Oh, is that what you want?" Ali asked Jamila, ready to ruin the moment. But she stood her ground.

"Yeah," Kathmiya said, trying to reinforce the chances. "That's what we want."

Ali stared. Took a long sip of his drink. Looked up at the ceiling. And then answered: "Fine."

"Really?" Kathmiya asked. She couldn't believe it had been so simple. He's not such a bad father, she decided. It took a while, but now he was going to let her marry, and pretty soon she'd be able to replace the balled-up rags in her pockets with soft wraps for her baby. "*Abuyah*," she cooed, "that's great! I mean . . . thank you. Thank you so much."

Ali's wide smile showed his brown teeth. "Don't thank me yet," he said.

Kathmiya basked. She was even tempted to hug him.

Chapter XXII

I f Shafiq were the king or the regent or the ruler or the president or the colonial power or whoever was in charge, his first decree would be that teen-aged boys should marry before girls, not the other way around.

Because there they were again, thanks to the marriage broker, sending another one of his sisters out of the house and into a matrimonial bed, when he was the one with all the curiosity.

The groom-to-be was one Moshe Khabazza, a very fancy individual, to hear the parents brag. At their house, Shafiq was subjected to an unending monologue about the Great Virtues of Moshe.

"He graduated top in his class," Moshe's mother repeated for the third time.

"Electrical engineering, from one of the best schools in India," the father echoed. Shafiq practically expected Moshe's parents to promise their son would end the Second World War, cure malaria and dump all the *jinn* into the Mediterranean Sea without even hurting the fish.

He picked up a magazine and stared at a picture of Stalin, Roosevelt and Churchill surrounded by men in uniform at a place called Yalta.

After his family left, Roobain sounded as put off about Moshe as Shafiq felt. "They talked too much. And did you hear what they said about earning a living?"

"'The only way to make real money is through gambling or inheritance,'" Naji repeated. "Bad sign."

After his next encounter with his potential son-in-law, Roobain decided to cancel the match. "Came to the warehouse and here is the first thing he said: 'All this and the dowry is still so small?'"

Wow. It was like bringing dung to a party instead of pastry. Nothing could be more offensive to Shafiq's father, who always taught his children that a *dinar* earned honestly went a long way.

"But the electrical engineering . . ." Shafiq's mother tried.

"I don't care if he's the king of Persia," Roobain spat. "Naji's right: the family has no values."

After hearing about the cancellation, the marriage broker insisted they go over for one last visit with the Khabazzas. Approaching the house in the warm evening, Shafiq was grabbed by a manic energy in the air. And when the door opened, there was the source: dozens of guests, swarming around a buffet, forks full of herbed rice, succulent meats, salty lettuce leaves.

Before Shafiq's family could back out, Moshe's father threw one arm around Roobain and the other over Marcelle's slender shoulders and pressed them toward the living room filled with couches and chairs and all those guests who had been raiding the spread of food.

"Please, please," the father quieted the room. "I present to you my beautiful future daughter-in-law!"

The men cheered. The women ululated. Marcelle looked fascinated. And Shafiq's parents stared in ashen shock.

"In honor of my new family, I present this gold necklace my son has bought for his lovely bride!"

Moshe, who had stringy fair hair and a sniveling manner, stepped up to drape a chain over Marcelle's neck. Something like a yoke.

"What do we do?" Shafiq's mother whispered.

"We stop this," his father said.

But she was adamant. "A broken engagement would ruin her."

So there it was. The frightened teenaged girl would marry some lout who was soaking the family for a bigger dowry, while Shafiq could barely spend time alone with Kathmiya, let alone dream of touching her.

It would be good to be king, or president, or colonial power, or whoever took charge once the war ended. But even that might not be enough.

"Marcelle's getting married," Shafiq told Omar later that week. They were riding along the Corniche river walk, the smell of kerosene from the lanterns on each of their bicycles following them everywhere.

"What?" Omar stopped with a jerk.

Shafiq stared. "What?"

"Marcelle?" Omar repeated, looking pained, then embarrassed, then away.

It hit Shafiq like a punch in the gut: Omar had an unnatural interest in his sister.

"Come on," he said, pedaling ahead so that they wouldn't have to be near each other in that stupid, awkward moment.

Shafiq pictured Marcelle, just his sister with soft black hair and playful eyes. He remembered her as a young girl running under the legs of camels when caravans stopped to drink from among the many man-made canals, used to water date palms, that fed off of the estuary running in front of the house.

"This way." Shafiq led Omar to the wide road headed toward the governor's mansion where they could speed up. Maybe they could even go fast enough to shake off the awful desire that consumed their young bodies. They both pedaled hard.

Shafiq could picture the camels, who always looked proud even though they were loaded with giant date palm fronds, dried and dead and destined to be burned as firewood, while the little girl skipped underneath.

As the boys sped toward the official residence, its guards now coming into view, Shafiq thought of the camel handlers, who smiled when they saw Marcelle playing. She was just a kid, then and now.

Shafiq sped faster, revolted by the thought that anyone, even—maybe especially—Omar, would have forbidden thoughts about Marcelle.

"Watch it!" Omar shouted, and Shafiq swerved to miss a Model T Ford that had jumped out of nowhere into his path.

"Thanks!" But even as he was offended, Shafiq was also relieved not to be the only one who grappled with this dreadful desire. He wanted to turn around and tell Omar everything about Kathmiya, even if that meant he would have to hear some version about Marcelle.

Omar caught up with Shafiq, his smile as wide as ever. "I'm happy for your parents—they must be so glad, right?" he said. It was a great effort at covering his unintended confession.

Shafiq figured Omar was right to pretend nothing was going on. Instead of admitting to any crush, he told Omar about the trick engagement as they jumped off the bikes and started walking through the café-lined streets.

"We should get revenge!" Omar was a man on a mission, and if it had anything to do with selling pigeons or taming desire, Shafiq was in.

"Sure, but how?" There would be no way to convince his parents to call off the engagement, and if he ever did, Marcelle would be unmarriageable, miserable, as ruined as a glass smashed at a wedding.

"I don't know, but let's figure it out."

It sounded like trouble to Shafiq, but trouble plus Omar usually equaled success. "Let's," he said.

And he pretty much forgave Omar for thinking about Marcelle. No difference between that and his own impossible, obsessive dreams for Kathmiya.

They were in Salim's front yard soaking up the yellow light of day when Kathmiya announced her news. "I'm getting married," she told Shafiq.

"Well, you know," he stammered, trying to calm his speeding pulse. "*Mabruk.* Congratulations."

He wished hard it would rain. If his life were a movie, there'd be dark clouds and pelting storms. Basra's clear, inspiring skies just showed how little his own moods mattered.

Instead of going home, he went to Omar's, but no one was there except the father. "Should I read to you?" Shafiq asked. Poetry was the only medium that had a shot at untangling this mess.

Hajji Abdullah asked to hear "A Song of Death." As Shafiq read the verse, the old man dropped off to sleep.

Shafiq turned to "A Life of Love," but Omar came in before he could read it. And even though they both needed whatever answers Khalil Gibran's verse held, Shafiq just closed the book.

"Carefully," Omar cautioned.

"I know," Shafiq answered, wrapping it up gently.

"What do you say we get this guy who's trying to infiltrate your family?"

"Sure." Better to ruin someone else's chances than brood on the death of his own.

Chapter XXIII

Kathmiya sang a song that didn't exist. She twirled around like the dancers pictured in Leah's magazines, who moved to the rhythm of music she would never hear. And she embraced this fresh, unbelievably sensational feeling called hope.

Uncle Haider was coming over. He'd make it all right. Better than the time he'd given her an extra blanket—Fatimah even saw, what a look in her eyes. Better than the time he took Kathmiya hunting so she could see how they skinned the buffalo. And better than that connected feeling whenever she visited him and he called out her name before he even saw her.

Uncle Haider had three sons, and only one was married. That left two others who were eligible.

The lapping water sounded musical. The rustle of the wind in the reeds was like a song broadcast over Baghdad Radio. The buzz of mosquitoes was a cheering victory parade.

Jamila didn't look nearly so happy.

"What's the matter?" Kathmiya asked, her face lit by the glow of the heated dung-bricks. "Aren't you glad to get rid of me?"

Her mother sighed. "I'm happy that you'll be back home."

"And?" she challenged in that stubbornly direct manner which, though it set her apart, was one of her indelible features, like wild hair or large eyes.

"And," said Jamila, exasperated, "I'm just like you—relieved that you will finally have a husband!"

"So now you admit it's about time?" Kathmiya asked. But Jamila didn't answer.

Uncle Haider's skin shone reddish brown and he wore a plain *dishdasha* as gray as the sun-baked clay pots. The muted earth tones all around relaxed Kathmiya, who still sometimes felt overwhelmed by the harsh colors and slick textures that seemed to coat every surface of the city.

When he greeted his niece, there was nothing about the words he spoke that she could point to in explaining how secure he made her feel, but everything in the way he said them. The simplicity of his wholesome love was like a canoe on the river: everyday and essential.

As the two brothers discussed a neighboring tribe—despite how they were viewed by the rest of Iraq, the Marsh Arabs didn't think of themselves as all one "*Midaan*"—Kathmiya imagined being closer to her uncle after the engagement. Maybe he could get Ali off the *arak*. Maybe instead of causing so many fights, Kathmiya would be the one bringing the family together.

Haider seemed extra tender toward Kathmiya, praising her cooking and her manners and her kindness. It threw her off just a bit, this excess show of affection, but she served him tea with sweetened buffalo milk, still hopeful that there would be good news by the end of the night.

Ali never raised the subject, so Kathmiya spoke up.

"How is Abdul?" she asked. That was her first-choice cousin to marry. His eyes, while not as warm as Shafiq's, were at least friendly.

"Very well, thanks be to Allah." They had already gone over this ground when Haider arrived, but Kathmiya wasn't asking out of formality. She nodded toward her mother. "Anything you wanted to ask Uncle Haider?"

Finally, the words: "Have you thought about finding him a wife?"

Uncle Haider shifted on the reed mat where they all sat.

Kathmiya felt her face go red.

"No," he said.

"But he's getting older, time for a family, right?" Kathmiya asked, training her black eyes on Haider, so fierce he wouldn't look back at her.

"Jamila . . ." he said. Meaning, *Jamila, stop your daughter before she makes this situation worse.* But Jamila only stared in response. "Yes—I mean no. We want him to marry. But not—" Haider tried to look away from the women, but his eyes flickered toward Kathmiya almost involuntarily, as if to apologize without words.

Her heart was pounding. She wanted to disappear back to when her worst problem was working as a maid in Basra, not being openly rejected in her own family. More than anything, Kathmiya wanted to end the conversation.

But Jamila was suddenly, awfully, painfully singing her praises. "Kathmiya is a fine girl, very hardworking, she even earns money. And don't worry about the bride-price—" Haider was already shaking his head, looking down, the firelight casting shadows on his conflicted face.

"Thank you," he said, to cut her off. Even when he was killing Kathmiya, Haider was compassionate. He knew she wanted this over and was trying to end it.

But he didn't manage to stop Ali from saying, "Abdul will not marry Kathmiya."

Kathmiya burned. Her father knew all along, and he still set up this charade of a dinner.

Tears as hot as the tea she had just served stung Kathmiya's eyes as she walked outside. They wet the front of her best dress, the one that Jamila had just that day said made her look pretty.

She was too angry at first to listen to her mother and Uncle Haider whispering outside, on the other side of the hut. But slowly, she tuned in to their conversation over the sound of the nocturnal marsh insects.

"You of all people should help," Jamila was scolding.

"I couldn't," Haider answered. "He knows."

Knows what? Kathmiya held still. "He" must be Ali, but what he knew she couldn't guess.

"Look at it this way," Uncle Haider said to Jamila. "I had right of first refusal, and now that I've turned you down there are even more options."

"How can you say that?" Jamila pleaded softly. Kathmiya felt like she was walking on a narrow bridge over a deep river. If she could just grab hold of what she did to make her father so angry, she might reach the other side.

Gathering her courage, she edged out of the darkness and faced her mother and uncle. "What does he know?" she asked. "What did I do?"

Haider started. "Go back inside," he said, but so kindly, so gently, Kathmiya had to obey. She turned to leave.

"Your life is blessed," Jamila called after her.

"She's right," Haider agreed, but Kathmiya just shook her head and retreated.

Chapter XXIV

A large copper sign engraved with the seal of the government of Iraq greeted Omar and Shafiq when they got to the Basra Electricity Department. From a crown at the top hung two unfurling curtains that framed a standing lion on the left and a standing horse on the right. Together they flanked the Tigris and Euphrates rivers flowing down both sides of a palm tree.

"I'm not sure this is such a good plan." Omar was hanging back, as though that government seal could read through their subterfuge.

"We've been over this a hundred times," Shafiq said. "And besides, it's your plan. So let's go." Some people drank wine for courage; Shafiq had Omar.

"I'm thinking we need a little more time to prepare," Omar said, shrinking into the slender shadow of a palm tree.

Shafiq was always the timid one, so he knew this routine. *More time* meant "I'm chicken, let's forget it." "What are you saying?" he asked. "We're here, let's go."

"Look." Omar pulled Shafiq toward him, as though the tree's skinny shadow might hide them both. "This is life we're talking about, not some way to get pocket money for a Ping-Pong ball. Think about it. People's futures."

Nothing had ever given Omar one second's pause about diving into any caper until now. "So you're afraid?" Shafiq challenged.

"You said Marcelle will be ruined if the engagement is called off. I don't want to be the reason for that."

"First, I didn't say that, my mother did," Shafiq argued, stepping out of the shadow. "Second, it's not that Marcelle *will* be ruined, she *might* be ruined." He turned toward the door with its government seal. "And third," he said, looking over his shoulder as he headed for the entrance. "She will definitely be ruined if he's a liar, so we'd better find out now."

It was a bluff, going in alone, but Omar didn't follow.

Which left Shafiq with nothing but their plan.

He rehearsed it in his mind as he passed the noisy generators, shuffled across a wooden floor littered with wires, and climbed a staircase toward offices where the men wore suits.

Omar should have been there. Shafiq's usual role was just to boost the charade as a supporting actor. But before he was ready, the understudy was in the lead.

"Excuse me, sir," he began when he arrived at the large corner office where the manager sat behind a polished mahogany desk. And then it all flooded out—not the pre-planned lie about seeking a job at the plant, but the simple truth. About how his sister was supposed to marry someone employed there. About how the family needed to know if his credentials were real. And even the names. "She's Marcelle Soufayr," Shafiq said. "And he's Moshe Khabazza."

It was suddenly too late to avoid meddling in their lives.

But it worked.

"Say hello to success," Shafiq told Omar outside.

"What do you mean?" Omar bounced out of the shadow with his grin back on. "You found out the truth?"

Shafiq had done it all on his own, and he was going to make Omar pay for not going in. So he described the insides of the building, the walk up to the office, the man's shirt and tie, and even the pictures on the walls—"the king of Iraq and a map of the province"—before getting to the point.

"Wow," said Omar when Shafiq was through. "From now on you're the mastermind."

Unless, Shafiq thought, *it all goes to rot.*

Two days later, when the letter came from the Basra Electricity Department, there was that national emblem again.

The teens tumbled over each other reading it. "Moshe never even went to university!" Omar said.

"Just some vocational school in Bombay." Shafiq felt a looming sense of dread. Now they would have to actually do something.

"Looks like he just finished 'one year of a two-year power generation program' back in 'thirty-six," Omar said scornfully.

"Half the requirement."

" 'Moshe Khabazza is employed as an assistant technician at a salary of twelve *dinars* per month,' " Omar read.

"Not a bad living, but he told my parents he earns fifty," said Shafiq, wondering, *What am I going to tell them?*

His brothers were properly awed by the letter and its fancy, official-looking seal. But their father just crumpled it up on the spot.

"What did you do that for?" Shafiq asked. "That was proof Moshe's a liar."

"It was one of the finest universities in India," Naji joked, "if only he had really gone there."

"Enough," Roobain said, leaving the paper on the table and walking out.

Naji picked up the crumpled ball and started tossing it around randomly. Something like Marcelle's fate.

Shafiq dragged himself out to report the news. "I guess we messed up," Omar said, once they were safely inside his living room.

"I messed up," Shafiq said, dropping his body into the family's burgundy couch. "You tried to stop me."

"Yeah, but when it worked, you know, I guess I started hoping . . ."

Omar never finished the sentence. And Shafiq didn't ask. He had his own futile hopes and couldn't take on any more.

Chapter XXV

Arriving at the rooftop, where he knew Kathmiya would be folding clean sheets, Shafiq was surprised to find her looking disheveled. Her bouncy hair was matted, her large eyes were half closed, and distress held her smile down. "Is it your husband?" he asked.

Kathmiya glared. Shafiq, though, smiled, if only secretly. Something was definitely wrong—with the engagement.

"I guess you just seem . . . distracted?"

"Can we focus on the writing?" she asked, sharp as the pencil he'd given her.

Shafiq was ready with a lesson. "What did I tell you about *alef*?"

"Easy," she said. "A stick going up. Like the number one. I know that already."

"Okay, but what if *alef* is at the end of a word?"

Kathmiya thought. It definitely looked as though she was puzzling about more than her letters. Those great eyes became heavy again, and she took in a sharp breath. When she noticed him watching her, she shot out, "Just show me, okay?"

"When you end a word in *alef*, curve it around like a flag," he said. "And then sing the national anthem," he joked.

She didn't laugh.

Shafiq took a deep breath and scratched an *alef* on the lined paper he'd given her. By now it was filled with her exercises. The penmanship was deliberate, but somehow it still looked different from real writing, as though the scattered letters would never connect.

She copied his *alef*. Over and over.

Maybe the guy called it off. But what man in his right mind would not want to marry her? Maybe she was considered too poor. But her beauty is worth more than all the wealth in the Baghdad Central Bank. Maybe I'll be lucky, but even if it ends for them, there is no beginning for us.

"That's it," he said. "You've totally got it."

But she wasn't encouraged. "How long until I get the whole thing—the whole language?"

Shafiq shrugged. "You're so smart. Really soon."

Kathmiya rolled this information around like a pearl, as though she were checking to see if it was real. Maybe she decided it was, or maybe she was just testing him, but finally she asked, "Can I show you something?"

This is it, he thought dramatically. *She's either going to tell me good-bye or tell me she's free.*

They climbed down from the roof and walked to the small maid's-quarters end of the hallway. Shafiq held his breath, filled with a monumental sense of possibility.

"Look," she said.

As soon as she brought out the picture book, he nearly laughed at his own delusion. This wasn't a touching farewell or an announcement pregnant with possibility; this was an embarrassing little trinket.

At least to him it was. But when he took it from her, she snapped "Careful!" and he could tell that silly though it might be, she thought this book was something special.

"Well, I guess I'll have to start teaching you English," he joked.

Just a tossed-off comment, but it drew Kathmiya up, opened her eyes wide. "You mean you can read this?"

"Hey, I'm not the best, but if you let me open it—"

She wouldn't. Kathmiya turned the pages while Shafiq scanned the words. "It's about this girl. She's called Sally."

Kathmiya looked disappointed, who knew why. Shafiq tried to mine some gem from the text that might excite her. He settled on, "Sally is feeding these animals at her uncle's farm."

Suddenly Kathmiya was brooding again.

"Hey, don't worry, it's just a little story," he said. "I mean, I know you really like this book, but—"

"It's not the book," she fumed. "It's the uncle."

"Yours?" Shafiq tried to picture her family.

"He was supposed to make a match for me but now that's not going to happen."

Finally, some news.

Shafiq had two choices, leave her hurting to keep his nonexistent chances open, or try to help. "What about a matchmaker?"

"Well, yes!" Kathmiya brightened. "I can write an *alef*. I know practically all my letters, ten times more than anyone else back home. So what is going to stop me from going to a matchmaker?"

Shafiq had just shown her the door, and she was ready to walk out.

Chapter XXVI

The next time she went home, Kathmiya was determined to suggest going to the matchmaker. But the conditions were difficult; Fatimah was pretending to be weaving straw but really hoping for more of the drama that had been brewing for the past month.

"Why don't you check the sheets, see if they are dry?" Kathmiya suggested.

"You do it," her sister insisted.

"I washed them," Kathmiya countered.

There was an insidious little pause. "Okay, well, I'll go." Fatimah made too much of a show of walking out of the house to fool Kathmiya into thinking she was safe, but she had to use this sliver of a moment to press her parents for some action.

"Since last month with, you know . . . Uncle Haider and everything, I've been thinking," Kathmiya said. Ali ignored her. She hadn't bothered to pour him liquor because she was going forward whether he agreed or not.

"Yes, my sweet, but let's give it time." Jamila tried to put her off.

"Let's not. Let's just go to a matchmaker. Much more efficient, don't you think?"

Ali was startled by her directness, but not enough to go along. "No." He shook his lolling head on the grass-stuffed pillow where it lay.

"Please?" Kathmiya tried.

Ali didn't bother answering. "Your father said 'no,'" Jamila reported uselessly.

In came Fatimah. "No to what?"

"Nothing." Kathmiya didn't have to lose the fight and her pride.

"She wanted to go to a matchmaker," Ali revealed.

"Is that so?" Fatimah asked, looking Kathmiya up and down. "Well, I think it's a fantastic idea."

Kathmiya waited for the blow, but when it came, it wasn't that tough to endure. "I'm tired of everyone asking why my sister is single and working," Fatimah said. "It makes us look bad. People talk. She might not get the best husband around, but at least she won't be the subject of so many nasty rumors."

Ali could never say no to his older daughter. And once he agreed to visit the nearest matchmaker, Kathimya didn't care.

When they approached the large thatched tent the following day, hope was starting to thump a loud back-beat in her heart.

The old matchmaker, covered in black, peered at them. "What are you doing here, Sayed Ali?" she said, her astigmatic eyes shifting back and forth.

"Yes, well," he said feebly.

Kathmiya could feel the weight that dragged down his efforts on her behalf until they were stone dead.

Like a person dumping water from a sinking boat, she started unloading some of her higher hopes. *It doesn't have to be a sheikh; any dung collector will do,* she thought desperately.

"I am afraid your second daughter will be very difficult to match," the old woman croaked. Kathmiya felt that familiar pounding in her heart. Like with Haider. Like it wasn't bad enough that her circumstances were terrible—there had to be some mysterious reason that everyone knew except for her, something that made her smell bad, look awful, somehow repulse all good luck and even normal prosaic accomplishments.

But this was more serious than with Uncle Haider. Because as bad as Kathmiya felt, Jamila looked worse. Threatened, as though someone were scraping a blade against her neck.

The three adults, Kathmiya realized, were communicating without speaking. A raised eyebrow from the matchmaker. A nod toward Jamila from Ali. And then a look down—was it shame? contrition? regret?—from Jamila.

But Kathmiya's mother tried to carry on the transaction as normal. "She is a great beauty, good around the house, very devoted and totally pure," she trilled.

"True, she is beautiful—" said the matchmaker. Kathmiya wished she had one of her balled-up, stinking rags to throw in the woman's face, but she clenched her teeth against her anger.

Smile.

Look Interested and Attentive.

Sit Gracefully.

Charm is Key.

"—no one disputes that. But there is a feeling around here—"

Now there was a dead certainty, like the way thunderclaps always portend rain, that the mystery was about to unlock, right then.

"—that her beauty might carry some danger," the matchmaker said.

Danger? Kathmiya had always known she was unlucky, but dangerous? Was she diseased?

"The danger," continued the old woman, "of having—"

"That's enough," shouted Jamila, loud enough to cut off the answer to that perplexing, defeating question: Why?

Besides disease, the only way Kathmiya could be so unmarriageable was if she were impure. But she wasn't. She knew it, and even if they were wrong and they thought she was, they would have killed her a long time ago. Impure girls were disposed of with a rock to the skull.

And even if they had thought she was impure and miraculously let her live, that still wouldn't explain how she would be a danger to anyone but herself.

Jamila had whipped around and was racing out through the small open entrance of the thatched hut, where the sun poured in too cheerfully. Ali followed right behind her. But Kathmiya stayed behind.

Charm was Dead.

"What do you mean, danger?"

"Oh, you'll find out soon enough," taunted the matchmaker.

"Tell me!" Kathmiya commanded.

"Or maybe you never will, which is all for the best, but then you won't be married."

Kathmiya knew she would get nothing but riddles from this wicked purveyor of dreams.

When she got outside, though, she did catch a clue.

"How long has she known?" Jamila was asking.

"Known what?" Kathmiya grilled.

Jamila put her arms around her daughter and sent Ali off. "Go." It was impossible that a woman should talk to her husband like that, but Ali, hobbled by alcoholism and the hidden devils that inspired it, was barely a man, and retreated.

Kathmiya had never paid much attention to the evil eye, but suddenly she was terrified of it. "Do I have the *jinn*?" she asked, gasping out a tearless, dry sob.

"It is not because you are cursed," said Jamila, "but because you are blessed."

What a ridiculous contradiction. But when Kathmiya looked up, she saw a stern conviction in Jamila's eyes. "Really?" she asked. Against Kathmiya's better judgment, her tense body was starting to relax.

"Really." Jamila sounded so sure.

On one side was life in Basra. Kathmiya could despair and go back there. But on the other side were the wonders of the marshes, the water that cleaned everything, the tall grass, the bounty. Her mother's faith. Hope.

"But why did she say I was—"

"I tell you what," said Jamila, looking as worn as the bottom of Kathmiya's only shoes. "I promise you I'll find you a husband if you swear to me . . ."

"Anything!"

". . . that you'll forget about today and that whole conversation."

Kathmiya would always wonder. She might even try to find out. But she wouldn't tell her mother. "I promise."

Chapter XXVII

S hafiq was hoping to play backgammon with one of his brothers, but they were too busy arguing.

"We can change all the small-minded prejudice, unite the country," Naji was saying.

"Is that so, *rafiq*?" Ezra asked sarcastically. Shafiq remembered the word: "comrade."

"The Communist movement has room for all Iraqis—Jews, yes, but also Christians and Muslims and everyone else, from Armenian refugees to the grand-children of Turks." Naji sounded more in love than when he'd ever talked about a girl.

But Shafiq felt unmoored. Communism was illegal. At school they were taught that if they joined the move-ment, the police would lock them up and torture them. Naji was strong, but the prison guards had guns.

"The Zionist movement is the only one where you will never be in the minority," Ezra said.

"What's your point?" Naji asked, cool as the evening breeze. "I don't need a majority—I want a plurality for my country."

"Until your country attacks your people. Again. When that happens you'll be glad some of us organized to defend the Jews," Ezra persisted. "The Zionist movement is about that and so much more."

Zionism. That philosophy that Salim was always denouncing as a danger to the Jews of Iraq.

"Ezra, religion is separating us," Naji pushed back. "Communism can bring us together; Muslims, Jews and Christians in a new Iraq where religion doesn't matter. Then we'll all be equal."

It sounded perfect, except for the parts Naji didn't mention, like being beaten senseless by the police.

"You completely missed the point," said Ezra. "Shafiq, you have to ask yourself, am I an Iraqi who happens to be Jewish? Or a Jew who happens to live in Iraq?"

Shafiq didn't answer. What he really wanted to be was a man of honor, true to his whole heritage. If only being an Arabic Jew weren't splitting him in half, and dividing his family in the process.

There was nothing honorable about Shafiq's glee when he saw Kathmiya next at Marcelle's wedding and realized she was too miserable to be engaged and on her way to a new life without him.

It wasn't that she watched the bride with envy; it was the way she held Shafiq's niece Aziza so close, as though only the simplicity of a child could comfort her in this impossibly complicated world.

After the ceremony, Shafiq's family paid respects to the rabbi, who took the opportunity to lecture them. "Our ceremonies unite us, they strengthen our community, and they protect us from the pollution of the outside world," he intoned.

Shafiq took the measure of his family. The new groom had wormed out of this little formality, but even without Moshe, Marcelle was glowing. Salim just paced. Ezra nodded while Naji shifted against the natural soccer instincts that seemed to always urge him to toss something in the air.

"Today we see many Jewish families trying to 'modernize' by sending their girls to French schools," the rabbi went on. "But the people running them are not Jewish, and they look down on our customs."

Shafiq's parents had sent Marcelle to the French *Alliance* school, but they didn't seem bothered by the old man's approbation.

"Never be fooled. We must preserve our culture or we perish," the rabbi warned.

Marcelle was admiring her new ring. Salim and Naji had wandered away. Shafiq took a cue and sidled off, hoping to confirm his happy suspicion about Kathmiya's sadness.

He found her sitting on the ground outside the reception hall with Aziza, who was crawling around.

"Moshe's a rotten guy," Shafiq said.

"Yeah, maybe they'll be miserable," Kathmiya replied.

He liked her stinging tone. "Who needs marriage, right?" he asked. "Stupid matchmakers don't know anything."

It was as obvious as the attraction pulsing between them that Kathmiya had gotten nowhere with hers.

"I did realize one thing, though," she said after a pause.

"From the old lady?" he asked, grabbing Aziza while she wandered away and switching her direction so she crawled toward Kathmiya.

"That matchmaker has never been married, you know? And I looked at her lonely little hut and the carpet she wore for a dress and the way her ankles were thick like tree trunks and I decided, whatever happens, I'd better find someone, because I don't want to end up like that."

In his mind, Shafiq dressed Kathmiya in a carpet and covered her legs in bark, but no luck, he still wanted to kiss her.

"You could marry anyone you want," he whispered.

"Oh, please." She rolled her eyes. And he was out of arguments, because he knew that no matter how much he might want to marry her, kismet had other ideas.

It took only one week for Moshe to come charging into the Soufayr home ranting about a new business and demanding that Roobain loan him five hundred *dinars.*

"We're going to be rich," he'd said at first.

"Take it slow, my brother," Naji replied. "There's more to life than money."

But Moshe pressed on about "a ship . . . a business . . . moving goods across the river . . . over to Iran and back."

"Like hashish and black-market carpets?" Ezra taunted, and Moshe wasn't even smart enough to deny that he had illegal trading in mind. He just plowed ahead, trying to excavate their father's pockets for cash.

"I'll give you a gift," Roobain finally said. "But I'm not into investments."

He offered fifty *dinars*: bribe money to get rid of the pest.

Moshe looked stunned, like he'd been slapped in the face instead of promised enough money to retire for four months, and started murmuring to himself about business, money and professionalism. The family stared.

"Say something!" Shafiq whispered to Naji, the only one with the good nature to burst any tension with laughter.

"Hey, I'll give you a million *dinars* to let it go," Naji tried, but he was more bitter than funny.

"Don't you know I graduated top in my class from one of the best . . ." Moshe began.

Shafiq couldn't take it. "Stop lying," he mumbled.

"Oh, you want the truth?" Moshe spat. "Are you ready for it? Your. Mother. Is. A. Filthy. Whore."

"Out," Roobain said with quiet fury, pressing his fists together until they turned white.

"You are stupid not to appreciate this business opportunity," Moshe shouted, backing out through the arched open doorway.

"Leave," Naji commanded.

"Now," Ezra added.

"Or else," Shafiq put in, hoping Marcelle would finally be free but suspecting she would stand by her corrupt husband.

He thought of the Jewish girls who ran off with Muslim boys and broke their families apart. They always seemed possessed by some crazy idea bigger than the tribe, which was already the biggest idea of all, the one organizing principle everyone understood.

Marcelle was like that, but her crazy idea was really, really small.

She could at least run off with a Muslim boy, one who was good. One whom we know and trust. One who was—

But Shafiq didn't follow the thought. Like an anchor, it led straight down to the darkest depths.

Chapter XXVIII

"In the Name of Allah, the Merciful and Compassionate."

The writing was uncertain, but it was hers. Kathmiya began her literate life the way any Muslim should, by invoking the name of God.

Next she wrote her name, which was also the name of one of the holiest Shi'a mosques in Baghdad.

Then she wrote, "Aziza." Her little bundle.

Finally she wrote, "Thank you, Shafiq."

The paper nestled in her pocket the next time she went home to the marshes. The blows she suffered there were never physical, so its flimsiness was not a failing. They were strikes against her worth, and literacy was her smashingly powerful weapon to fight back.

"How is everyone?" she asked her sister.

Fatimah was carrying her youngest, a jumpy girl who always seemed to bounce away from her. When Kathmiya brushed the toddler's arm, she reached up.

"I guess she remembers you, even though you're gone most of the time," Fatimah said.

The insults were getting boring. Kathmiya almost wished her sister could come up with a new attack. Every chance she got, Fatimah reminded Kathmiya that she lived in the city, and Kathmiya fought back by flaunting her sophistication and pretending she preferred life there. The crowded streets, foods like watermelon, music on the radio . . . Kathmiya held up these shiny little trinkets, trying to deflect the fact that only life in the marshes was truly brilliant.

But now she had new tricks. She was beginning to connect the words on signs with the goods in stores. Shafiq would draw pictures, intentionally poor renderings of things she would never guess except that he wrote the words underneath: dam, lamb, swam. Words and pictures she could match. And then letters and words. The little girl Sally and her uncle's farm might always be a mystery. But then again, maybe Kathmiya would unlock it someday.

"I think," she began, trying to calm her jumpy little niece, "your life is so much better than mine."

Fatimah didn't take the bait so easily. "Well that's a first! You, who are always talking about how much fun you have in the city, eating weird desserts and making money."

"Yeah," Kathmiya said, and the words slid out like gelatin off a spoon, "but I need to get married, have children. You know, it's scary."

Fatimah was enjoying this. It was obvious from the way she leaned in, raised her eyebrows, and said, "Tell me what you mean. I don't understand."

Kathmiya's histrionics were impressive. Partly she wanted to satisfy Fatimah's thirst for dominance, but mostly she was happy to finally get it all off her chest. ". . . living in the maid's quarters where no one talks to me, feeling like I'm getting too old to ever marry, wondering what I did to deserve this . . ."

It felt like a burden was lifted—but a protective shield was also gone.

Except one last bit of armor. There was still the reading and writing. She hadn't told Fatimah about that, and even if she did, it would still be hers—not so much the ability to read but the confidence that came from confronting such a mass of tangled confusion and straightening it out in her head.

"Well," Fatimah said. She took the girl back and let her scamper off. Then she put a hand over her sister's. "I tried, I really did."

That was unexpected. "Tried what?"

"To find you a husband. I mean, I think I found one, he's interested, but our parents said no."

"Our father, you mean."

"Actually," Fatimah said, "it was our mother."

Kathmiya stared. A lifetime of rivalry with Fatimah had taught her to see through a bluff. But this wasn't one. Jamila was standing in her daughter's way.

Instead of confronting her mother with tears dripping off of her lonely chin, Kathmiya asked Fatimah for the name of the potential mate-for-life-and-escape-to-stability, paid a local boy two mesh bags of sugar-coated almonds to row them over, and went straight to the home of one Baaqir Zain.

"Tell me everything you know about him," Kathmiya asked her sister as they glided across the water. She'd had to bring Fatimah's husband along too, for safety and cover. Even in her willful rebelliousness, Kathmiya wasn't reckless enough to destroy her already bruised reputation.

"Rich," Fatimah said.

When her husband saw Kathmiya's eyes widen in skeptical surprise, he confirmed this. "Wealthy, that one."

The sisters had almost grown . . . if not close, at least civil since Kathmiya's heart-rending confession.

"Are you wondering why he would want to marry you?" Fatimah asked. That was much gentler than she might have put it before, but it still stung. Mostly because Kathmiya really was wondering.

"Guess he has good taste," she replied, lapsing back into her defensive bravado.

"Guess so," Fatimah said sweetly. Now that was alarming.

They got out in front of one of those impressively sturdy estates, three separate reed homes grouped around a fire pit. The sisters waited while Fatimah's husband went in to make the introductions.

"Baaqir Zain," Kathmiya repeated with fixed determination.

"At least if you marry him," Fatimah suggested in that undermining way she had perfected over a lifetime of petty jealousy, "that will stop the rumors . . ."

"Will you drop it?" Kathmiya mumbled.

". . . that you are too old to marry and you never will, that you were sent to the city because that was the only way to get some use out of you, that you might carry the danger of—"

"Just stop," Kathmiya said, trying to regain her composure, trying to put on that gracious face that would win her a home, trying so hard to be likeable she forgot all about her own likes.

Until Baaqir Zain came out to see her. Old like a wrinkled turtle. Worse than that, he was creepy, pinching her arms and shoulders and touching her face.

"Hey," she started, pulling back before his reptilian paw got any closer.

"If I take another wife I have to make sure she's good," he said, smile all gummy and wet.

So other women endured this. Kathmiya wanted to talk to them. For the home, she'd take it. But the husband . . . "Where are they?" she asked.

"She has questions," he said to Fatimah's husband. "But it's okay."

"Where are your other wives?" Kathmiya remembered that eerie feeling during the riots—an absence of women. And now again. Besides Fatimah, she felt there was no other female in the whole area.

"She might as well know," Baaqir Zain said to Fatimah's husband. "She might as well hear this." He turned to Kathmiya. "All of them were bad and so they're gone. One was barren, one was greedy, two lost all their feminine charms and my last—she was just useless. Anyway, you know the law . . ."

Gone?

". . . I'm entitled to a full refund on the bride-price if I send the girl back."

Not dead at least, but out there, somewhere, in that terrible land of women who had been married and then abandoned.

One level of hell below Kathmiya's own station in life.

"We're leaving," she told the canoe boy, and stepped in, not bothering to check whether Fatimah and her husband would follow.

"Can I keep it?" Shafiq asked Kathmiya when he saw the paper she had written.

"Sure." She could always write more. Words would come to her. Letters would form on the page. Sentences would emerge. And maybe meaning would follow.

Chapter XXIX

Shafiq had nothing but disgust for Marcelle as she stood by her greedy husband. That and guilt for not having insisted on stopping the wedding when he and Omar suspected and then confirmed and even proved what a liar Moshe was.

Shafiq could live with losing Marcelle until she came to her senses; he didn't even want to see her before then. But he felt stabbed when he thought about the sincerity of his parents handing over a dowry of family jewelry that Moshe was going to recklessly sell off to fund his greedy scheme.

And Shafiq felt, along with the rest of his family, devastated when he saw his mother mortifying her own flesh every chance she could as penance for provoking the insult that tore her youngest daughter from her embrace.

She beat herself and cried until she fell asleep. Shafiq thought of all the times his mother used to put salt in his pockets for good luck before he left for school. The way she would talk about the *jinn* like it was a real force of nature, as ubiquitous and burning as the sun. And how peaceful and content she looked when she was putting a little amulet on a baby for good luck.

"How about that rabbi?" he whispered to his brothers while their mother slept.

Ezra started nodding before he even knew what Shafiq meant. Naji seemed to hesitate until Shafiq pointed out that Reema wasn't in line to join the young Communists anyway.

"We're going back to see the rabbi," Shafiq informed his mother later that afternoon. He would have rather listened to Kathmiya telling Aziza stories about princesses all afternoon than hear the rabbi's droning lectures about customs and traditions, but if that would drag Reema out of her delirium, he had to try.

Shafiq leaned back on a pillow on the floor, resting his feet on the bare brick wall and looking up at the blank ceiling, trying to recreate times he'd spent with Kathmiya: watching her study, reading her note, the word "Shafiq" in her handwriting.

Reema sat at the rabbi's feet while he rattled on about lost Jewish traditions.

"Turmoil in the outside world, but not to worry—our ways can save our people."

Shafiq tried to ignore the conversation, but he couldn't help but notice how rapt his mother was, listening to the rabbi's elaborate instructions.

"Never sweep after sunset," the old man said as though he were teaching hard science instead of delving into the realm of speculation and mystery. "It will disturb the jealous spirits."

"Perfumes harm children," he rasped in a voice as coarse as his beard. "If you find clothing from a dead criminal, take it immediately."

Good one, Shafiq thought, imagining raiding the corpses of thieves with Omar.

"That always brings luck. Especially if it comes from the left side."

It was going to be some scavenger hunt in the graveyard.

"Learn," the rabbi continued in that voice meant for fifty people even if he was just talking to one, "from our Muslim and Christian brothers, for they share many of our powerful traditions that must be respected and preserved."

He opened a small wooden drawer and pulled out an amulet made from bits of blue china and straw. "This is very powerful for conflict in the family," he said. When he gave it to Reema, she radiated joy.

"Against the *jinn*?" Shafiq's mother's voice revealed the naked, pathetic hope that Marcelle's estrangement came down to some evil force that could be conquered with a broken-off piece of blue china.

If only.

Walking out, they passed a government building with a large, handwritten announcement scrawled on the wall above a water tank.

Shafiq read it once, and then again and again.

The first time he understood completely. The second time was for confirmation. And once more, just to exult, he went over each word.

GERMANY SURRENDERS UNCONDITIONALLY

The rabid dog was dead.

When Shafiq told his mother, she broke into a wide, irrational smile and he knew she thought the rabbi had ended the war.

"See?" she said, pointing down at her skirt. Sure enough, she was turning out pockets full of salt.

The next day, as if by magic, Moshe showed up at the house.

But it was some kind of cursed spell.

He looked more unraveled than ever, his stringy hair separated into gritty strands, his fake-rich suit obviously borrowed, his tie stained.

"Thank Allah you're back!" Reema said. "Where's Marcelle?"

"She doesn't want to see you," he replied with sadistic glee. Before Reema could start to hit herself again, he added grandly, "Oh, I tried. I told her, 'You only have one set of parents in life. You'll feel nothing but regret when they die.'"

"Inheritance," Ezra whispered, and Shafiq nodded.

"What do you want?" Naji asked, stepping in front of Moshe like a goalie blocking the net.

"You are always welcome," Roobain said, "but no insults."

"Except you are wrong about that—I never insulted you. I just wanted to give you a great chance to invest in my business." Moshe picked up where he'd left off with an alarming lack of self-awareness. Shafiq marveled at his disconnection from the rest of the world. Him and Reema, but at least she was placid, harmless.

"I don't want a piece of your business," Roobain said. "Let's not talk about this anymore."

"Oh, I don't know," Moshe sang brightly. "You wouldn't really want to make me angry."

"No, you're my daughter's husband. I want you to be happy. But is that something I have to pay for?"

"Well, let me put it this way," said Moshe, working up to a foam. "Let me just say it straight. Your son there, Naji, well he's crazy getting involved in Communist activities. If the government finds out, they'll hang him. And, oh yeah, angry people don't keep secrets. But a rich businessman might."

Shafiq watched the color drain from Naji's ruddy face. His parents stared, trying to absorb the shock. They all understood Moshe's meaning.

It amounted to a death threat.

As soon as Moshe left, Naji broke the silence. "Don't ask. The less you know the better. Just please trust me: I never wanted to cause you any trouble. I believe in the equality of all people. There's nothing criminal about that."

The sun seemed too bright, like it would cast a light on Naji and get him thrown to the dogs of jail . . . and not any prison, but the one where they reserved the truly brutal treatment for political types accused of crimes against the state.

Shafiq was furious. With that dreamy, risky, impulsive choice, Naji had handed Moshe the keys to the cell where they ruined altruistic young lives.

"I am sure you have done nothing illegal," Roobain said. "We"—the Jews, they all knew who he meant—"never break the laws of our country."

"Our country?" Ezra said quietly.

What about it? Shafiq wanted to scream. *Of course it's our country.*

Naji looked down. Shafiq suddenly choked on an outflow of love for his second brother, the one with the roped-up muscles and ready laugh and cures for the world. "Naji," he said with the last drop of his true boy sweetness, "we understand."

The look in Naji's eyes changed. Fear was gone. And it took his inhibitions when it left.

"At our meetings," he said to Shafiq, as though only this young, pure soul could understand, "we talk about being revolutionaries. We want to build an ideal society. But when do you get the chance to actually do that? When you give up what you really love for the cause?"

Something was wrong. His eyes didn't look normal. Moshe was infected by some garden-variety greed, but Naji was completely overtaken, and he was trying to engulf Shafiq too.

"I'm proud to be a Communist. It is the only way out of the materialism of this world. I'm sorry you had to hear it from Moshe, but I can't compromise my beliefs—"

"Naji!" Ezra had never sounded so uncertain or so disturbed.

"Moshe will hold this over our heads no matter how much money you give him. You'll owe him your life savings until I leave the Communist party. And even if I quit today, he can still tell the government that I was a member. They don't need much evidence to lock me up, or worse."

Reema had started reciting some superstitious prayer, scratching around at her sides as though she were looking for blue china or salt or the left cuff of a dead criminal.

"So," Naji said, shining with an external glow, as though he were illuminated by someone else's light, "I have to go."

"You are not going anywhere." Roobain tried to state this as a fact, but it sounded more like he was pleading.

"This is blackmail," Ezra pointed out.

"Naji, I don't care if we lose all our savings to Moshe . . . how can you go? Where are you going?" Shafiq was desperate to break the spell.

"Stop worrying. I'm smarter than Moshe. I'm not going forever, just until the rest of society comes to realize that this is the future for Iraq. Then I'll be back. Meanwhile, Moshe can't hurt me, or any of you."

"You can't run because of him," Roobain spoke quickly, trying to dam the flood of Naji's raging fanaticism.

The fervor looked so celestial, Shafiq almost envied Naji's rapture. He might have followed Naji underground, to a secret Communist meeting, to the Soviet Union, to wherever he was going to build this perfect world—but then Shafiq saw his parents looking devastated as a second branch broke off the battered family tree.

Roobain appeared feeble, opening his mouth to speak and then coughing on his own dry spit. And Reema just looked unhinged.

"I'm not running because of Moshe," Naji said calmly. "I'm following my true path. He's just an excuse to get me there. For the sake of the family and for Iraq."

"I don't care about Moshe." Roobain was begging. "I care about you. Shafiq's right, I'll find five hundred *dinars* for him. I'll pay whatever it takes."

"No." Naji was firm in body and mind.

Shafiq realized that Moshe was not even the danger anymore; it was this outsized cause that had stolen his brother's soul.

Naji packed a few shirts and slacks into a small rucksack while Ezra tried to stop him. "You are killing your mother. Is that how you save the world?"

"You'll understand someday," Naji replied, so oddly serene.

"The Communists will never protect us if we suffer another attack. You know as well as I do that the police did nothing during the riots—they even participated in the killing. Killing and injuring and robbery and all kinds of other crimes against our people, just because we're Jewish—"

"And it was the Muslims who saved us—our brothers! Isolating yourself from the rest of Iraq instead of trying to build an ideal society—is that what you want?" Naji asked, his olive skin glistening not with sweat but conviction.

"I don't want to be isolated, I want to be free to defend myself if I'm attacked. You know," Ezra tried, "it's completely selfish to expect the Kurds and other good people to protect us. We have to be prepared."

"By preparing for a confrontation you are creating the conditions to engender one," Naji declared.

Shafiq, overwhelmed by powerlessness and gloom, didn't try fancy arguments based on some geopolitical logic—he just begged. "Don't go, Naji," he said, hugging his brother's strong chest. "Please. We need you. We'll miss you."

"I'll be back, probably sooner than you think. And anyway, if you ever really have to find me, just ask at *Al-Wattan* café."

Shafiq looked into his brother's eyes and found a measure of reassurance when Naji nodded with a lively smile.

Okay. It will be okay. Naji might be dreaming of going to Moscow for training, but as long as he could be found through *Al-Wattan* café, he'd never be out of reach.

Al-Wattan. It meant "The Nation." Everyone loved Iraq but no one knew how to help her.

It only took one day turning to night before they knew Naji was really gone, maybe already very far. And when Ezra went to the café, he came back defeated. "They said we'll hear from him in time. And they tried to recruit me to their misguided movement."

"Then," Roobain said, "I don't want you going back. I've lost too much already. We wait for Naji and in the meantime don't get mixed up in this business."

"I'll never buy their arguments," Ezra said.

"Shafiq." Roobain took him by the shoulders. "Never go there. Ever."

Naji's departure left more than an empty stretch of life ahead without him. It was murderous, but Shafiq kept telling himself there was an ending where he'd find Naji and they'd be together again, either in an ideal world or a corrupt one, where they could play soccer and laugh about movies.

But his brother's absence also created a gaping distance between Shafiq and everyone who didn't know the truth, including Omar. The official story was that Naji had headed to school in Lebanon, and Shafiq wasn't going to expose his best friend to the truth and endanger him in the process, so their conversation stayed superficial and dull.

It was as if Naji had rejected his own family for some worthless, diseased whore.

The more Shafiq thought about it, the more furious he was that even in self-destruction, Naji was easy and graceful. He hated that Naji was so talented and resourceful that he could leave behind his whole life in one stroke. If only he had been more selfish, less good, less brilliant even, he might not have pulled it off. But Naji was Naji, and everything Shafiq loved and admired about his favorite brother had been used in the service of something so destructive the only comfort he could salvage was rage.

Chapter XXX

Kathmiya might be just a single girl, but she was learning to think like a woman. And she knew well enough that Shafiq was relieved that day she had told him the old marriage broker didn't come through with a match. She saw two expressions from most people in the world: pity in the marshes, and pity in the city. But Shafiq—she could make him admire and laugh and wonder and worry.

Nearly all of her clothes had washed out colors like dark gray and pale black, but when she pushed around a teenaged boy's emotions she felt for a second like they were threaded with gold.

"My sister found a husband for me, finally," she told Shafiq the next time Leah brought her to his house. Lying forced Kathmiya to strain against images of the

man-turtle in her mind. The hardest part was forgetting his slippery hand against her skin.

"That's nice," Shafiq said. "I hope he's good."

"There could be, you know . . . others, so it's still
being decided," Kathmiya said, trying to draw out the
charade, but Shafiq's once-responsive moods had gone
limp.

"You need the security, right?" he asked. "That's important. Listen to your sister. Keep close to the family."

He was completely impassive. It was enough to make
her long for pity. "Won't you miss me?"

Shafiq shrugged. "You can write me a message."

That sentence, just months or even weeks before,
would have elevated Kathmiya to the tops of the heavens, but now it sounded dismissive. "So where do I send
it?" she challenged.

"My friend and I used to do this all the time," he said,
walking over to a crevice in the back wall. "I'll go first."

After jotting down a few words on a scrap of paper,
he folded it up and stuck it in the hole. She went along
and pulled it out. " 'Write me, not a kaf—' " She didn't
much like the game and didn't feel like puzzling out
the meaning.

"Write me messages, don't just tell me to ask for you
at some café," he recited without even bothering to look
at the paper.

"What is that supposed to mean?"

"Keep your family and your friends close."

At least he wants me close.

"But especially your family," he added.

Or maybe not.

Alone with her thoughts later, Kathmiya felt an unfamiliar hunger. She had never consciously wanted Shafiq's attention before, but now she realized how much it meant to her. She could barely admit it to herself, but a dream was starting to take root in her mind involving them together as a way out of her lonely life.

It was a delicious fantasy, but completely forbidden, and she vowed to never to act on it.

That evening, after Aziza was safely asleep, Kathmiya wrapped herself in a black *abaya* and slipped out of the house. She had never been to the port so late and when she got there she was rewarded by a restful sight: men reeling ropes up into boats, donkeys sitting on their hind legs, porters who'd spent the day carrying groceries for other people finally eating their own meals of kebab and long-grain rice.

Jamila had given her the address—no, more precisely, the directions, but only from the water's edge: walk down the ramp toward the big warehouse, past the corner coffee house, up to the edge of the street with the lead-colored building, through the narrow alley, across the open market to the area where goats were sold, then two estuary crossings over, look for the third house with a brown door.

Along with the directions was this warning: "Don't tell the old widow anything." According to Jamila, her employer was ten times as nosy as the Iraqi police, and twenty times as merciless.

Kathmiya thought about knocking on the front door and drowning the woman in so many questions she wouldn't have a chance to ask any of her own. "What would you do without my mother? Wear smelly clothes and wash in a moldy bathtub and eat off of dirty plates?"

If it got Jamila fired, so much the better. Kathmiya didn't care how angry her father would be if she unlocked the gate that kept her mother inside.

But she had to save her spiteful energy for her own cause, so instead of banging on the front door as stuffed with attitude as an onion filled with spicy meat, Kathmiya took measure of the building, saw the lace curtains on all the windows but one, and threw a pebble up to hit it.

She missed, and missed again, and a couple more times after that until the old widow screeched, "What is going on out there?" Kathmiya almost screamed,

"It's me!" but just then she saw Jamila peeking out from behind one of the lace curtains.

"Over here!" she shouted. Jamila held up a hand to make her stop, and seconds later she was at her disruptive daughter's side.

"What do you think you're doing?" Jamila demanded. "She nearly caught you."

"Really?" Kathmiya asked boldly. "Because I'd like to meet her, finally, ask a few questions, like why she can't let you see me more."

Jamila pinched Kathmiya's arm but it didn't work, those little hurts that used to keep her in line.

"Well, I tried to find my own way out of this life," Kathmiya announced.

"I heard. Baaqir Zain has been asking about you. I made Ali tell him you moved away."

Kathmiya had been enjoying her bitterness like the last drops of thick coffee, but that ruined it. "Thanks," she mumbled.

"Please," Jamila said with the profound push of her convictions, "trust me. I'm trying."

This unassailable affection just reminded Kathmiya of everything that was missing. "But why?" she asked. "Why is it always so hard?"

"Go," Jamila said, as always cleaning everything up when Kathmiya needed her to spill.

"No," Kathmiya said. "Not until you answer me."

"Shh," her mother hushed. "This weekend. I promise."

"Now."

"Not here," Jamila insisted. "At home."

But Kathmiya didn't wait until they got home. They were back on the same boat that had taken her to and from work since she was thirteen, but now her feet didn't dangle off the edge of the trunk; they planted squarely on the wet wooden floor.

"So?"

"Here . . . ?" Jamila asked.

". . . and now."

It all came back to that book. Jamila explained that years before, she had brought Kathmiya as a baby to her job in the city. "We lived with the American missionaries until you were three. They read to you and indulged you and doted on you. You were even learning words in English! No wonder Ali didn't feel close to you, but I just couldn't leave you at home, I loved you so much I took you along."

"What are 'missionaries'?"

"It doesn't matter. The point is you should be glad. I brought you because you were my baby. But your father didn't see you so much . . . so, well." As if that was an explanation.

"I want to know what missionaries are. And don't tell me he won't let me marry because I was away when I wasn't even old enough to help out around the house. Like he even would have missed me then!"

"They are people who spread the Christian faith," was Jamila's partial and useless answer.

"So why does he make sure all the matchmakers and even his brother are afraid to arrange a marriage for me?"

Jamila's eyes looked anxious, but Kathmiya felt lulled by her mother's clear tone, as even as the voice of an announcer on the radio.

"You picked up some customs, back there in that foreign household. Asking a lot of questions and expecting lots of attention. Getting your way all the time because they spoiled you. You were—"

Kathmiya recognized her toddler self, wanting a little attention, some answers, the attention she deserved. "I was spoiled? Are you saying I'm so wretched now because people used to answer my questions?"

"There! You just did it again! I was only saying you were different. Ali never got used to it. Eventually, he made me leave that job. The old widow I work for now, at least she's Iraqi. She had a husband back then, but she was already mean; she wouldn't let me bring you."

"So the missionaries ruined me but the mean Iraqi woman didn't help?"

"Oh, Kathmiya. It wasn't the job. It was the way they fussed. Let you ask questions and be in everybody's business and have the run of the whole huge house. They didn't have their own children, and so you were it. You were the little princess."

It almost would have been a pleasant story if only Jamila could have stopped right there.

"When I took you home, you weren't used to our life, never wanted to do chores or keep quiet or know your place. Ali finally swore that as soon as you were old enough, he'd send you back to the city, where you belonged."

There was only one other person who might help piece together some of this wayward history, and the spoiled, willful, determined girl that Kathmiya was would never get anywhere with her, so she came at Fatimah from a completely different angle.

"You have no idea what it is like to be out and alone while everyone else is embraced by their family," she began.

It seemed so simple and surefire, like catching a chicken, all squawk and pride when it was really at the mercy of its butchers, but Kathmiya drew only a confused stare.

"Me?"

This wasn't coy Fatimah, wanting Kathmiya to follow up with, "Of course you, the one who is so much more lucky and cared for than I ever could be." This was a whole new type of sister than any Kathmiya ever had: hurt and wondering.

"But you're the one . . ." Fatimah began.

"I'm the one?" Kathmiya couldn't even muster a hollow laugh.

". . . who our mother worries about and fusses over and always did."

"Our mother? Our father watches over you and let you marry. Who cares what she does . . . it makes no difference in a person's life." If Fatimah couldn't understand that, she was worse than a squawking chicken—she was about as smart as the shell of an egg.

"That's just because he has to make up for, you know, the way she treats me."

Kathmiya covered her face in her hands before looking up again. "How can I explain this?" she asked. It was like trying to make little Aziza stop from crawling under a bus, the consequences were that enormous and clear to Kathmiya but invisible to her sister. "You got married on the first try. I have a choice between becoming an old maid now or having Baaqir Zain use me up and then send me out to the land of old maids later!"

"I never really thought of it that way," Fatimah confessed.

If Kathmiya didn't need information from this woman, she might have smacked her ignorant face. *Of course you thought of it that way—you never stopped rubbing it in.*

"I mean," Kathmiya said slowly, "you always, well, bring up the fact that I have to work in the city and sometimes"—*sometimes I think you are twisting the dagger that our father stabbed me with*—"sometimes I think you know how painful that is. It's tough being single and working all the time."

"Yeah, but besides all that—"

"That's all there is! Don't you understand? Nothing else matters!"

"—you and our mother talk, you are so close, she fusses about you constantly . . . I'm back here with crying children and you two are in the city riding horse-drawn carriages and everything."

"You two talk just as much!"

"Not hardly." Fatimah sniffed.

Kathmiya threw her head back and stared at the open sky. Had she made watermelon and taxicabs sound that fun?

"Fatimah, I'm so sorry it's been horrible for you. The truth is, we are very close and we talk a lot."

"I know!" Fatimah gurgled, trying to evolve up from egg to chicken.

"But there's one thing she's never told me, and I was hoping you might know."

Silence.

"Because you see the world so clearly, you're my big sister and you understand so much."

"About the book, right?"

Thanks be to Allah, finally. "Exactly that. What do you know?"

Fatimah shrugged. "Unlucky blue eyes, did you notice?"

Kathmiya remembered Shafiq—the recent Shafiq, who didn't seem moved by her anymore. The last time they'd said good-bye, she was pouting, and he said, "Don't worry, there's nothing in life that can't be cured with a bit of blue china, or so my mother says."

"Blue?" she'd blinked. "That brings the *jinn*."

"Takes it away," he corrected with all the conviction of an oarsman who was too tired to row but went through the motions of trying to get a passenger anyway.

"Brings," she said.

"Whatever," he'd conceded.

"Whatever," she'd agreed.

But she couldn't explain this to Fatimah, so she just asked, "Where did it come from?"

"Those people, those missionaries. I guess they wanted to get rid of the bad luck."

If blue was good luck in Basra, orange and green paisley might as well be lucky in their land, Kathmiya knew, but try explaining that to her never-left-the-marshes older sis.

"And the bottle?"

"Must have come from someone else—she hated it," said Fatimah. Kathmiya remembered the sound as it smashed against a rock. So many splinters later, no clues left.

"But don't lose that *dinar*," said Fatimah. "She's very attached to that."

Except one. Kathmiya waited.

"She told me it was the 'only thing she has now.'"

"When did she say that?" Kathmiya asked. And then, before she could stop herself, the words escaped. "And why did she tell you?"

"It kills you, doesn't it?" Fatimah's indignation was lit. "One thing she told me that you don't know, and that's too much."

"Sorry—sorry—all I meant was—"

"And that's all I have to say," Fatimah announced petulantly.

"Right," Kathmiya replied, giving up. "I guess we're even now."

"Not quite," her sister huffed.

Kathmiya might be able to read numbers, but she'd never be able to add that one up.

Chapter XXXI

Every time a ball bounced that hadn't been kicked by Naji, Shafiq felt it. During the dead pauses at dinner when Naji would have come up with some easy joke, Shafiq knew it. Searching the newspaper as though there might be a hint about his ideological brother buried in the headlines of the day, Shafiq understood that this terrible, invisible pressure of absence was real.

And then the cries started next door. As though Shafiq was destined to be in rhythm with Omar, in mirth but also in painful, bruised-purple sorrow.

"It's Hajji Abdullah," said Reema, who also had a best friend on the other side of that wall.

Shafiq wanted to run over, but his father stopped him with that commanding authority on the Arab way.

"You give them privacy the first night. There will be a right time to pay respects. Not now."

Shafiq didn't even try to block out the crying. He heard Salwa's open wailing, but also Omar's sobs. In his own head, Shafiq joined the mourning.

The death of the old man.

The loss of the young man.

Everyone else left bereft.

He wanted to punch Omar's shoulder, just to feel that energetic life they shared. There may never be anything to laugh about again, Shafiq thought, but at least they could be sad together.

As the night wore on, he heard invocations to Allah echo through the wall. Omar's father was called "Hajji" because he had been to Mecca. *That would send him to heaven.* Shafiq might not believe in blue china or the *jinn*, but he needed a little comfort now, and he took it where he could.

The body was being prepared for burial. "What do they do?" Shafiq whispered to his father.

"They lay him so his head points to Mecca," Roobain said solemnly. "They wrap him in a white sheet."

Shafiq wished he could write Omar a letter, like the one he had received during the riots, but he didn't have the book of poetry. Which was okay, because Hajji

Abdullah loved it so much, and he was going to need
that wisdom on his way to the other world.

The next day, Reema broke out of her cloud of
tribal superstition to become his mother again. "I'll be
there every day to help when the Imam comes," she
said.

"Doing what?" he asked.

She just shook her head. Like the answer was
anything—everything—but still not enough.

There were scores of men gathered around the funeral procession as it made its way through the streets.
The plain wooden casket was all that remained, a box
holding a corpse headed down into the ground. Shafiq
made his way over to Omar, restraining the urge to
run for a hug. Tears streamed from Omar's eyes and
that was a moment Shafiq could never undo—those
minutes, right there in the daylight, surrounded by
men, wearing a black suit and a stiff shirt, feeling
his friend's face go wet with tears and knowing there
was no way to stop them. You could say "passing"
or "end" or even "going to heaven" but from here it
was all just death, so over, beyond repair, way beyond
hope.

"My brother," Shafiq said quietly. Omar's frown
twisted into a full cry. Shafiq pressed his shoulder

forward, so Omar could lean on it, and when he pulled away, the shirt was wet.

Their eyes held one last contact before Omar left to catch up with his brother Anwar at the front of a line of uncles and cousins and other neighbors and friends and people just following their religious compulsion to mourn the dead.

Men of every faith joined their voices to proclaim Allah's Holiness, Greatness, Compassion and Mercy. The prayers mingled like wildflowers—no pattern, no plan, still beautiful.

The air around them was silent. Shafiq was glad that all activity stopped at each café they passed. Muslims, Christians, Jews—all quietly stood up out of respect for the dead. Just like they had during the procession for the king. In the end, Shafiq thought, everyone is important, the founding monarch and the school janitor.

Waiting outside the Mosque, Shafiq already missed the times he and Omar read poetry to the old man. Behind that sadness was his brother Naji and his sister Marcelle and the wars and riots and bullies and hurts that just nicked at life, leaving behind little scars that never went away until the smooth, happy times were all scored with reminders of pain.

He joined the crowd again after the men came out carrying the plain wooden coffin to the graveyard.

There, Shafiq watched from a distance as Hajji Abdullah, wrapped in a stark, white shroud, was laid directly into the ground facing Mecca.

For three days following the funeral, the living room in the Abd El Hamid home was transformed into a reception area where visitors streamed in to pay respects. Shafiq and his family joined in bowing their heads and hearing the prayers of the mullah. Roobain, who had been to the funerals of other Muslim friends and associates, had explained it all: the special *sura* they recited from the Koran, the way to bow your head, the chance to reach for the hands of the family. "But they may not respond and you shouldn't expect them to," he'd said. "Sometimes solidarity is louder in silence."

Reema proved that. Her head covered with a veil, she got up and went to the kitchen, where she stayed for sixteen hours. And returned the next day for longer. And the next. No salt or blue china. Just making coffee and cooking meat and chopping vegetables and baking bread and cleaning, cleaning and scrubbing and washing the house so that Salwa, all she had to do was cry.

Sometimes solidarity came in silence. And sometimes in shaking rice in a pan to get all the little pebbles out. Shake, shake, a sound like a rattle, the pebbles separate and the rice is clean.

Shafiq thought of Salwa saving his life when his mother's milk ran dry. She was a widow now, but like Reema, he would never desert her.

"I miss him," Shafiq said a week later.

Omar looked away and Shafiq worried that it had been a mistake to raise the subject. But soon his friend looked back again. "There's something I wanted to show you," he said.

Usually so blustery and carefree, Omar was extra careful opening the copy of *A Tear and a Smile*. The reverence Hajji Abdullah had taught them to have for the book had only intensified with his death.

"He loved the poetry, *rahmette Allah a'lay*," Shafiq said, blessing Hajji Abdullah by invoking God's mercy.

"It means so much," Omar said, turning the pages as though this paperback were an original edition instead of the copy sold from Baghdad to Beirut. "Do you want to hear?"

Shafiq hardly had to answer. They were close again, and it was more refreshing than any philosophy, or maybe it was the only philosophy Shafiq could really believe in.

"Chapter Twenty: The City of the Dead," Omar recited. The verse described a funeral, complete with a wooden casket and a dog "with heartbreaking eyes."

Shafiq wondered whether Hajji Abdullah could see them. In a way, he hoped so. The old man would be comforted by the words. Maybe more than that, by the boys carrying on the tradition.

"Oh Lord, where is the haven of all the people?" Omar read. "I looked toward the clouds, mingled with the sun's longest and most beautiful golden rays. And I heard a voice within me saying, 'Over there!'"

For a few silent seconds they absorbed the verse.

And then Shafiq spoke. "Naji's not really in Lebanon." Omar listened. "Communism. He's underground."

"You should have told me . . ."

"Why? I didn't want you to have more trouble."

"We already have heaps of trouble. What's a little more? We should sell it."

"You could." Shafiq felt a smile forming.

"Only if you back me up," Omar prompted.

"Yeah, then we'll get more trouble."

"So, we'll corner the market."

"Be richer than kings."

Chapter XXXII

The next time he saw Kathmiya, Shafiq brought a note.

"How are you?" she read off the paper.

"Well?" he asked.

"Fine, if you don't mind being misunderstood and all alone."

"You'll always have me as your teacher." He smiled.

"You know what I mean."

"No husband still?"

"He had money but no soul."

"Oooh . . . that's bad. What about another match-maker?"

"Won't work. All this time I've spent in the city apparently ruins me at home."

Shafiq didn't believe in much, but he had learned that you could lose someone at any time and once you did, all you had left were memories, sweet with satisfaction or filthy with regret. "Come on, Kathmiya," he said. "You have to realize there are more matchmakers than just in the marshes. We've got about a million in Basra. It wouldn't take you two seconds to find a husband here."

It felt good to knock on the door where Jamila worked, even if Kathmiya's heart pounded much harder than her knuckles.

She could feel the old woman who answered judging her—feel the time slip in that split second when she went, in someone's eyes, from being a person to being a lowly *Midaan.*

"Please, ma'am," she said. "My name is Kathmiya. Your maid, Jamila, she's my mother."

The door closed.

Kathmiya's cheeks burned, but she had come prepared. No need to throw a rock at the wall this time. She knocked again.

"Please, ma'am," she started again. "I thought you might want this." The glossy magazine had been in Leah's garbage; Kathmiya could only hope the old widow didn't already have a copy. "There's a wonderful article about the newest movies from Cairo. Please, if you like."

The woman didn't bother to notice that Kathmiya could read an article enough to recommend it. But neither did she bother to stop her maid's daughter from coming in while she started flipping through the colorful pages.

Kathmiya knew enough to pick up a dirty tea-cup from the dining table before heading toward the kitchen, where the sound of running water, like the theme song on a radio drama, announced Jamila the Maid.

"Here's another one," Kathmiya said, placing the cup in the sink.

"What are you thinking, walking in like this?" Jamila's face flushed.

"You're my only relative in the city. Where else should I go?"

Jamila shot her daughter the is-this-an-emergency look and when Kathmiya just shrugged in response, she said, "Nafisa—that's the widow—she sleeps late in the mornings . . . we could plan it if you tell me next time before showing up."

They could hear someone approaching, so Kathmiya pulled one of the rags out of her pocket. She was pol-ishing the tiled floor under the garbage barrel when

Nafisa peeked in. Satisfied that she was being serviced, the widow left them alone.

"I've been thinking," Kathmiya said.

"No more questions," Jamila replied.

"I wasn't going to ask you anything. Just suggest that we find another matchmaker. One outside of the marshes, maybe here in Basra. Less complicated, you know?"

Jamila silently wiped a tall cup, so that for a few seconds all they could hear was the squeak of fabric against glass. "Fine, my sweet," she said. "If you want to we can. But it will take some money."

"You must have enough, don't you?"

"How much have you saved?"

Kathmiya stared. "You're not asking me for the money I've put aside for my father's funeral at Najaf?"

"It's for your engagement . . ."

That little vase where Kathmiya dropped all but a few *fils* from her weekly pay contained more than her savings.

". . . to help pay someone to find a good husband . . ."

Not that she could have written the word for it but in there was something like redemption.

". . . to secure your future."

A chance to make it right with Ali, even if he'd be dead by then. "No," she answered flatly.

"Why do you have to make this so hard?" Jamila asked.

And Kathmiya thought, *Why don't you just try a little harder?*

It took three weeks, but Jamila finally promised that they were headed to one of the most successful matchmakers in Basra.

Kathmiya had been through the ritual more times than most women would survive, but now she was determined not to let that dangerous little hook of hope catch her heart.

This was a battle, especially when they approached the impressive-looking home, so much more official and reassuring than the one that held the musty old marriage broker in the marshes. Its door was solid, the knocker brass, and Kathmiya could just smell the metallic scent of possibility glittering near.

"Maybe it's your destiny to live in this sophisticated world," Jamila suggested as they entered a clean, bright room and sat on an upholstered sofa.

Kathmiya knew that whatever curse was haunting her had not been lifted, but she felt her dreams pounding away at her doubts. *This could be my escape,* she thought. Instead of her usual fantasy involving a match in the marshes where the sheikh's tent would be spread with food and filled with cheering relatives, she pictured herself on the grand balcony of one of Basra's largest mansions surrounded by blooming flowers and adoring crowds.

The matchmaker was not a shriveled old lady but a robust man, with a smart, skinny moustache like a movie star. "*Mabruk*, it is time for your child to marry," he said, offering congratulations.

Kathmiya felt strangely at ease. There had to be one good husband in the crowded city of Basra.

Even Jamila seemed relaxed as she answered the broker's questions about her daughter. "Beautiful, educated and excellent around the house; knows how to cook and sew better than any chef or seamstress," she boasted.

That's close enough, thought Kathmiya. *And if this works, I'll learn all the home arts to perfection. I'll devote myself, day and night, to my husband, my children, my new home, not because anyone pays me; they won't have to, it will all be mine. Not only the home and the family but the freedom.*

"Tell me about yourself," the man asked Jamila with an open sincerity.

"I'm just a humble woman," she replied.

"She's very good and kind," Kathmiya chirped. "Mother of two, grandmother of two, all girls, all healthy, thanks be to Allah."

"The father?" the matchmaker wanted to know.

"Her father, well . . . "

Sailing confidence fell still.

". . . her father has left this world." Jamila looked down.

Why lie? Ali was contemptible but not completely gone . . .

"*Allah yi-ruhmah.*" Jamila added a prayer for God to have compassion on him.

All of a sudden, Kathmiya felt that familiar dead certainty about the imminent collapse of a marriage negotiation.

As if to confirm her dread, the man cocked his head slightly to the side. "Oh?"

"I'm afraid so," Jamila said. "*Allah yi-ruhmah.*"

"*Allah yi-ruhmah,*" the matchmaker agreed, but he definitely looked skeptical. "Where is he from?"

"North of here . . . to the north . . ." What a painfully ridiculous answer, Kathmiya thought. She wondered if she should take over the conversation, but decided that might be too forward, too assertive, altogether too ruinous.

The marriage broker looked annoyed. "You are *Midaan,*" he noted, without any of the usual sneering prejudice, but with an emphasis that said, *I see through the obfuscation.*

"I have money!" Jamila blurted out frantically. Her panic just rang more alarms, but she didn't stop. "Here!" she added, flinging her meager savings on the small wooden tea tray between them.

The crumpled *dinars* only served to make Jamila look more corrupt. Kathmiya wanted to crawl out of the room . . . her skin . . . this life.

"You have money," said the matchmaker, quiet and firm, "but you lack honesty. Had you come here in truth, I would have been happy to find a wonderful match for your daughter, whether she is as cultured as you say or not. But since you are lying to me, I could not, in Allah's name, ever connect another family to yours."

The words had been spoken in a perfectly measured tone, but they boomed in Kathmiya's ears: ". . . a wonderful match for your daughter . . ." *Had it been so close, only to be snatched away?* Kathmiya wanted to beg but the matchmaker's hand was pointed straight at the door and she knew she had no choice but to leave.

Outside, on the sunny street that had offered so much promise just minutes before, Kathmiya hooked her arm through her mother's. There was no point in attacking Jamila. Better to accept fate. It went against everything in her resolute, determined, raised-by-spoiling-missionaries character, but that hadn't gotten her far in life anyway. So she just sighed and walked her mother back to work, sneaking in by the back door instead of defiantly storming through the front.

Chapter XXXIII

"*Moon Over Miami* is coming to Ashar—finally!" Shafiq boomed as he crossed the threshold into Omar's home. "Do you realize it's been out for five years . . ."

They were all in the living room, or at least the shell of the family that was left: Salwa, Anwar and Omar. The soft maroon couches were in their usual corners, the framed Koranic verses kept their places on the walls, but there was an unfamiliar grim mood hovering over it all. Not the grief of death but the fear of something less clear but more disturbing, like slow torture.

Salwa's hospitality was as Iraqi as Roobain's, so she invited Shafiq in.

"That's okay," he said.

"Please," she pressed.

Leaving would only make it worse, so he nodded toward Omar and said quietly, "I was just wondering, do you want—?"

"Go ahead," Salwa said, and Omar left with Shafiq through the arched entrance, the familiar blast of sun-heated air hitting their skin when they got outside.

"What happened?" Shafiq asked.

"My uncle, remember from the funeral?"

Shafiq couldn't recall and didn't pretend to.

"Right," Omar continued. "Why should you know him? He disappeared the next day. It looks like he's not going to marry my mother. No respect for tradition. And so we're in this kind of situation. Anwar may have to come back from Baghdad."

"But law school . . ." Shafiq began.

And then he stopped himself. There were plenty of intractable problems—getting Naji back, undoing Marcelle's marriage, the paradox of an unwanted Kathmiya whom he wanted so much—but then there were difficulties that could be conquered through the human solidarity Shafiq had been raised to revere. "My father can take care of it."

"We know," Omar said. Shafiq's feelings had been so injured by loss he had almost forgotten what it felt like to be clear and happy. But now he remembered. They were all in this together, at least that much was understood.

"So let's go," Shafiq insisted.

"Not yet," Omar said. "My mother has one more person to ask first."

"I'm going with her," Shafiq decided. "That way I can make sure it works. Any problems, I'm taking her straight to my father."

"I can come too," Omar offered.

"It's okay," Shafiq said. "I'll be there."

If he had learned anything from Roobain, it was that in Iraq, neighbor leans on neighbor and friend on friend; these ties of intimacy were all that was meaningful. Without them, society's fabric would be completely torn.

Salwa allowed Shafiq to accompany her to the mortgagor on one condition: "Don't be friendly to me. That will make him less sympathetic."

The office was located in a choice spot on the second floor near the front of Roobain's warehouse. Shafiq stood in the doorway and watched Salwa enter.

Salih Al-Zubairi, the man who held the secured interest in the house, sat behind a small desk that had a large log book, an ink bottle and—a sure sign of status—a black telephone with the earpiece hanging on its stand. A small table fan whirred rhythmically. There were two chairs, but when Salwa entered, he invited her to sit with him on one of the pillows arranged neatly on a Persian carpet reserved for receiving clients and visitors.

"Welcome, welcome," he said. When they were settled on the floor, he sent a servant to bring them tea from the merchant's café.

Salwa began by asking about the Al-Zubairi family, and he replied in kind. She seemed to be trying to control the pace of the conversation by dwelling on the subject of his relatives. "Your mother is in good health, *In-sha Allah.*"

He nodded, then asked about her family again, but before telling her story, she repeated, "I am glad that your mother is well, *Al Hamdulilah.*"

Shafiq was getting restless. *Help the woman,* he wanted to demand. *What is it to you?*

After the gentle back-and-forth wore out, Salwa mentioned Hajji Abdullah. "You know that my husband, *Allah yi-ruhmah,* has passed away," she began.

Just then, the servant returned carrying tea in small clear glasses. Salih Al-Zubairi passed one to Salwa with a sympathetic nod.

"*Shukran, shukran,*" she thanked him, before continuing: "He worked hard all his life, but it was never easy. First, we lost the store in a fire—"

"There is no strength except in Allah," said Al-Zubairi, repeating a well-worn phrase commonly used in response to a calamity. But Shafiq knew Salwa was hoping for the solidarity of man.

"Anwar is finishing his studies in Baghdad. He is a fine son but he's not yet established," Salwa said, cupping her hands around the warm glass.

"May Allah help you," replied Salih Al-Zubairi.

But will you help her? Shafiq wondered.

"I have still my youngest at home," she continued. Shafiq's ears burned at the mention of Omar, who should not have to be trotted out for sympathy from this businessman.

"Omar is studying hard and hopes to complete high school, but now that his father has died, *Allah yi-ruhmah,* it is not so easy." Hearing this hurt. Shafiq had not wanted to admit that Omar might really leave school. Not when he was so close to graduation. And without the hope of even becoming a railway clerk.

"Life is hard nowadays."

At least help until Omar graduates, thought Shafiq.

Salwa, too, pressed on. "Just one woman, I cannot imagine how to take care of them under the circumstances." She put the teacup down so gently it didn't make a sound.

"Yes, we are all struggling."

Al-Zubairi was ignoring her special circumstances, Shafiq knew. He wanted to step into the room and tell the man that his father owned the whole warehouse, but he respected Salwa's request.

She began appealing to the mortgagor's religious obligation for charity. "*Tamam, Ammi,*" she said. True, my uncle. "That's why we need to help each other in this world. In the eyes of Allah we are all one family."

Salih Al-Zubairi looked like he knew exactly what the desperate widow was hinting at. Clearly, she could not keep up with the payments.

"There are many suffering people in the family of man," he said.

"Allah rewards *sadaka,*" she replied, referring to acts of giving to the poor, "and compassion."

"You are very wise," Al-Zubairi agreed in a sweet voice. "But if you can't pay the mortgage then I will have to foreclose on the house and buy it back."

At a huge, dirty profit, Shafiq thought, deciding it was time to leave. He was moving toward Salwa when she started crying. "I'm a poor widow," she whimpered as Shafiq put his arm around her gently. Then, as though his kindness gave her a last burst of courage, she added plaintively, "but my sons are good and will someday earn enough to satisfy the loan."

"I am sure they will," the mortgagor agreed in his friendly, patronizing voice. "They will probably earn enough to buy you a brand-new house if you ever need it," he added in a warm tone that made his cold words all the more chilling.

"Let's go, auntie," Shafiq said. "My father is probably in his office," he added. "You know, keeping track of the rents on our warehouse here." He shot the mortgagor a look but the man just smiled in return. Salwa left with her head against the young chest of her "nephew."

Shafiq walked toward his father's office, but Salwa was pulling him in a different direction.

"Please," he implored. "We're telling my father now."

"Just one more place—one more," she asked meekly. "Please, come with me."

She had already been so harshly rejected, Shafiq could only agree. They walked together to one of the better neighborhoods in Basra, stopping at a large home with arched windows and ornate wooden balconies. "Madame Sadiqi, my mother-in-law's sister," she explained.

The elegant façade did not inspire hope in Shafiq, who had learned early that most of life's serendipitous rewards came from unexpected places, not those blinking with ostentatious displays of wealth.

Before Salwa knocked, she took a turquoise seven-eye bead out of her pocket and started rubbing it. Blue, salt, beads . . . everyone had a different way to fight the *jinn*. And none of them worked.

In the distance, Shafiq could see *Al-Wattan* café. He was not tempted to go in, partly because he promised his father he wouldn't, but mostly because as long as he held the trip in reserve, he might still hope that he'd find Naji there, brown skin glowing and muscles flexing and wide grin flashing. *Al-Wattan* café empty of his brother would be worse than nothing.

"Years ago," Salwa told Shafiq, "we went to the country with these relatives, and their servant rinsed our hands with rosewater." Shafiq hoped it would be the same person who greeted her now, a familiar face to soothe Salwa's anxiety.

He was two steps down from the front door, but he could see easily enough that even after introducing herself as a relative, Salwa was not welcome.

"I will let the madame know you are here," was all she got.

Salwa turned around and gave Shafiq a smile, ever the mother, concerned that he was uncomfortable when she was the one being treated like a suspect instead of a sister.

When the servant returned, Shafiq immediately felt the atmosphere relax. Instead of being indifferent, the servant looked warm and solicitous. He expected the door to swing wide open, but it closed a bit and he heard the servant whisper, "*Umm Hamad* said she cannot see you now."

"We have all day," Shafiq prompted Salwa.

"Please," she implored, "may I wait until she's ready?"

Seeing Salwa looking small and desperate in the grand, arched doorway, Shafiq felt uncomfortably adult; Salwa, his protector, needed protection. She was alone in a society where security depended on the kindness of relatives. "She must have heard that my husband died. His name," she said plaintively, "was Hajji Abdullah."

Shafiq could tell this wasn't working. The servant didn't seem comfortable either, barely coughing out the words, "*Umm Hamad* says to tell you there are babies in this house."

Everyone knew a recent widow could not enter a home with infants because of the *jinn*, but Shafiq chafed, this time not against the superstition, but because he could tell from the servant's shifty tone that she was lying.

"Come on," he said putting an arm around Salwa. "I'm taking you home."

The heavy door closed.

But Salwa wasn't ready to leave. "I brought this," she said. It was an old picture of a young couple. "I don't want it anymore."

"Belongs in the garbage," Shafiq agreed.

Salwa shook her head. "I'm giving it to them."

Shafiq knew that door would only slam again, but how could he stop her? "I'll be right at the corner," he said, leaving enough distance so that he wouldn't have to watch her fail again, and more important, so she wouldn't be seen.

Watching her mother send away the poor woman with a weak lie on the instructions of the callous old widow, Kathmiya felt disgusted.

"How could you?" she hissed at Jamila, who had just closed the door on Salwa.

"You heard! Nafisa forced me . . ."

"You have to help her!"

"I want to, but how?" Jamila asked.

And then, as though Kathmiya had commanded it through sheer willfulness, there was another knock at the door.

Jamila looked first amazed and then contrite. "I am so sorry, my sister," she said after welcoming Salwa in. "I lied."

Kathmiya watched from the side, cheering the spark of bravery. Her mother might never influence a matchmaker, but at least she had some fire left.

"There are no babies in this house," Jamila continued, struggling to bring her voice above a whisper. "Please, forgive me."

Salwa just shook her head in confusion. "Don't worry, my sister," she said after a pause. "It's not your fault."

"If it is money you need—" began Jamila. And then, jolted by a sudden decision, she thrust the small purse containing her life savings into Salwa's hands.

Salwa looked even more baffled. "Why are you giving me this?"

Kathmiya knew her mother looked crazy, but at the same time, she had never been so proud of Jamila. They were poor but not completely impoverished. Emerging from the background, she said, "God rewards *sadaka*."

The woman looked stunned. "But how did you know?" she asked. *Sadaka*. The same charity she had just sought from the mortgagor.

"To be honest," Jamila said, "we have many problems of our own, but none that can be solved with this." Kathmiya experienced a little death as her mother pressed the purse firmly into Salwa's hands. It wasn't the money she wanted, but the illusion of believing that her problems could be solved.

"Your health?" Salwa asked. "Maybe you can use this for a doctor." She tried to return the gift.

"Please, take it," Jamila said, opening the door again.

After she closed it behind Salwa, Kathmiya hugged her mother. There was nothing left to say. There wasn't even any money. All they had was the knowledge that not every stranger in the world was turned away for being desperate. And in that moment, it was almost enough.

When Shafiq saw Salwa again, he found her completely changed. "God rewards *sadaka*," she said in a transcendent voice, as though she had experienced some kind of religious revelation.

He noticed she held a small pouch of *dinars*, but they were barely enough to cover two months' rent.

"Allah is great," she said with conviction.

"But—" he began gently, "let's go to my father all the same."

Salwa nodded, aglow with new hope. "With Allah's protection, we will survive."

At the warehouse, Shafiq found his father walking around the main floor with a set of wooden prayer beads in his hand. "Our neighbor needs help," he said. Roobain brought them all up to a small office where Shafiq used to fan his father while he calculated accounts.

"What can I give you?" Roobain asked directly.

"We don't have money for the mortgage," Salwa began. "My brother-in-law refused to help us, and my only other relative with means, Nafisa el Saddiqi," she looked down as she said the name and finished the rest of the sentence staring at the dusty Persian carpet under her feet, "refused to see me."

This was a surprise to Shafiq. Salwa had met him at the corner with those few extra *dinars*. If they didn't come from the old widow, then who?

Roobain nodded. Shafiq knew his father remembered all Salwa had done for them. And beyond that, Roobain was an Arab man of honor who would not refuse the request of any guest. A Bedouin in the desert, he always taught Shafiq, would kill his only camel to feed a stranger.

"*Umm Omar,*" he said, "*ala al-aynn wo-ala al-rass.*"
Consider it done—my pleasure.

Since Salih Al-Zubairi's office was located in the
warehouse, Roobain saw him regularly. "I will pay
the mortgagor directly—you won't ever have to trouble
yourself."

Moved by this kindness, Salwa repeated over
and over, "*B'issim Allah wi'bissim awladi*—we will
repay you." Bless you in the name of God and my
children.

She then leaned forward, attempting to kiss Roobain's
hand.

He was embarrassed by her genuflection, however
authentic, and gently gripped the string of worn prayer
beads as he pulled away. "We're not strangers; we're
relatives," he said with quiet feeling.

"Still, we will repay you—" Salwa insisted.

"Shhh . . ." Shafiq stopped her.

There could be no debt between them, or rather,
what they owed each other continued to grow through
the years, not in the form of a balance due but as a
credit to both.

Buoyed by this flash of light, Shafiq felt ready to
celebrate even Kathmiya's luck with a Basra matchmaker.

Instead, he found her disconsolate. When he asked what was wrong, she looked at him with tender surprise, as if to say, *Oh, at least somebody cares.*

"It didn't work—my family, the matchmaker, nothing works for me," she said in that sweet, low voice through tears that reminded him of the first time he ever saw her.

"I don't get it." Shafiq squinted at her.

Instead of answering, Kathmiya guided him to her small room, where she pulled out the last item he ever expected her to own. "A dollar?" he asked, having seen enough in American movies to recognize one.

"You know what it is?"

"Money," he answered. "But where—?"

"My mother was hiding it."

"Hiding this? Why?"

"I was hoping you would know."

He turned the bill over in his hand. What a distance it had traveled. "This is from America."

"America," she considered. "Is that why she loves it?"

Shafiq knew the answer was important to Kathmiya, even if it seemed a bit remote from the reality of her situation. One lousy dollar would not alter her fate. Maybe it would be better to let her think she had found a magic genie. But then what?

"It's not much money, not enough to change your life," he said, braced for a wave of hysterics.

"I figured that," she said, more annoyed than undone.

"Your mother couldn't spend it; not in the marshes, not even here. It must have been some kind of gift, something that made her happy because of the person who gave it to her."

Kathmiya looked at Shafiq intently. "I wish someone would give me a gift." She blushed.

He wanted to give her anything, but the price was too high—not of the object, just the intimacy. After a pause, he said, "This dollar—if she hid it, there must have been a reason."

"Yes." Kathmiya sighed. "A rule against it."

"Right," he said. *The same rule that forbids me from being with you.*

"What's the point of these rules?" Kathmiya's wondering eyes, fringed by thick bangs, turned to Shafiq.

He wanted to sweep aside her coarse locks and kiss her, but a fierce determination yanked him back.

"I lost one brother already because he doesn't believe in society's rules," he said, trying to navigate the journey from impetuous and imperiled to wise and safe. "I have to live by the rules." He stood to leave. Kathmiya was there on the bed, a pulsing temptation that could ruin his future. She was all the more unstable for remaining unmarried, despite her outstanding beauty and the keen intelligence that only he seemed to appreciate.

"It would be great to break out and do what we want," he said stoically, "but life doesn't work that way."

Walking out was easy; if Shafiq gave in to his desires, he would have committed a crime punishable by death. It would have been harder to act on his feelings. No one did that.

Except Naji. That stubborn courage.

Shafiq went outside and started wandering aimlessly up the quiet street.

But not really. He knew his destination, just couldn't quite admit it to himself until he got there.

From the outside, *Al-Wattan* café looked like all of the other places where men went to smoke water pipes, play backgammon, and trade rumors about everything from commodities prices to scandalous women.

Shafiq had rehearsed so many conversations since Naji left that he would have expected to hear the imagined dialogue in his mind as he entered, but it was gone. He couldn't remember a word of his planned greetings, could only remind himself to be careful not to say anything antagonistic. Who cared about Communism as long as they could be together?

Inside the smoky room, it took less than a second to feel Naji's absence, but Shafiq had braced himself for the fact that his brother was probably not hanging around Basra so he wasn't too disappointed. The dream had always been to have someone acknowledge Shafiq as the brother of such a selfless comrade. They would trust Shafiq for that. He could learn. He could know. And he could see Naji again, watch that grace and hear that laugh and smile like they were young.

And then, serendipitously, Shafiq saw a familiar face.

Complete with an invitation: "Well, hello!" Sayed Mustapha motioned for his former student to join him on a chipped, dark bench at the back.

This was perfect. Sayed Mustapha already trusted Shafiq. He must know Naji. And he could help put the two back together.

The old principal was still going on about politics. "Everywhere in the world talented workers are oppressed by those in power." Sayed Mustapha wore the same glazed expression Naji had when he waxed on about Communism. *They must issue rapturous looks to all people who join the movement,* Shafiq thought, restless for information.

"The best baseball players in America are kept out of the major leagues because they were brought as slaves from Africa," the principal continued. Shafiq felt like he was back in grade school sitting in a little desk-chair. "In Rhodesia, the natives are not even educated to read books, just taught to build furniture."

This was interesting but not useful information. "Can I ask you something?" The moment had arrived.

The principal put down his cup. "Now or tomorrow. I'm always here, every day."

"Do you know my brother Naji?" Saying his name felt equal parts subversive and empowering. "Do you know where he is?"

"I can't answer that, sorry."

"But—"

Sayed Mustapha leaned in close.

Shafiq strained to absorb whatever clue he was about to get. The name of a city? A mysterious stranger? A coded underground hiding place?

"Your brother is living for a cause greater than himself," Sayed Mustapha said with self-satisfaction. "I hope you'll understand someday, and do the same."

Useless! "My mother is so worried, please!"

"It's safer you don't know."

"Do you?"

The principal refused to answer, but finally, probably just to get Shafiq to stop clinging so hard, he promised that he would always be there to help. "In fact," Sayed Mustapha said, "let me give you some advice now. Don't expect good grades. You know about the quotas against Jews. Forget about college here."

Shafiq wished he could end this lecture. Bad enough to leave without any information about Naji, that much worse to get this gloomy forecast about his own future. "I understand, I know," he tried to brush off the warning.

But Sayed Mustapha was not used to being dismissed. "You'll need to study abroad . . ." the principal began.

Shafiq imagined the co-ed school in Beirut Omar was always going on about.

". . . in the Soviet Union, where they don't discriminate against Jews."

Shafiq pretended to consider the idea, but really, he was wondering whether Sayed Mustapha was hinting that Naji might be somewhere in Russia.

Shafiq was brooding back at home when Omar's brother came over.

"*Amoo Roobain*," Anwar said to Shafiq's father, calling the older man "Uncle." "With your help I'm doing well, advancing at the court, always aware of—"

Shafiq shuffled, not wanting to be reminded of the debt.

Roobain didn't either. "*Ala al-ain wu ala al-raas*," he said. At the eyes and at the head. He gently held Anwar's shoulder to say it had been his pleasure to help.

"I want to repay you, if only with a little," Anwar tried again, producing a thin envelope that no doubt contained a bit of carefully saved cash.

"Listen, my son: there is no need to pay me back," Roobain said. "We need each other and we help each other. In fact, I need a favor right now."

Anwar looked at pains to grant whatever it was. Shafiq held his breath.

"We are not strangers, we are relatives," Roobain said. "Please take this envelope and give it to my sister Salwa," he instructed, passing it back to Anwar.

Shafiq exhaled.

Chapter XXXIV

So many people visited Salim's buzzing living room, Kathmiya was used to opening the door and seeing everyone from wizened old professors to suspected gangsters. Leah welcomed each visitor with a smile—until the day Marcelle showed up.

"She must be after money," Leah mumbled. But Kathmiya recognized the keen desperation in Marcelle's eyes and knew she wanted something more valuable and more elusive: reassurance.

After all, Kathmiya had seen her mother fling a bundle of *dinars* at a matchmaker only to be sent away in shame.

"What do you want?" Leah asked sharply.

Maybe it was the good feeling from having helped that strange widow who showed up at her mother's job, maybe it was sympathy toward Marcelle, or maybe it was just human decency that prompted Kathmiya to invite her in. "Please," she said, "come this way."

Leah shot her maid a look but Kathmiya just shrugged as she saw them to the sewing room, where baskets of fabrics were stacked next to small bins for threads.

"Would you like some tea?" Kathmiya asked, since neither sister was talking.

"I'm fine," Marcelle huffed. "And that's exactly the problem. Not sick, like my sister was when she got pregnant." She fell back into a claret-colored chair.

"You mean . . . ?" Leah asked gently, suddenly tender. Marcelle nodded, trying to cover her anxiety. "I never should have left the family," she whimpered, the shell of her pride cracking under the pain of childlessness.

Kathmiya picked up a shirt and started mending a button. She was utterly sick of these spoiled people and their petty problems. Leah was telling Marcelle about the tricks their mother was using to keep the *jinn* out, like pouring sesame oil on the ground to appease the devils.

"She's doing this for you—for you to have a baby," Leah insisted.

"Is it helping?" Marcelle asked, as though she didn't already know about her own success.

Kathmiya could almost taste the rising hope. She knew it all too well. It had a rich but fleeting flavor, like that chocolate Shafiq had once brought her. Nestlé, it was called.

Tell her the truth, Kathmiya willed toward Leah. *If you lie, it only gets worse.*

"I think it's helping," Leah said.

The hope was so powerful it even pulsed through Kathmiya. She decided she had to at least see those rituals Shafiq complained about so much.

When Reema showed up a week later, Kathmiya brought her to the same sewing room. This time, Marcelle was waiting there with Leah.

"The chief rabbi wrote this prayer for you," Reema said, reverently holding a small square of stiff paper, inky with Hebrew letters. She barely seemed to notice Kathmiya, who was wiping the ornate iron sewing machine for an excuse to stay and hear the rest.

Marcelle was overdressed as usual, this time in a raw-silk outfit garishly patterned in green. "This is all you brought me?" she asked bitterly.

Kathmiya stared at the mystical-looking wad, wishing someone would offer it to her.

"Eat it," Reema instructed.

Or maybe not.

"Eat it?" Marcelle repeated.

"It will bring you children," Reema insisted. She had none of the suppressed greed of market hucksters, only an alluring sincerity.

Watching Marcelle chew the thick paper, Kathmiya wondered whether there was a prayer she could eat to get a husband, a home, an escape. *Maybe if I got one with Hebrew letters it would work on Shafiq . . .*

She knew that would be impossible. Futile to even hope for such a buried wish. But she'd be watching Marcelle all the same.

It only took a few weeks before they got the answer. "Some gift I received," Marcelle complained, brushing past Kathmiya as though there were no one there. "I guess Nana was too cheap to give me a real present. All of her money goes to the boys.

"If she loved me," Marcelle prattled on, "she would give me something really valuable. Not an old piece of paper that tasted like chemicals and stained my teeth."

Kathmiya wondered whether Marcelle's husband was thinking of abandoning her. It was bitter comfort that some people had it even worse than a single girl.

"She gave you what she valued most: her traditional remedies," Leah said defensively.

"You know what she values most, because you have it," Marcelle prodded.

Kathmiya had the definite sense she was about to hear something she shouldn't.

"That piece of jewelry again? You're still after it?"

And yet she was gripped by the conversation. With Marcelle ignoring her existence, and Leah too absorbed to care, it was easy for Kathmiya to sew herself into the background.

"You got all the luck and all the heirlooms," said Marcelle. "I'm not the only one who knows," she added.

"Moshe, right? What does he want? My whole trousseau?"

"At least you should share the good luck piece. The one that's blessed."

"Fine!" seethed Leah, sliding out of the room.

Marcelle waited with her arms folded across her chest. Leah came back with a tiny cloth sack, barely big enough for a pin. "Nana gave it to me with her blessing, just like she gave you plenty when you married."

Kathmiya expected Marcelle to be grateful, but instead she said, "I like it because it's lucky. But I'm not sure if it's enough to make my husband happy. He's very angry, you see. And when he doesn't get his way, well, you don't want to know."

Her veiled threat reeked like poisonous smoke.

Chapter XXXV

Just days after Marcelle's warning, the year 1947 began with a crack.

When the policeman's baton landed on Salim's radio, it shattered the beveled shell to splinters. Leah and Kathmiya stared at the copper wires inside: beautiful, twisted and torn. Little Aziza started wailing. Leah was trembling. Kathmiya just held her breath. She didn't know why the police had arrived, but she knew they would either decide she was not to blame because she was an ignorant, impoverished maid—or they would use that to hold everything against her.

She scooped up Aziza and pressed the child's crying mouth into her own shoulder, trying to muffle the sobs. Then she turned so that Aziza wouldn't see her father being led out by the two officers, whose black holsters cut a sharp diagonal line across their backs.

But Leah saw. Urine pooled under her feet.

"Well, you won't be using this to communicate with the Zionists anymore," the policeman who had smashed the radio said with satisfaction as his partner pushed Salim to the door.

Zionists. The people who were against the Jews of Iraq, or so Kathmiya had gathered living with Salim. Why would he communicate with them?

He was swaggering out, totally confident, practically exulting in his innocence.

But Leah was just begging, "No . . . No! NO!"

One of the policemen turned around, his gun heavy at his side, and Leah choked on her words. Kathmiya wanted to rush forward and protect Leah, but she was holding Aziza and thought they might all get beaten if she did.

The man picked up a few twisted wires from the floor. "Evidence." He smirked.

Leah fell to her knees. "Please, no, please, where are you taking him?" Her voice was hoarse, as though she had already sobbed it all out. "He's completely innocent," she croaked. Finally, she drew herself up. Kathmiya moved close to Leah, supporting her clammy body and Aziza's warm one while trying to be invisible.

"We never did anything; please, in the name of Allah," Leah said, her hands clutched together in a fisted prayer.

The policeman looked down at the tear-streaked and terrified woman at his feet. "It's okay, calm down," he said. "It's only for a little while. Then we'll bring him back."

These words, or some version of them, had been spoken throughout centuries and across continents by lying thugs trying to placate noisy would-be widows. And like the myriad other innocents left behind, Leah, no matter how much she wanted to believe them, still looked terrified.

"I'm an attorney, and I'm innocent," Salim thundered as they pushed him forward. "The law is supreme."

Kathmiya put Aziza down gently and supported Leah, who was starting to collapse. "You see?" she whispered. "He'll be fine."

But in the time it took for her to say that, he was gone.

Leah's eyes rolled back in her head. "Please, dear Allah have mercy!"

Kathmiya knew there was nothing that could get Salim back now, but she couldn't tell Leah that. And suddenly she realized there were people in the world with graver problems than her own.

"I'll bring his things," she said. Grabbing a straw mat, she put on her best I'm-just-the-nothing-maid pose and shrank into her loose *abaya*. Rich people had servants follow them everywhere. And so she headed to prison.

When Leah ran into Shafiq's house, he knew from the terror in her eyes that something unthinkable had happened. She was carrying Aziza too tight, like she was the last drop of water in a vast desert.

Naji had escaped on his own—courageous, proud, obstinate. Salim shared those qualities, but he never wanted to fight the state. His lapel pin—he wore it every day—showed a picture of the founding ruler, King Feisal. The handsome, proud, stern profile of the king, Salim's hero, right there on his chest.

That should help him get out, Shafiq thought with irrational hope.

But Leah's sobs, fractured by hyperventilating breaths, drowned out Shafiq's optimism.

Someone has to go save him, Shafiq knew.

Naji. He was the only one who was fearless and charming and magic enough to spring a man from jail.

Shafiq felt like every nerve in his body were pulled as taught as a slingshot, and the rock inside was aimed at Naji's head.

Not anywhere near as fast, not hardly as brave, but at least Shafiq was there.

"I'll go to the prison," he offered. Leah looked up.

"I'll go!" Ezra insisted.

Their father stared at one and then the other. Obviously, Ezra was older and readier. "You," he said quietly.

"Of course me," Ezra said, moving to the door. "This is an outrage against the Jews. We'll organize a rally if we have to. I can have dozens of people there in a matter of hours—"

"Stop," Roobain said.

Shafiq saw an opening. "I'll reason with them, quietly," he said. "I'll pay them. No trouble. Just get Salim out."

"That won't—" Ezra began, but Roobain had already changed his mind. "Allah be with you," he told Shafiq, who wished he could take the tremendous weight of responsibility and pile it on Naji as punishment for having left them like this.

Outside, Shafiq ran through a Basra that was completely changed. Not like during the riots, when the city was physically ravaged. Instead, the very order of the sights seemed to laugh at Shafiq's pounding anxiety. Old brick buildings still sat placidly side by side, as solid as ever, even though Shafiq felt so shattered.

Markets bursting with food that once might have tempted him—fat oranges and vats of salty feta cheese and barrels of black olives—all of it now no more appealing than dirt. Stone-tossing fortune-tellers who used to pique Shafiq's interest, back when he might wish for a future, now portending nothing but doom.

It was too outrageous, Salim being arrested for Zionism. He was the one who took every chance he could to preach against it. Shafiq ran on. Trying to chase his thoughts away, he stared at the sun-flecked river until spots filled his eyes.

Soon, his mind was as blurred as his vision. What was he supposed to say when he got to the prison?

Beneath his feet, the ground looked like it was cracking apart.

He stopped by the river to refocus. *If I can just convince them,* he thought, *if I am absolutely solid and soaring in my testimony, like an American airplane, they might let him go.*

The passing seconds were breathing down his neck, but Shafiq was trying to mine his memories for the key that would open the iron gates. He concentrated until he was back at Leah's house listening to Salim lecture about Iraq's recent history.

"The Young Turks came to Baghdad calling for a tolerant and brotherly society and we supported them."

"The Jews, you mean." Shafiq had heard this "we" all his life.

Salim got annoyed. "No," he said, rising from his chair as though he were arguing in court. "The people of Iraq. The Jews, yes, but also the Muslims, Christians and Kurds."

"Okay, yes, that's what I meant." Shafiq was just a kid. What did he care?

"Do you know who selected Sassoon Heskel for Parliament?" Salim challenged.

Only Jews would choose a senator named Heskel, Shafiq figured, but to be on the safe side he said, "The people."

"Wrong!" Salim pounced as though this small mistake, the misunderstanding of a disinterested teenaged boy, was the most fundamental fault endangering the country and the region, if not the world.

"The Jews, I mean." Shafiq backtracked.

"More Muslims selected him," Salim shouted in exasperation. "Muslims also appointed Abraham al-Kabir to a prominent finance position, and he helped establish Iraq's national currency. They sent his brother Yusef to represent Iraq at the League of Nations!"

Shafiq didn't know all these details, but he understood that they came together to form a picture of Muslim support for loyal Jews.

Salim continued. "You know what King Feisal said at the reception held by the chief rabbi?"

Shafiq had read the words, posted at synagogue near a picture of the king and local Jewish leaders, during so many long prayer services that he had them memorized. " 'There is no meaning in the words 'Jews,' 'Muslims' and 'Christians' in the terminology of patriotism,' " he recited. " 'There is simply a country called Iraq, and all are Iraqis.' "

Salim completed the quote, adding more that Shafiq had never heard. " 'I ask my countrymen to be only Iraqis because we all belong to one stock, the stock of our ancestor Shem. We all belong to that one race and there is no distinction between Muslim, Christian and Jew.' "

Shafiq looked up, not at the blinding river but at the road to the prison. There was no time to waste. It was not much fuel, but it was enough to keep going. *There is simply a country called Iraq, and all are Iraqis.* No one knew this better than Salim.

The prison was enormous—not tall but longer than five train cars lined up, surrounded by a huge fence with an open entrance at the front that led to a cave-like hole in the center. The walls were all bricked shut. It must be cold inside. Like nowhere else in Basra, it must be cold. The iron bars, the darkness, the dank center.

Shafiq knew that everything good and right had
rotted into vile and wrong when he saw, in this place
not fit for the most diseased street dog, Basra's most
beautiful pair of eyes peeking out from a heavy black
abaya.

"He's gone," Kathmiya said quietly. "They wouldn't
even let me give him this," she added, holding out a
crisp, rolled-up mat.

"Why are you here?"

"Shh . . . what are we going to do?"

Shafiq's confidence was all but gone. Would it help
to have a maid there? A friend? Would it put her in
danger?

Kathmiya resolved all of these questions by standing
close to Shafiq. Her body said it all. She wouldn't leave
even if he pushed her. They'd probably both end up in
a cold, dark room if he even tried.

Through a silent exchange, they agreed to fight for
Salim's release.

Shafiq walked up to the official at the front of the
room, experiencing a fleeting hope that if he freed
Salim, Kathmiya might jump into his arms. It was no
incentive, just another source of nerve-rattling anxiety.

"Sir," Shafiq addressed the man, who had uncom-
monly bad skin, blotched and reddish. "Thank you for
serving the great state of Iraq."

When the official spoke, his mouth moved but his eyes were dead of any flicker of feeling. "That's a new one."

"I'm here about my brother-in-law, Salim Dellal, who is also a servant of Iraq. I'm sure there has been a mistake."

The laughter that rang from the blotchy guard was like a dust storm darkening the sky. Each scornful, mirthless peal nourished the dormant scarlet flower in Shafiq's chest. It bloomed again, scattering its poisonous pollen into his blood.

"A servant of the state?" The guard laughed. "Not anymore. He's a prisoner of the state now."

Shafiq felt the weight of his failure; of course he shouldn't have tried invoking patriotism! What a stupid, liberal-minded approach to take with this shallow prison guard. But there was one plan left. "If it's money you need . . ." he stammered.

"Now you are making a little sense," the man replied with a hand out to grab the ten *dinars* Shafiq emptied from his pockets.

Shafiq and Kathmiya waited.

"Now leave," the guard said with quiet menace, the bumps on his cheeks quivering. "Before I have you arrested too."

Shafiq felt like he had been knocked to the ground. The blow was so vivid Kathmiya had to pull him. "Let's go," she said sharply.

They walked out in helpless silence. Which only got louder when they reached Leah's empty house. So much there they had taken for granted. Salim. The happy sounds of a child playing. Boring, old, wonderful, irreplaceable, vanished life.

"She must have taken Aziza to my place," Shafiq said.

"Don't leave me," begged Kathmiya.

Shafiq brought her up to her room and put his arms around her. "I never want to leave you," he breathed into her thick hair. He couldn't figure anything out. Trying only made matters worse. Nothing to do but act.

"I never want to be alone," she breathed back.

Shafiq felt a mix of fear and excitement, a pounding adrenaline that urged him to live for this moment. Kathmiya was not moving toward him, but just by not pulling away she was closer than ever before.

"Salim will be fine." He tried to focus on the reality around them, but it was so, so hard.

"How can you be sure?"

"He's an attorney. He lives by the laws of this land. They have to repay him now." But Shafiq didn't believe this as much as he had only an hour before.

"The law is what they used to arrest him," she pointed out, and he couldn't help but wish for just one moment that Kathmiya were not so smart.

The law. The rules. The ways of the world. Shafiq felt a throbbing in his head.

A world where devotion to tribe was put above pure love.

Where Marcelle was lost to a petty thief because she had to be married off to someone Jewish before she turned fifteen. Where Salim, the most vocal anti-Zionist Shafiq had ever known, was in jail on charges of Zionism.

Where Kathmiya, the most beautiful girl he had ever seen, could not marry. And where he, deeply infatuated with her, no—in love with her—could not do anything but leave. The pounding struck his heart. He stared at her exquisite heart-shaped face, her pomegranate-red lips, her mysterious eyes. Enormous black eyes, staring back at him as though—he could almost feel it—she wanted the comfort of his company.

For years, it seemed, Shafiq had thought of nothing besides this moment. And now it was here. He squeezed his eyes shut. Whatever happened, his life would never be the same.

And then he opened them again. "The law is what we live by," he announced. It was not his own voice speaking, but he had to obey. Still, he felt terrible abandoning Kathmiya in that empty house, echoing with absent souls. "I have to go now, but I promise to come back."

Kathmiya's black eyes were magnified by a coating of tears.

When Shafiq returned home, he had to rush to his mother to stop her from raining a new wave of blows down on her own head.

"The paper didn't work, our traditions are failing . . ."

If Leah knew what paper their mother was talking about, she didn't let it show, just sat listlessly, offering no words of comfort.

"They took the money, then sent me away," Shafiq said, struggling against the invisible wall of Naji's absence.

"We're going to save our traditions," Ezra said gently to their mother. Shafiq did not let his mind go to how "we" would do this. Only more trouble there.

"Marcelle has no baby," Reema gasped incoherently. "The spirits are angry. This proves that old remedies have lost their power." She let out a mournful wail.

"What it proves," said Ezra darkly, "is that Iraq is not safe for any Jew, even one as stubbornly anti-Zionist as Salim."

The spirit of Naji in Shafiq's head answered Ezra: *It is Zionism that makes Iraq unsafe for us.* Shafiq was not interested in either argument, just frustrated that

Naji was not there to make it, that both his brothers had gone from banter about philosophy to fanatical attachment to ideology.

"Forget your politics," their father scolded. "I don't care about the religious or the political or what have you. Salim is in prison. Leah is here with her little one." He had their attention. The entire family was depending on Roobain to pull Salim back from the precipice.

"Salim is innocent," Shafiq seethed through gritted teeth. "I can prove it! Everyone who knows him knows he hates the Zionists! It was only a radio . . ."

But his voice trailed off at the memory of the broadcasts, which they'd all listened to closely during the war. Everyone shifted nervously, feeling complicit in a crime that didn't exist.

"We need a lawyer," said Ezra after a pause.

Shafiq watched his mother twisting her fingers together. He wished he were as distracted, thinking about mythical papers and babies instead of the cold, enormous prison.

"My husband loves all people," said Leah through a daze. Everyone knew that any time you visited Salim you were as likely to find a Jew as a Sunni, Shi'a, Christian, Turk, Persian, Armenian, whatever friend trafficking through the home.

"They could speak for his character," Shafiq urged.

"As soon as a man defensively protests his innocence, he is known for the shadow of guilt," Roobain warned gravely. "The more people who hear, the more disgrace will attach to Salim."

"But . . . he's innocent!" It was a rare burst of clarity from Reema.

Shafiq shuddered to realize this likely made no difference.

"Everyone who knows him knows he's not a Zionist—can't we gather testimony?" he asked, thinking of the sadistic, joyless laughter of the blotchy official.

"There's no logical response if you've been framed," Ezra said flatly.

Shafiq said, "We need *wassttah*." Literally, it meant a connection, but everyone knew he was referring to someone with influence.

Roobain silenced them all. "Business associates and even colleagues can change their tune when the authorities are involved."

"Baba," Leah started to cry. "Baba, are you saying there's nothing we can do?"

"*Binti*, I am saying that we are alone but for the people we trust most."

And with that, he sent for Salwa.

———————

Shafiq felt a spark of hope as he rushed to his neighbor's house. Omar wasn't home, but there was Salwa. He didn't have to say a word; she asked, "What happened?" as soon as she saw his face. Then added, "*Allah yistir.*"

God forbid.

Quickly wrapping an *abaya* around her loose dress, Salwa held Shafiq's hand as they left her home. He was startled to realize how small her fingers felt, how much he'd grown.

When they arrived in the living room, which now had the air of a bunker, Shafiq watched as his family stared at the poor widow who represented their only hope. Salwa instinctively put an arm around Leah, who just sobbed harder.

Roobain explained what had happened. No one needed to apologize for disturbing Salwa. No one needed to tell her not to tell another soul. Nor did they need to ask for her help.

"Two seven one," she said.

It was Anwar's phone number in Baghdad.

Shafiq insisted on biking to the post office to make the call. He had failed to free Salim but he could definitely reach Anwar. Still, as he pedaled, it seemed that everywhere he turned, there were cars or horse-drawn carriages or children in his path, and the slowness of this most important ride of his life only increased the pressure in his head.

Finally, he arrived at the post office, a two-story building on the main street, which ran along an estuary near the center of Ashar. The clerk was in no hurry to help, but Shafiq could hardly shake him and say, "This is an emergency—my brother-in-law is in prison!" Instead he fought to look casual. *Watch the walls. Wait like you are bored. Don't lean in with desperation.*

A mother in front of Shafiq scolded her child. The clerk did not look up from the counter. The sun shone brightly. Everything was off.

Delay, delay, delay, delay, de-lay, d-e-l-a-y. Shafiq swallowed hard and stood stiffly. When his turn came, he forced a smile and handed the indifferent clerk ten *fils* and Anwar's number.

Two. Seven. One.

The clerk nodded to Shafiq, who picked up the black earpiece. He didn't bother to rehearse a speech. Anwar would understand.

But the phone just rang, maybe twenty times before Shafiq gave up.

The ride back felt even slower than the ride over, not for all the donkeys blocking the streets but the brakes that had been put on their plans.

When Shafiq shared the news—or lack of it—he saw the family's anemic optimism starting to fail. Every moment that Salim remained in jail seemed to increase the chances he would stay there.

An overnight train to Baghdad would leave the Margeel station in less than two hours. "Omar will go," Salwa said.

"I'm going with him," Shafiq insisted.

"No," Roobain was firm. "We have to stay together now."

All Shafiq could do was scribble a note.

My brother,

May Allah be with you.

Shafiq

When he stuck it in the hole in the wall, he felt like it was a wire that would connect the current of power between them.

Chapter XXXVI

The house was finally peaceful.

Everyone was gone.

No more Aziza hugging at her legs.

No more Leah or Salim to clean up after.

No more Shafiq, either.

Just the sound of a car passing outside and the shouts of a group of boys playing.

Kathmiya slept.

The next day, she shopped for too much food at the market and cooked too many orange lentils with rice for one person. After dinner, she ate a few of the narrow pistachio nuts from Turkey that Salim favored.

But he didn't come back.

No one came back.

The following day she went out just for air. Only to walk. She couldn't remember the last time she had felt so free. But it was an uncomfortable gift, purchased at the cost of Leah's pain.

Kathmiya stopped at different booths in the market-place, pausing to look at the goods she could never own: the glowing copper pots, the sparkling silver, the books she might hope to read but couldn't afford to buy. In the dingy gray dress she wore, she was obviously too poor, too *Midaan*, too outcast to be a customer.

Day after day, she meandered further through the city, watching men in cafés, purchasing a sour yoghurt drink on the street, picking up a newspaper some-one else had left behind. Her mind was filled with thoughts of all she'd seen by the time she got home, but it was not full yet, and she flipped through Salim's magazines, imagining the world beyond. Could she go to Baghdad someday? Kathmiya had left the marshes against her will, but now she wondered whether she might one day strike out just to travel. To busy cities where people didn't know her past and would let her have a future.

The ability to read letters and write phonetically did not exactly translate into literacy, but Kathmiya could make out some signs in shop windows. One said, "Dresses from Baris." She wondered who Baris was.

The styles were classy; beautiful but not overstated, not strange.

She walked by the shop a half dozen times, trying to appear casual while she studied the dress she liked best, with its bell-shaped sleeves, high neckline and long, flouncy skirt. Modest but still fun. She would have liked to buy it but that was impossible.

Oh, well, she thought. *It's ugly anyway.*

But she couldn't forget the dress. The next day she purchased three yards of a deep burgundy-colored cotton, evenly hued, with none of the light and dark washes left by the vegetable dyes used in the marshes.

All the sewing she'd done her entire life, never once had it been for fun. For herself. Kathmiya was starting to see that on the other side of solitude lay freedom.

Chapter XXXVII

When Omar came back, Shafiq asked for the straight story. "What are the chances—really?"

He got a tense smile in return. "Good."

Shafiq looked right into his best friend. "Just tell me everything, please. I know your brother wants to help. I know that. But what can he do?"

Omar sighed. "He's a judicial clerk. When I got there he was interviewing a goat owner who didn't pay the shepherd."

"So no influence."

"Not a lot."

After a pause, Shafiq began to ask, "Did he—"

"He's going to try everything, but the first judge he approached was useless."

Of course this established old official would never care about a nameless Jew in Basra, Shafiq thought, anger rising at the discrimination.

"But he's going to another one, Muhamad Jawdat—"

"Wait." Shafiq had to know. "What did the first judge say?"

Omar just said it: "That the best way to help members of his community was to stay out of their affairs."

"Members of . . . he's Jewish?"

Omar nodded. And Shafiq was crestfallen. This heir to Salim's heroes—the Jews who served the government of Iraq—was too busy protecting his own career to get an innocent man out of that massive, bricked-shut jail.

"What was the judge's excuse?"

Omar looked like he didn't want to answer, but Shafiq widened his own eyes as if to say, *I'll figure it out anyway.* "Basically, he expressed sympathy but wouldn't go near the case. Said, 'There's no use getting us both in trouble.'"

But who will get us out? wondered Shafiq.

Days stretched on with no news. The distance between Marcelle and the rest of the family could be measured by the fact that no one told her what had happened. Moshe's dangerous game of blackmail seemed even more deadly now. "We are alone but for the people we trust," Roobain had said. The family circle was closing in tighter.

Shafiq threw himself back into his studies. He tried to ease his constant worry by picturing Salim charming the guards and inmates.

No one is as resourceful as Salim, Shafiq told himself. *No one makes as many friends. People just adore the guy. He'll probably find all kinds of new clients in prison, and grow rich when he gets out.* Alone with Leah in the courtyard, Shafiq tried his weak joke out loud. "He's drumming up business in there, representing half the inmates by now."

Leah just looked pained.

"Anwar is working on it," he said, trying to console her. "Omar said he's going to the top judge—"

"It's all my fault!" she suddenly confessed.

"Leah, stop," he protested.

"Marcelle can't have a baby," she said.

"What is all that? You sound like Nana. Don't get all crazy now, please."

"Nana's right this time," Leah said, and then she told him about the paper that Marcelle ate, her demand for a certain ring, the threat she left behind.

"That one piece of jewelry was special," Leah said with a wistful sadness. "Marcelle knew it. Nana said it was lucky when she put it in my trousseau. I thought it was beautiful, with a pink stone and a twisted gold band—but I guess it wasn't enough gold to stop Moshe," she added ruefully.

"You think he actually did this?" There was no motivation—Moshe hadn't made a demand first. And yet. It sounded just like him: ignorantly vindictive, randomly destructive.

"He probably told her to get more," Leah said. "I've thought about it a million times. I think he expected Marcelle to come back with a ton of gold, everything we own, and maybe she lied and said we refused so that she would be safe. Why else would the police show up just a few days after she left?"

Shafiq turned the story over in his mind. "Moshe is dangerous," he acknowledged.

"I know," Leah said bitterly. "I should have seen this coming. I should have stopped it. If only I knew how serious he was."

"Don't blame yourself," said Shafiq. "He's responsible."

One relative had done more harm to their family than all the rampaging mobs during the riots.

"I'm going over there," he decided.

Although Shafiq should have stopped to think, to consult, to plan, he bolted out the door, afraid that if he hesitated, he would lose his nerve entirely. Obviously, Moshe was capable of the most dangerous behavior, and Shafiq might well end up following Salim to prison. But whatever Anwar was doing in Baghdad had not budged the situation in days, and even a failed attempt seemed better than the agony of this endless wait, watching his mother prepare supposedly protective concoctions of water and salt, seeing Leah smother Aziza with a frantic love, knowing Salim was alone somewhere behind those impenetrable walls.

In the street, a gang of boys played stickball unaware of the vagaries of the world, even unaware of their own bliss. Men shopped in the busy *souk*, cars rode over the rough streets, and vendors shouted to passing customers, but Shafiq was miles away.

Almost unconsciously, he headed toward Leah's house. *I'll go see Kathmiya to find out if she knows any more*, he told himself.

But really, he was thinking, in his overwrought, adolescent heart, *And also, maybe, to say good-bye forever.*

When she opened the door, he could see Kathmiya looked different. As though she wanted to hear his news but didn't need to see him. Instead of being put off by this startling independence, Shafiq was mesmerized. As they walked inside, he indulged in the mad fantasy that this cozy house was their home. That they could go up to her room together and leave the rest of the world behind.

They sat on the living room couch as they never had before, perfectly alone.

In the silence, his eyes wandered to her small, rough feet, her arms with their dusting of black hair, the ringlets and curls that dripped down her shoulders. He deliberately avoided her eyes, which drew him in so inextricably he might never get out.

She seemed to know he was watching her without looking, seemed to almost welcome it.

Shafiq felt crushed by the pressure. Sitting across from this beauty in rags, he wanted to escape his family and their troubles, forget entirely about Moshe, and run off with Kathmiya. But he wrenched himself from this pointless daydream and spoke.

"Leah told me she gave a ring to Marcelle," he began, relaying what he knew. "Did you hear anything about it?"

Kathmiya shared her side of the story, and then added a detail: "Marcelle came once after that, with the husband." Her eyes flashed. "No one was home and your sister just plain ignored me."

"Sorry . . ." Shafiq whispered.

"I could have been the chair to her. But the husband, he spoke."

All the nerves from Shafiq's wrists to his shoulders went taut. "What did he say?"

Her face disappeared behind her black curls as she looked down. "He claimed Salim had all the money."

Shafiq was trying now to look into her eyes, but she wouldn't meet his gaze. "What else?" he demanded, feeling the sweat rimming his hair.

"That's all," she said, glancing up at an angle, her light face shining through a mass of dark curls.

Softly this time, he asked again. "You can tell me."

"That 'Salim must be rich to have such a beautiful maid.' "

Shafiq's anger burned so brightly he was momentarily blinded.

The greed, the jealousy, even the insult to Marcelle were nothing compared to the image of Moshe inside of Shafiq's head, leering at the beauty he held so sacred, tossing off a comment that, instead of elevating her with honor, only reinforced her degradation.

Fear about confronting Moshe disappeared. Shafiq's teeth were on edge. He couldn't wait for this fight.

"I have to go," he said, backing toward the door. "I'm going to make sure he never comes near you—ever."

Shafiq had forgotten about Salim, about prison, about the reason he had set out to see Moshe in the first place. Nothing mattered but getting the slimy film off of himself.

Marcelle answered the door looking puffier than their petite mother, like a distorted version of Reema.

"Do you know what Moshe did?" Shafiq asked without a word of greeting, brushing past her into the living room.

Marcelle flinched. "It wasn't him."

This was as good as an admission of guilt. "So you know!" Shafiq roared. All this time, waiting, wondering, discussing, hoping, trying to find a way out, the family thought they'd been hiding their trouble from Marcelle, when she had a fat little hand in plotting it.

A flicker of vulnerability crossed her features. "How is Leah?" she asked, guiltily timid.

Shafiq was struck dumb. There were no words to justly describe the terrible fear and anguish that had consumed not only Leah but the whole family these past ten days. He thought of how his worn sister strained to hide her sadness in front of Aziza, how sometimes a tear would escape from her swollen eyes and she would brush it away quickly so her little girl wouldn't notice, how her brave, pained smile fooled no one.

And then Moshe walked in, chest thrust out like he was the Big Man. "So, you've decided to come ask for my forgiveness," he guessed.

That was the original plan, before Shafiq saw Kathmiya, back when he was ready to say—or pay— as much as it would take to get Moshe to recant the accusations that had landed Salim in prison. Revenge, Shafiq had thought, would have to wait until everyone was safe.

No way to be practical now, though, when just looking at the stringy-haired creep reminded Shafiq that he'd insulted both Marcelle and Kathmiya with his lecherous compliment. It was rash, probably insane, and would definitely only make everything worse, but Shafiq could not appease Moshe.

"I've come to warn you, actually," Shafiq said, a cruel snarl on his lips. *Warn you that I'm going to throw you to the dogs for calling Kathmiya beautiful when you're married to my sister.*

"Oh, really?" asked Moshe casually, though there was a note of defensiveness in his voice. "What can you do to me? I'm just a poor man trying to make an honest living."

Shafiq recognized the tone; Moshe sounded like every swindler at the market trying to con an extra *fils* from a customer.

Shafiq had dealt with these types all his life, and he relaxed, starting by offering Moshe good wishes. "I hope you're innocent. That will be very helpful for you, and for Marcelle, of course. Because we have a judge"—Shafiq knew next to nothing about Anwar's efforts in Baghdad but went out on a dare—"the most powerful judge on the Supreme Court of the state of Iraq."

Moshe's already slouchy posture slumped more.

"His name," Shafiq said, "is Muhamad Jawdat." He flashed this detail like a policeman's badge, never taking his eyes off of Moshe.

"And how do I know you're telling the truth?"

"Don't take my word for it," replied Shafiq calmly, leaning back all indifferent like a shopper at the market who doesn't want to buy. "You'll see Salim released soon. And when you do, you'll know how much influence we have. The power to get people out of prison—and to put them in." Moshe looked unsure, so Shafiq added, "From what I hear, the only thing they hate more than a Zionist is a stooge who uses the system for personal revenge."

Moshe fussed with his cuff. "Yes?"

"Yes," Shafiq replied, amused at how simple it was, like walking away from the tangerine salesman to force down the price.

He was ahead. He should go. But thinking of Kathmiya, Shafiq couldn't resist twisting the knife. "When he gets out, let's hope that they don't lock you up for false testimony."

"I never actually said Salim was a Zionist," Moshe protested stupidly, like a huge, brainless fly buzzing deeper into a little spider's web.

"Let's hope," continued Shafiq with a smile, "that Muhamad Jawdat believes you." He emphasized the name, enjoying how its specificity rattled Moshe.

By his side, Marcelle had tensed to stone. He still hadn't answered her question about Leah, and he owed it to both his sisters to reveal the truth—but not in front of Moshe. "Marcelle," he said, "I need to speak to you alone."

A year or even a month before, Shafiq would never have dared send Moshe out of his own living room. But Naji was underground, and Salim was behind bars, and Ezra was nearly completely lost to his own infatuation with ideology, and it fell to Shafiq to act. "Please," he added, gesturing to a curtained doorway leading to the back of the house.

Moshe, debased from practically admitting that he had sent an innocent man to jail, obeyed.

"Marcelle," Shafiq said once her husband was gone. "Can I trust you?"

She nodded. He wondered. The bluff had worked, but could he take this chance? "It's been very hard on Leah," he began, trying to hedge his bets.

Marcelle looked down. "I guessed that," she said quietly.

"Then how could you—?"

Through bow-shaped lips she sucked in her breath hard, as though if she let it out there would be a flood of tears. Shafiq thought of his parents and put a tentative hand on Marcelle's shoulder. The tenderness punctured her defenses, and she began to weep. "Leah had everything. She got pregnant. And I'm still not."

Shafiq remembered his mother ranting about Marcelle not having a baby. His unhinged mother who had never been the same since Naji left. But there was a grain of truth in her perception. Moshe hadn't cooked up this plot on his own; it had simmered in Marcelle's jealousy. For petty envy, she robbed Salim of his freedom, Leah of her peace of mind and Aziza of her father.

He wanted to hate her, but it was obvious from the dark half-moons under Marcelle's eyes that her nights were haunted. "At first I didn't believe in spirits and all of that," she began, "but now I think I'm hurting myself by not believing."

"You are killing your family, but they still love you," he said. "We do, I mean."

Marcelle's face spread into a quivering smile. "I don't want the ring anymore," she said suddenly.

Another impulsive, superstitious decision. They all might as well trade their minds for amulets. "No, Marcelle." Next she'd be grafting onto a political ideology or looting clothes off of dead criminals.

"It is cursing me—don't you understand?" Again, that fanatical look. "I've made the lucky ring unlucky by my vindictiveness."

Eyes shining with an overcharged gleam, Marcelle opened a small silk pouch and pulled out the delicate gold ring, which glowed rose from the oval pink stone at its center. "Here," she insisted.

The trinket would never bring back Salim, but there was some logic to Marcelle's contrition, and Shafiq wanted to accept. Still, he didn't answer, just nodded toward the room where Moshe was waiting.

"I have," Marcelle said, reading his thoughts, "a bit of money he doesn't know about. If he ever asks, I'll say I sold it and show him the cash. He'll take it all from me someday anyway, but if I give this back, maybe Allah will forgive and bless me with a baby."

She held the ring out to her brother.

He hesitated, thinking, *If Salim is not released, Moshe will go after me next.*

But he took the delicate band, feeling a contagious shiny hope that maybe, just maybe, Marcelle's redemption would free them all.

The next day a pebble rolled off the cliff, the first sign of an avalanche.

Shafiq was sitting in his living room across from a portly brown-haired man he recognized as one of the attorneys Salim socialized with through the Lawyers Guild.

"They asked if he is a Zionist!" the guy's belly shook while he laughed, but Shafiq's family sat still as though posing for portraits; in Iraq, no one smiled in them. "I said, 'this guy is no Zionist! He's more patriotic than the flag.'"

If Naji were there he would have smiled. So Shafiq did it for him. The grin turned to a giggle, then a laugh, and soon everyone's incredulous guffaws were swirling around the room. Salim was not free, but something had shifted.

Later, when Shafiq tried to give Leah the ring, she frowned. "I can't take that," she said, backing away as though it were a malarial mosquito. "I gave it to

Marcelle with spite. That's why we have all of these problems."

Shafiq was fed up with the quack diagnoses. "Moshe is why we have these problems. And Marcelle regrets taking it from you," he tried.

"It's tainted by my anger as much as her greed." Leah turned away.

"Please." Shafiq had no more use for jewelry than the salt his mother sprinkled into his pockets whenever he wasn't looking.

But Leah just pressed the warm gold ring into his hand. "If you heard how Nana talks about this you would understand. It won't work for me or Marcelle—but it will for you. For your future wife, I guess."

The thought was so far-fetched he knew he had to get rid of the supposedly lucky stone, and fast.

Shafiq counted on Omar to tell him what had really happened in Baghdad.

"Anwar told the judge he needed help," he explained. "So the guy asks, 'For whom?' And Anwar says, 'It's my sister—her husband is in trouble.' Suddenly the judge gets really mad. He nearly kicks my brother out of his office. 'I'll never give anyone special treatment just because they're your relative,' he screams. 'That's an abuse of power.' So Anwar quickly confesses the truth:

his 'sister' is really his neighbor, and her husband is in prison on false charges of supporting the Zionists."

Shafiq remembered how the Jewish judge didn't want to help. "Then what?"

"He said, 'In that case, I can investigate.' I guess he realized Anwar wasn't trying to get a favor for his relative, but get justice for an innocent man."

"Still . . . investigate?"

"Said he won't act until he gets the facts," Omar replied. Then he added tentatively, "Too soon to say, but the facts—"

Omar couldn't contain his smile, and Shafiq couldn't help but finish the sentence, "—are on our side."

When the sun hit the top of the sky on Saturday, Kathmiya heard the familiar creak of the door and knew Salim was back.

Gaunt, gray and haggard, but home.

She hadn't expected it, but she felt welling up an irrepressible feeling for him, this gruff man who barely spoke to her. Maybe she was relieved to learn that life didn't always end in horror. Or maybe she was just glad not to be alone anymore.

"Where is everybody?" he asked. She could tell from a grain of defeat in his voice that Salim had lost more than weight in prison.

When he heard that the family was staying at his in-laws' house, Salim ordered Kathmiya to go there with him. "We'll be having a party and there will be plenty of work for you."

As usual, her affection was returned with nothing. Less than that—with a demand. She didn't begrudge him a party after surviving prison, but she had tried to get him out of there. She wished for once she might join the celebration, instead of just cleaning up the detritus of everyone else's fun.

She knew better than to dream of a celebration with Shafiq or to think about wedding the one young man she cared for who could also set her free. But no matter how hard she tried to block it, the idea took hold on its own.

As soon as Salim came barreling through the large front door, the flood of relief that washed over the Soufayr home could have swelled the Tigris and the Euphrates and all of the marshes in Kathmiya's village and beyond.

There were stretched smiles and tight hugs and raucous cheers and fine food and even better company. Salwa was at the center of the party, smiling like she hadn't since Hajji Abdullah had died. The family also sang Omar's praises for rushing to Baghdad. And they toasted Anwar above all.

"I'm naming my next child for that judge, Jawdat," Salim declared.

"You always used to say your boy will be called Feisal, for the first king of Iraq," Shafiq teased playfully.

"Iraq?" Salim repeated. He was squinting uncomfortably, like the light in the room was too bright. It was then that Shafiq noticed what Kathmiya had seen right away: Salim was back, but he would never be the same.

Shafiq took advantage of the general excitement to steal a trip to the kitchen. "Everything's normal again," he told Kathmiya with a smile.

"For you and your family, yes." He could hear her disappointment and was desperate to empathize and make it right. "The future's still pretty confusing," he began tentatively.

She looked up. "I've been walking around a lot, and practicing my writing."

"Me too!" he said, forgetting that her little pages full of longhand phrases were leaves on the tree of his formal schooling. Now that the very grave danger of Salim's imprisonment had been resolved, Shafiq was free to address the much more ordinary concerns that had seemed too petty to contemplate for the past two weeks. "I've been studying, but the more I study, the more I wonder—what should I do? I don't know if I'll get into university in Baghdad. Ezra had no luck. So what's the point of working so hard if the system is against me?"

Just then, Leah called Kathmiya, who turned sharply to leave. Shafiq didn't notice her quiet fury. He was too busy contemplating what to do with his wide-open future now that prison was no longer a prospect.

This time, Leah didn't ask Kathmiya about dishes or laundry. "Our auntie would like to meet you," she said, pointing to the plump mother who had been at the center of the celebrations.

Kathmiya looked more closely, and then she recognized that face: kind, and worn like a favorite dress tattered from too many washings.

Salwa thanked Leah and put an arm around Kathmiya, guiding her to a small, scruffed bench in the hall where they sat alone.

"I remember you," the two women said at once, and then both laughed.

"Are you okay?" Kathmiya asked.

"Allah is great," Salwa replied. "But you . . . your mother . . . that problem . . ."

"Yes, that," Kathmiya confessed, trusting Salwa wouldn't judge her for skipping the euphemisms.

"I would do anything for your family," Salwa said, gently taking Kathmiya's palm as if to press this pledge onto her flesh. "Just tell me, how can I help?"

Since she could remember, Kathmiya had wished for the day when someone—Allah or the people who gave her the red barn book or the village sheikh—would ask that question. But now that the dream had finally come true, she went blank. Being unmarriageable was frightening enough, but not knowing why tortured her more. It was like watching a disease progress without ever having a diagnosis. Clearly, she was destined for loneliness, but without knowing the cause, she had no idea how to find a remedy.

Salwa broke the silence. "I live next door," she said simply. "Anytime you need." Kathmiya didn't look up until she heard, "You or your kind mother, of course. She's welcome in my home, and everything I own is hers."

At the mention of her mother, Kathmiya finally let herself hope. *Maybe I'm not so alone after all.*

Shafiq had gone straight from the kitchen to Reema, who was on the upstairs balcony looking out at the city through shutters that were thrown wide open after two weeks of being sealed shut.

She smiled when he produced the small gold ring with its sparkling rose gemstone.

"Leah said she gave it to Marcelle in bitterness, and Marcelle said she accepted it in greed. So," Shafiq lied, "they asked me to return it to you."

He tried to hand his mother the ring but she pushed it back. It was like an invisible lasso kept pulling it to him. "This is the pink sapphire," she said, as though that were an explanation.

"What do you mean, Nana? Pink or not, I don't want it."

"Sapphires are blue," she continued in the entranced voice she used when talking about the magic of the world he never saw: the danger of jealous spirits or the *jinn*, the power of a pinch of salt or a gallnut charm, the fading ancient traditions that had to be upheld at all cost.

"You see," she began, "it only becomes pink because it tries to be a ruby. It doesn't succeed, but it doesn't fail, either, because in the process it becomes even more rare and beautiful."

Shafiq turned the ring gently to the side so that its facets sparkled in the light. He had only ever heard of blue sapphires. *You tried to be like the others and failed—and along the way became more precious and more treasured.* Despite his skepticism, the story reeled him in.

Reema was speaking in her usual breathy, enchanted voice, but for once Shafiq was listening. "It's too special to be given to just anyone, and it will have no power— it could even have a bad influence—if it is given lightly or taken under threat."

He nodded, for the first time transfixed by his mother's old folk wisdom.

"You haven't told me the whole story about your sisters, but I know you were trying to help. They were right to insist that you take it. So this is yours now. Give it away only with a pure heart. Then it will bring you even more happiness."

Salim was free, and Shafiq could almost, almost, believe in magical gems.

Chapter XXXVIII

It turned out the old principal was right. One by one, Shafiq heard the Jewish students at school talking about leaving Iraq. Europe was devastated and dangerous but Beirut was safe and modern. Even the Soviet Union would be better than competing with the top three Jewish candidates in Basra for maybe two slots at a college.

Shafiq told Salim he planned to take the civil service exam, hoping for some of his brother-in-law's famously contrarian optimism. "Maybe I can, you know, follow in the footsteps of Senator Heskel," Shafiq said. He was in Salim's study, where the Holy Koran sat on a shelf right next to the Old Testament.

Salim didn't look up from the papers he was shuffling. "Heskel was the finance minister. The senator was Daniel."

"Well, you know what I mean," Shafiq said, trying to sound cheerful even if his future was melting like the frozen water his mother bought each afternoon at the local ice factory.

"You'll need to get your history straight if you want to go into government," Salim added, still mulling over the documents.

"You taught me a lot already . . ."

At this, Salim looked up. "I don't only mean past history, Shafiq. You'll need to anticipate the future. And Iraq—" he shook his head, looking down again. "Iraq—"

"Okay, I get it." Shafiq stopped Salim, whose patriotism had already been ruined; no point in making him admit it out loud.

"Shafiq," Salim was undeterred, "they didn't beat me in my cell."

"Thanks Allah," Shafiq breathed.

"They took me to the latrines so I could smell the urine while they hit my back with straps." Salim turned in his chair and hitched up his shirt to show the welts cutting like tangled branches on his skin, so startlingly crimson, they looked painted on.

If only. "Allah protect us," Shafiq whispered.

"I told myself it was good, because at least on the way to the beatings, marching with my head pushed down, I would look at the light on the floor near my stinking feet to see whether it was day or night," Salim continued. "The guards scared me, I admit I even thought about confessing to make the beatings stop—I might have but I was innocent, completely innocent of all charges!—but what really terrified me was not knowing whether the sun was out. There was no way to measure time. There was no way to tell how long the nightmare had been going on. And that just seemed to mean that it would never end."

"Allah have mercy." It was all Shafiq could manage.

"I know what the floor of a prison bathroom smells like, what it is like to retreat from the blows by ramming my face even closer to the stench, to feel like I will never be clean again. I wish I could forget but I never, never will."

After escaping Salim's study, Shafiq looked for Kathmiya. She was basting top sheets onto blankets in the living room, surrounded by soft fabric on the yielding couch.

"Hello," he said.

"Yes?" she muttered.

"Is everything okay?"

"The same," she said, fingers flying through the wide stitches. "Which is not good."

"I know," he began. Seeing those blindingly beautiful eyes, he blurted out, "Everything is wrong."

"Right," she replied quietly. He stood tall. When she looked up at him he didn't look away, just abandoned himself in her shining gaze.

"If only we could escape." His thoughts spilled out of his mouth. Terrifying.

"I wish," she said. Even more scary.

Shafiq was overwhelmed. But he knew she understood. "If we could just fly away, like my pigeons . . ." he said.

Njum, njum. He thought of the birds soaring skyward as he urged them to reach for the stars.

Walking through the dusty streets to *Al-Wattan*, Shafiq reviewed in his mind the articles he'd been reading about the Communists. Naji's name was never mentioned but the movement was growing. Strikes. Protests. Demands. And imprisonment. He tried to assure himself that Naji was probably instigating trouble instead of being punished for it. But he knew he had to find out.

The place was as crowded as ever, but two black teas later, Shafiq still didn't find Sayed Mustafa.

Same the next day.

And the next.

"I'm always here," he remembered his old principal promising. Finally, Shafiq asked the waiter.

"Sayed Mustapha—skinny guy, wore a suit, used to sit over there?" Shafiq gestured to the bench where the principal had made a second home.

The waiter's eyes narrowed. "Never heard of him!"

Another man leaned in and Shafiq could almost taste the smoke on his breath. "Gone," he said. "Don't ask."

But before Shafiq could follow the advice, a man in a cream-colored suit started asking questions. "How did you meet Sayed Mustapha?"

Shafiq's mind raced but came up with only one answer. "He was my school principal."

"That was years ago," the man said, wielding the details of Sayed Mustapha's life like a threat. From an inner pocket of his smooth jacket, he drew out a notebook and a pen, which he pointed at Shafiq's chest. "And are you now his associate?"

Shafiq wanted to run out but that would only make him look guilty. "No," he said, trying to relax. Years of theatrics with Omar were worth something. "I haven't seen him for ages," he said lightly and yawned.

The interrogator jotted down a note. "So," he demanded. "What's your name?"

A certain muscular fear that had been instilled in Shafiq from a young age prompted him to answer right away. "Khaled Hamadi." He made the name up on the spot.

Self-consciously sauntering out through the café's open archway, he tried not to think about what had happened to Sayed Mustapha. Shafiq's nightmares were already crowded with fates for Naji: Moscow, prison, worse. *Wherever they are,* Shafiq prayed to himself, *let them find their way out soon. And let them know enough never to return to* Al-Wattan.

The Nation.

Shafiq's lanky legs carried him away as fast as possible, but he was too disturbed to go home.

Determined to shake the fear from his bones, he continued walking. He crossed the small bridge that ran over the main estuary between Basra and Ashar, trying to calm his restless mind. Each foot on a different slat of wood in a pattern, trying to unrattle his nerves as he stepped.

He breathed in the breeze from the river as he moved along the Corniche toward the business district in Ashar. On the Shat al-Arab river, passengers rode in the long, narrow canoes pushed by men with tall bamboo rods. Larger ships transported everything from apples to donkeys. Fishermen cast their twine-colored nets while boys rowed around them in tin boats, the sounds of the waves magnified by the metal surface.

Wandering up to the noisy markets, where the coppersmith's banging competed with the squawking chickens, he saw the Kurdish porters wrapped in headscarves, promising to carry shoppers' groceries for just twenty *fils*.

A chain of men passed crates in a line; Shafiq noticed the boxes were stamped with the official government seal. Spices went upriver to Baghdad, and documents came back down to Basra.

There was no more sparkling city imaginable. Shafiq thought about Iraq, the Garden of Eden, home to the greatest civilizations since recorded history began. He felt this geography and culture to be part of his very being, the soil from which he sprang. Second to Kathmiya, Basra was his true love. Her many waters, majestic palm trees, homing birds, sweet dates and warmhearted, generous people were his hearth and home. Under the brilliant stars that sparkled over Basra's unpolluted skies at night slept all members of his family, immediate and extended, together forming the only protective network Shafiq had ever known.

But the inexorable tug of his own ambition told Shafiq there was little point in staying in Iraq only to hope for one of the few places available in the pharmaceutical school. Beyond the country's borders, he could get a better education, maybe return as a professional, set up a life, and then rejoin his family.

Sayed Mustapha believed in his students, whatever their religion—believed in a pluralistic Iraq. Salim put this doctrine into practice, mingling freely with anyone interesting—to him that meant everyone. Both loved Iraq, and both had encouraged Shafiq's future there.

One way or another, each had been silenced. He couldn't adopt their models of promoting Communism or opposing Zionism. He could share their nationalism, but only in his heart.

It was time to leave.

Once he accepted that, Shafiq continued his walk with a bounce in his step. He was too young to give up all hope. Maybe Naji would come back soon. Maybe they could even meet overseas.

Shafiq headed to Ashar. As he passed the American consulate, he saw a young man with hair shaved so close he looked bald. Buoyant with a newfound sense of purpose, Shafiq smiled when their eyes met.

"American?" Shafiq asked in his best movies-and-magazines English.

The man, who looked like he was Ezra's age, stopped to face Shafiq. "That's right," he said, bright as a floodlight. "Hi."

"America is so great country," Shafiq responded, hoping to keep the conversation going.

The stranger laughed. "I sure miss it."

"You miss it?" As soon as Shafiq repeated the phrase, he understood what it meant. "Where is home?" His cousin Fouad used to have a pen pal from Akron, Ohio, and Shafiq hoped the American lived there so he could mention this.

"Ever hear of Fitchburg, Wisconsin? Just outside Madison."

"Oh, yes!" Shafiq pretended to know. "Your home is here?"

"Not just my home—my girl's there, too."

Shafiq understood this to mean "daughter," and sweetly replied, "Oh, small girl," as though he were fussing over his niece.

"No, no," the man laughed, clearing up the confusion with a raunchy emphasis, "my *girl.*"

Now Shafiq understood. "Yes, your *girl.*"

"You won't believe how pretty she is." The American, casually dressed and rugged, seemed completely different from the porcelain Brits who had chased Shafiq from their pool so many years before.

"She is your girl, she is beautiful," Shafiq complimented the American, who had opened his wallet to show off a photo.

"Sure is."

The slim girl with brown hair in the cracked photo was remarkable and unremarkable, beautiful and common. Not Rita Hayworth, not so remote, but a breathtaking woman who was ordinary and available.

"Beautiful," Shafiq said. "America is so many beautiful girls."

The young man chuckled roundly. "You would love it," he said.

I'm sure I will, Shafiq thought, no longer wondering where he would go.

His mind filled with images from American movies— the modern buildings, cars everywhere, and especially the array of pretty girls—Shafiq approached his English teacher, who had learned the language at a college in the United States.

"Can you help me to apply?"

"To Hope?"

Shafiq had never heard this short English word. "Hope College is where I went," the teacher explained.

"Yes, Hope," Shafiq affirmed.

The teacher promised to help, and then he explained what that word meant. "When you wish for something, you want it, you know it might happen."

Hope. Shafiq felt nearly there.

It took three weeks to receive the application, but Shafiq filled it out immediately. Writing from left to right felt strangely promising, as though this backward movement could undo all the madness of the East. He pressed three red twenty-five-*fils* stamps featuring the Kirkuk Oil Field onto the envelope, hoping he could follow the images of the petroleum installations all the way to America.

Chapter XXXIX

As Kathmiya walked to the brick house that Jamila cleaned, the city shimmered in the light of Salwa's promise to help. The men everywhere, in thin suits headed to government offices, in loose *dishdashas* milling about the market, in khaki shorts loading boats— she imagined that one of them would get her out by taking her in.

Kathmiya threw a pebble at her mother's window.

"I told you, she sleeps late in the mornings, you should come then!" Jamila said after rushing down to stop the noise.

"I'm getting too old," Kathmiya began bluntly. "If we wait any longer I'll be a spinster for sure."

"My child, I am trying, believe me." Jamila hustled Kathmiya into the house and up to her small room. Even after so many years of working there, she had nothing on the walls except for a small woven amulet, like the one Kathmiya had given Leah when Aziza was born. Colored threads twisted around two perpendicular sticks, art made out of nothing but string and faith.

"Well, I have good news," Kathmiya said, sitting on the mattress. It was much thicker than any they had in the marshes but would never be as comfortable because this would never be home. The marshes had exiled her, but they were still "home."

Kathmiya told her mother about the serendipitous encounter with Salwa. "It must be the will of Allah," she concluded breathlessly. "She promised to help!"

She waited for the smile, the encouragement, the plans. But instead, Jamila just breathed in and exhaled slowly.

"I know exactly where she lives—you can go there as soon as you want," Kathmiya prompted.

Jamila's lids were heavy. "That woman is poor, worse off than us," she said, looking down at the rough brick floor. "Imagine—me, a *Midaan*, had to give her money." Kathmiya was crushed, but Jamila didn't stop. "I don't regret it, of course not. It was *sadaka*, a charitable act as Allah wills. But I have no illusions that she'll be able to help us."

"You have to at least go and see her!" Kathmiya felt her cheeks tingle. To miss this chance would be like finding ten *dinars* but refusing to spend them.

"Of course not, no." Jamila shook her head. Then she started offering the usual promises to find Kathmiya a husband.

"You've said that so many times—why should I believe you?" Kathmiya glared. "Why?"

"Quiet!" Jamila pinched her daughter's arm, but this only amplified the volume.

"I am almost nineteen and I have no husband and the matchmakers in the marshes won't help me, not the ones here either and—"

"Hey! You!" Old Nafisa.

Now Jamila slapped Kathmiya across the face. "You have to make a scene here? Is that going to help?"

Nafisa stood in the doorway in a navy dress with a high lace collar that guarded her neck like she was royalty. "So sorry," Jamila groveled. "I've beat her and I'm sending her away."

But Nafisa just shook her head. "Make her some tea," she instructed. "The girl is distressed. But I have a few words of advice that will ease her mind."

Kathmiya felt immensely relieved.

In the kitchen, hands cupped around a hot glass filled with black tea, Kathmiya repressed the memory of how Nafisa had turned Salwa away, instead contriving similarities between the women. Both were older, alone in the world with nothing but kindness for those less fortunate. Humbled by circumstance, maybe. Or just good-hearted.

"You will have to learn," Nafisa said, "your place in this society."

Kathmiya nodded and smiled. It occurred to her that this woman was wealthy, and maybe she could help. She put on her best find-me-a-home posture, hands folded in her lap, fluttering eyes attentive, eager for advice and open to charity.

"Some of us may not have so much, but we learn to enjoy the little things," Nafisa went on. "Flowers are free, and so beautiful! Sometimes just a warm cup of tea can be simply delicious."

"Mmm, yes!" Kathmiya smiled. *And a home of my own would be nice.*

"Your mother has told me all about your situation," the widow went on. *So now you've decided to help,* Kathmiya willed.

"She's asked me many times to use my influence to find you someone to marry," Nafisa said. Kathmiya felt warmed by this information. Jamila really had been trying.

"I must say I thought about it," Nafisa continued, gesturing for more sugar cubes. Kathmiya noticed the ones

Jamila scurried to bring were real little blocks, instead
of the big single cone Leah bought to chip into her tea.
Further proof that Nafisa was not just magnanimous,
but also rich. "And I'm going to tell you what I told your
mother: it is much safer to stay in your class. A girl like
you is adequate, some man somewhere might take you
in. But you would never truly be happy. Because you are
a *Midaan*. You should know your place and stay there.
Otherwise, society will fall apart. And think of the
husband—he would have to sacrifice so much to be with
you. His family would cast him out. If he died, you would
have absolutely no one. And husbands die, take it from
me. No, you are best off accepting the ways of kismet."

Kathmiya was crying now, but Nafisa's concern was
genuine. "Trust me," she said. "It is better this way."

No one had ever spoken to Kathmiya so directly.
She felt endlessly grateful.

The next time she saw Shafiq, she was as calm as the
lazy water in the marshes, and let him follow her to
the small maid's quarters. It might have been a dangerous place for them to be alone back when she was
dreaming of a life with him, but now that she was resolved to accept her fate, they were safe.

"I've been thinking," she said. "Life here with Leah
is fine. I can smell the flowers and drink tea and be
happy."

"That's great!" Shafiq acknowledged her major revelation only briefly before moving on to his own news. "Guess what? I applied to go to college in America." Kathmiya knew nothing of the country and even less of how Shafiq might get there, but she understood that he was leaving. "At a college called Hope."

As he explained the meaning of the English word, she felt her face sting worse than when her mother slapped it. There she was, all passive and accepting of fate, while he was planning to actually get on an airplane and fly to another country. To live, study, learn.

"How can you do that?" she asked. She meant it in so many ways: how dare you, how is it even possible, how could I?

"I didn't get in yet," he said, sounding defensive.

"So you go flying out to America and all I get is to drink tea and smell flowers?" she fumed. Suddenly, Nafisa's advice was not tough and loving, but just tough and unsavory, like overcooked meat.

Now Shafiq looked angry. "Kathmiya, I don't know how to tell you this, but I don't feel so sorry about your whole situation here."

"Oh, no?" She was furious. Little spoiled schoolboy who never even made his own bed pretending to understand her life when all she did was make beds—for others.

"No! If you don't mind, why are you so worried about being alone? Any man in this city would marry you if he could. You act like you have no idea that you are brilliant and beautiful. Oh, poor little Marsh Arab maid. I might have thought that when I first met you, but I never saw anyone learn to write so fast. I never met anyone who has such intelligence and," he hesitated and then blurted out, "such beauty!"

They were staring, face to face. "The old widow told me to give up," Kathmiya confessed, relaying Nafisa's advice.

"The old widow doesn't know you like I do," Shafiq said.

"But she said even if I found someone, he would have to abandon his whole family for me," she said, the dream Nafisa had helped her to relinquish coming back into focus.

"So, why wouldn't he? You're way more beautiful than Cleopatra. Armies could fall for you. And so will some very lucky man."

Shafiq. It was Shafiq. "Would you?" she asked with shy but irrepressible hope.

"Me . . . ?" he stammered.

It was enough. Kathmiya understood, in one terrible blow, how completely deluded she had been to even hint that they could be together. Nafisa had warned her that she should not try to escape her destiny. Shafiq would never abandon everything he had just for her.

"Good luck in America," she said, thinking, *You live your life and I'll manage a way to live mine.* There were tears welling in the corners of her eyes—not from sadness; she was too hard to feel sad—but frustration that she couldn't even storm out just then because she had absolutely no place to go.

Chapter XL

Shafiq was the one who left, but she was so embedded in every crevice of his mind there was no getting away.

That evening, Shafiq shut his eyes and tried to remind himself about college in America, the breathtaking excitement of going to the capital of the world: the triumphant winner of the war, the place to realize his dreams . . .

But instead of feeling excited, he felt empty. What an utterly selfish choice. He would be abandoning his country and his family for his own personal glory.

The image of Naji burned in his mind, telling Shafiq to live for something bigger than himself. It was a pure sentiment, noble and great. But Naji had thrown it away on the wrong cause, like a man who loves an unfaithful wife. Communism was an abstract theory that led to nowhere but prison.

Kathmiya might only be a single individual—but what was worth more than one human life? Saving her felt like a calling.

His calling.

It would mean leaving his parents, but he would still have Omar. He would still have Basra. And he could rescue one lost person.

America or Kathmiya? The more he thought, the more he was convinced of his decision. *If she needs me, then I have to stay.*

Kathmiya did not greet Shafiq when he arrived the following day while she was hanging laundry on the roof.

"I brought you a present."

Against her better judgment, she smiled. *He's back.*

"I wish you would face me so I could give it to you," he continued.

She turned toward this tall boy, nearly a man, the sheet in her hand rippling slightly in the breeze, the clear blue sky overhead the only witness to their encounter. He moved closer. "Give me your hand," he said gently.

Kathmiya let the sheet fall on the brick roof and held out her work-reddened palm, watching as Shafiq placed a ring on her finger. She stared, the glint from the stone reflected in her black eyes. She had never received a gift, unless you counted a tattered children's book whose origin she did not even fully understand, and here he was giving her something precious.

"It's beautiful," she said, catching her breath.

"Just like you," he confessed, taking her decorated hand in his.

They walked together back to her small room, moving quietly so as not to rouse any attention. This time he sat close to her on the bed. "This is very unique," he began. And then he explained the story of the pink sapphire.

Kathmiya experienced something she never had before: she felt understood. Because the story of the ring was her story. She had been trying so hard to fit into a society that couldn't accept her, with no success; just utter, abject failure. But the ring held the promise of a lofty perspective: she may never have the rewards that society prized, but rather than becoming less worthy, she could be more rare, more precious, more beautiful.

It was as close as they would ever come to a wedding night. Neither family would accept their union, but Shafiq and Kathmiya both believed in that moment they were making an eternal pledge, and so they came together as either had only barely imagined.

Even more sweet than the love was the sleep that followed. They nestled together in a deep, restful slumber. But when Shafiq awoke, she was gone.

PART THREE

Chapter XLI

It is all horribly wrong, Kathmiya realized as soon as she saw the watery pink streak on her dingy sheet.

There were no witnesses, there was no celebration, there was only a sticky desire that should have been resisted and a hollow, upside-down feeling like an overturned boat floating on the water.

She stared at her lover, who appeared more handsome than ever now that she was determined to leave him. But what choice did she have? Run off with him and live . . . where? She had already been driven out of the marshes. And now she could not even stay in Basra.

As she wrote him a final note, the magnitude of her shame burned at Kathmiya's skin.

Then she stumbled out of the house with nothing but the little ring in her worn pocket. When the sun-warmed air hit her face, Kathmiya knew there was only one place in the whole city of thousands of people where anyone would receive her.

She wasn't sure how to tell her mother, only that she had to see her. Jamila had to forgive and help her daughter. If not, Kathmiya would be good and truly ruined.

When Kathmiya knocked at Nafisa's front door, she was met with a rude look of surprise. "I thought you would be with your mother," the widow said. "Your father being ill and all."

Ali was sick and no one had even told Kathmiya! She wanted to sink back into her familiar, comfortable red world of anger, but how dare she? After what she had done? Jamila was her only lifeline to the family, and it was fraying. Heat and friction could break it completely.

Back at Leah and Salim's home, Kathmiya felt more empty than before: Shafiq had not waited for her. The message in her note kept him away. She wrote it that way on purpose, but she had also been testing him, mad, irrational girl that she was, hoping that he would find her after she left.

"My father is ill. I have to go home," Kathmiya told the family. Only she knew the buried secret: that she would never return. The ruse made leaving all the more difficult, because her good-bye was supposed to be temporary, not anguished. She hugged Aziza close and felt her soft toddler skin and thought, *Is that it?*

One last night in that little maid's room. Too late to appreciate the security she had enjoyed there, the safety of the small life she could have had if she had followed the old widow's advice.

Kathmiya had not been home to the marshes for months. She had never been openly ostracized but she had exiled herself, deciding to return only in triumph.

Now, instead, she was on the ferry again with nothing but her clay vase, her burgundy dress, her red book and oh, that ring. A reminder of the terrible cataclysm she had brought on herself, but also a keepsake that still promised there could be a way out.

As she approached the wetlands where she lived, she tried to summon her inner resources. Perhaps it was Allah's will that Ali got sick so she could see her family now. Torn and soiled she was, but home.

It was daytime when she arrived at the small hut, but the clouds overhead blotted the colors, as though the ash from the charcoal fires had settled on the green grass, the blue water, the pale straw.

Kathmiya suddenly remembered a little song that the weavers used to sing. The melody danced in her heart. *I belong here*, she realized.

It was right to abandon Shafiq, she insisted to the part of herself that lingered in his arms.

Natural melodies. Placid waters. Heart and home.

As Kathmiya approached the house, a child scampered forward, Fatimah's youngest, now walking, as little and light as a doll. The girl was barefoot and dressed in a too-big shirt, a sharp contrast to pampered Aziza with her neat jumpers. But in her niece's winsome smile, the innocence of her life, the simplicity of this world, Kathmiya found a measure of tranquility.

She was feeling calm despite her shame when Fatimah came out, stunned to see her. "What are you doing here?" she asked quietly.

Facing her sister, Kathmiya experienced, for the first time, a release from her perpetual resentment. The grave sin she had committed retroactively justified all of the ill treatment she had suffered. It was suddenly only natural that Fatimah should enjoy stability and happiness; she was the better woman. Eager to atone, Kathmiya was meek for the first time in her memory. "I heard *Abuyah* was sick, so I came to see him."

"He's fine," Fatimah said dismissively, but she looked curious, as though she noticed something was different. "Just a little tired."

"May I see him then?" The old Kathmiya would have barged in, but having sinned, she didn't dare.

Fatimah sighed. "We've moved back home, my family. We're looking after him. So just don't worry about us," she said softly. Then, as though she sensed her own triumph over Kathmiya's spirit and was more secure than ever, she managed a kind tone. "Another day, perhaps, you can come back. But leave us be now. Go with Allah."

But I have nowhere to go, Kathmiya thought. Still, she said nothing, just turned back toward the thick reeds and headed to the ferry. It would not leave again until morning, but for this cowed, disgraced young girl, the wait was just another penance she deserved.

The marshes didn't have a proper port like in Basra, only a shore where boats slipped by like they did everywhere, homegrown canoes rowed by local people who took passengers to the larger stops where they could board commercial ferries from far-off cities. Kathmiya made her way there by evening. She rested against her little burlap sack of possessions, but she couldn't sleep.

The yellow-headed blackbird's night song, like the sound of a rusty gate swinging open, didn't trouble Kathmiya; she was disturbed by the doubt tugging at her heart. Her rapturous acceptance of this suffering as just punishment for all of her wrongs was, in truth, wearing thin.

That old widow and her advice.

Although she wanted to cling to the simple belief that she was the worse woman, and that Fatimah had a right to a husband and home where Kathmiya did not, the chain of events told a different story. If Kathmiya had been safely married off in the marshes, she never even would have met Shafiq.

Yet, part of her wanted to be with him. *That is sin enough*, she thought.

Since waking up skin against skin and realizing she had to leave, Kathmiya had not indulged in self-pity. But now, trying to get comfortable on the small pack of belongings that was all she had in the world, she felt overwhelmed by a mushrooming sadness.

She tried to push her mind back to the idea of finding a place in society—of being humble, like the disgraced and undeserving woman that she was, but Kathmiya couldn't rest her thoughts there. Finally, she took out the pink sapphire ring and held it delicately. She could feel the smooth stone and twisted gold band. Still there, still hers, still with the ability to sparkle, even though she couldn't see that in the dark night.

Kathmiya was intuitive enough to understand what the ring stood for, but she was unable to figure any possible way its inspirational origin could lead her to safety.

Dawn broke over the horizon, sending a shimmering glow across the waters and reminding Kathmiya yet again of the heart-rending beauty of the world she was about to leave.

She turned over, then felt a quick panic until she found the ring between two pebbles colored gray like a pair of pigeons.

She hesitated before putting it in her pocket. Bury it in the moist ground? Accept her fate and forget that anyone had ever tried to love her?

She could keep it in her pocket . . . or not.

She put the ring on her finger.

Stared at its facets.

Admired it, really.

And then rummaged past her burgundy dress and few other clothes and one bar of soap and clay vase until she found the red barn book.

The *dinar* was inside, as inscrutable as ever, but now Kathmiya understood why it had fascinated Shafiq: it was from that place, that America where he was planning to go.

She turned the book's pages from back to front, thinking she was reading it forward, until she got to what she took to be the end. And there, above more indecipherable words, were two symbols: a flag and a cross.

Kathmiya had never paid much attention to these markings stamped in the book, and had no hope of reading the inscription penned underneath them. She had never, for that matter, noticed either symbol anywhere in the city. But she had always understood that the book came from a faraway country. And she had explored enough of Basra to know that there was one neighborhood where all the foreign people lived.

She still had no idea who had given her the treasure, but she was going to try to find out.

Kathmiya boarded the next ferry headed south and realized, for the first time in two days, that she was ravenously hungry.

Chapter XLII

Shafiq had a foreboding sense that Kathmiya was far gone, but he still hoped she might come back—until he read her note.

It was penned in the margins of a news article about the growing threat of Communism. Kathmiya never could have understood how this choice of paper would cut Shafiq even deeper, but he felt doubly wounded all the same, abandoned again by someone he loved.

"I am so sorry to my God," she wrote in her precise hand. "Please do not follow me or ever try to find me." Then, below, as though she realized he would, she added, "Shafiq, they will kill me if you do."

And now, the expression he had remembered on first meeting her was again ringing in his ears: *You applied mascara to make her more beautiful but ended up blinding her.*

Only it was so much worse than that. He had nearly gotten her murdered, and she might die yet.

The self-disgust was overwhelming. Shafiq was repulsed by his own actions, all the attraction and love he'd ever felt for Kathmiya transformed now into hate for himself.

Like Kathmiya, Shafiq had an overwhelming urge to connect to the person he felt closest to, but it was not his mother. He desperately wanted to confide in Omar, but when they met in the morning to walk to school together, Shafiq felt no more able to break through the silence with his adopted brother than his real family. Eerily, daily life resumed. Shafiq was crushed within but still whole on the surface, while Kathmiya, he knew, was running for her life.

In class the next day, while the teacher wrote algebraic equations on the chalkboard, Shafiq could not help but think about their brief time together, sweeter than all the dates in Basra. He missed the fleeting but endless possibility of the life they had almost embarked on, but more than that, he was terrified for her.

Strong as she was, and capable beyond what anyone had ever given her credit for, and extraordinarily beautiful, she was still in serious danger.

Shafiq tried to shut out the memory but all he could hear in his mind was Ezra scolding Naji when he asked about the beautiful maid: "They would murder her in a heartbeat."

Staying up all through the first night after she left, Shafiq was consumed by a droning anxiety that released him from its grip only after he'd given in to the inevitable: he had to search for her. He needed to know she was safe, to try to convince her to come back, to somehow erase this stain.

Even in his recklessness, Shafiq knew to postpone telling his family at least until he found her, so he made excuses about a school science trip to the marshes and then headed there, clinging to the maudlin thought that if he didn't make it out alive, they would know where to look for his body.

He missed the ferry but hired a fisherman to take him upriver in a small boat. Kathmiya had described her journey home to him in poetic terms, but these were of little use after he arrived at the edge of the wetlands and began making his way through the mud and reeds. Unbelievably, he had never learned her last name, and he trembled as he moved through the area, so obviously out of place, despite having thrown on one of his father's old *abaya* by way of flimsy disguise.

America was an abandoned dream.

He had lived near the marshes his whole life, but had never actually seen this other world. He stared at the brown reed huts clustered on small islands that nearly sank in the ubiquitous waters, watching the long, bent canoes used to travel among them.

Where do I begin? he wondered. Shafiq reviewed the few bits of information he had: there was a sister with three children—or was it two? Kathmiya's mother worked in Basra and would not be around. And she rarely mentioned the father, except to complain that he drank too much.

These scattered facts were useless. It was like arriving in Basra and asking for a man named Muhammad with a beard.

Only he wasn't in Basra. Shafiq could barely tell the land from the water in this strange place. Houses seemed to stand in the middle of rivers, while canoes navigated through passageways that looked like solid ground.

All he could think about was the next step forward. He tried to pay attention to the route he took but the landmarks kept shifting—a pelican that took off; a black water buffalo, slick and wet, that swam away; a patch of light on the sparkling grass cast by a shifting sun.

Making his way through the wetlands he tried not to think of what might have happened to Kathmiya, imagining instead carrying her away. The more his feet sank into the soft ground, the more despondent he felt, but who could he ask for help? Even if he could find a willing guide, he would only be courting death if he mentioned the girl.

Pangs of hunger were tearing at the walls of his stomach. Shafiq had a few *dinars* in his pocket, but there was no store to spend them in.

Still wrapped in his father's black *abaya*, he climbed on a small rock, trying to get a better overview of the lowlands. Scanning the horizon, his eyes fell on the majestic *mudhif*. Clearly, this was the center of town, the locus of power and the heart of the society. For a fleeting, breathtaking moment, he forgot Kathmiya and her lost virtue while he relished the symmetry and beauty of the massive reed building.

It drew Shafiq like it must have drawn countless people who were awed into thinking that magnificence could offer beneficence. Without a single brick or drop of mortar, the *mudhif* had more grandeur than Basra's most stately homes.

"Are you a visitor?" asked a man outside.

Shafiq wanted to duck away but knew this would only imply guilt, so he greeted the sentry in his best imitation of Kathmiya's backwoods accent. "Yes, Allah be with you."

"Come," instructed the man. "You must pay your respects to the *sheikh*."

Four great bundles of reeds as tall as trees flanked the front of the structure, which was curved on top. There were no windows, but slats in the weaving let the beams of yellow light through.

Entering through a beveled wooden door, Shafiq was even more awestruck by the interior of the large dome. It was like walking under the ribs of a lion, he thought, staring at the even golden-colored beams that curved from floor to ceiling on each side.

The servant led him to a mat on the floor, woven as perfectly as the walls.

"Kind sir," he said, trying to shake his fear and doubt. "I am trying to find a man from around here."

The *sheikh*, with his stern eyes and sunken cheeks, looked intimidating, but he nodded.

The servant brought rice bread and tea in handmade clay cups.

Shafiq knew he couldn't mention Kathmiya's name, and he didn't know her father's, but he tried combining theirs.

"*Abu Kathmiya*," he guessed. The father of Kathmiya.

The *sheikh* shook his head. "There are fifty men who fit that description here."

Worse, Shafiq knew that Kathmiya had an older sister, so surely he would have been known only as the father of . . . whatever her name was.

Shafiq tried to remember everything he had ever heard about the old man. "We have nothing at my home," Kathmiya would complain, "except the empty bottles of *arak* that he tosses in a pile behind the house."

Shafiq could hardly ask for the town drunk, so he danced around the subject. "Fine craftsman, but had a small problem of thirst. I'm sure there are not a lot around here who drink the way he does."

Now the man smiled. "Ali Mahmoud? Two daughters, a few grandchildren?"

"That's him," Shafiq said, jolted by the fear that he might actually find Kathmiya, and meet his death in the process. "Is he far from here?"

"I will have one of my boys take you," the *sheikh* offered matter-of-factly.

That reliable Arab hospitality. Shafiq's father always protected and helped anyone in his home. And now Shafiq received the same consideration in the heart of the marshes.

"Thank you, thank you, and may Allah protect you," Shafiq repeated over and over.

On the way there, he decided he would hide until she came out by herself and then convince her to run away with him. That way, even if they were alone together in the world, she would be safe.

He had no idea how the family lived, but it seemed like it would be easy enough to get Kathmiya out of there. She was naturally worldly, so why would she want to stay in this primitive environment?

And then he saw it: the sagging little hut with clear empty bottles piled outside.

Her home.

He thought about their last fight, when he'd challenged her, said he couldn't understand why she wasn't able to find a husband. But staring at this hopelessly impoverished little place, barely big enough for a few people to crowd together inside with no pipes or lights or any of the comforts of a modern home, he started to understand how far she had come. Even if she looked to him like she belonged in a palace, she was mired in poverty.

Shafiq thanked the oarsman, pledging to repay the sheikh's kindness someday. And then he approached Kathmiya's little bit of shade under the harsh sky.

Two small children sat outside, the oldest around Aziza's age, but ragged in used clothing and already working, pounding rice in a crude stone pestle. Now Shafiq remembered that Kathmiya had two nieces.

This was it.

When the boat left, he slipped behind a thick bed of reeds, the fresh smell of damp earth filling his nostrils. Whether it would take a day or a week, Kathmiya would go out alone, and then he would signal her. There would be no need to pack, since these people had no possessions.

Shafiq's lank limbs grew sore from crouching, and he gave in and sat on the moist ground. Soon his well-founded fear started to fade as impatience took its place. Night fell, but he couldn't sleep. Every rustle in the wind could have been a dangerous animal or a threatening *Midaan*. He was stripped of shelter, his hunger was raging, and he would never be able to rest, not until Kathmiya was safe in his arms.

And then?

Too far ahead to think about, too impossible to contemplate. Some kind of underground existence like Naji had, only without an illegal group to back you, just out in the open air like a Bedouin in the desert.

His future deprivations seemed even more pronounced knowing that Kathmiya's family was safe inside their house, tribe, world. And then he realized: *That's my advantage: to be up and alert while they are all lulled into unconsciousness. Now is the time to get her.*

Shafiq crept slowly toward the little home, hearing the sounds of quiet breathing as he approached. There were six people sleeping on little mattresses arranged around the edges of the open space.

Scanning the figures in the light of the moon, he thought for a second that he had found Kathmiya, but the wild, dark hair belonged to a woman twice her age . . . must be the mother. His eyes moved quickly past the two men, obviously the husband and father of a young woman sleeping near her three children.

But then he realized: it could not be.

It could not be Kathmiya's home, he knew.

The sister's stocky body, her eyes beady even when closed, her bulbous nose and weak hair—none of it added up.

Determined to be sure, he shifted his focus from the young woman to her father and saw there a coarse, bloated face that had even less in common with the girl that he loved.

So there are two town drunks, he thought, starting as a child stirred. *Or perhaps two different towns. Or ten or ten thousand.* The realization that he was in the wrong place fell on Shafiq like a sagging roof, and he skulked out, lost in the midst of the vast, unfamiliar marshes, trying to leave before trouble came crashing down.

Shafiq followed the water, moving away from the dry land until he came to a shore. And then he followed the shore, feet wet and body clammy and head aching, until he found a small dock. Fishermen arrived before dawn. Soon boats began coursing through the river, and Shafiq watched helplessly as the large ferry taking passengers to Basra glided by.

There was no way to catch it, and frustration roused him to action. Approaching an older fisherman, Shafiq faked his accent and asked for a ride to Basra, offering to pay two hundred *fils*. It was such an exorbitant sum that the man at first refused out of suspicion. But when Shafiq produced the coins, he was welcomed onto the boat. Resting his exhausted head on his arm, he fell asleep under the blanket of the hot sun.

Chapter XLIII

It didn't take Kathmiya long to find the flag. Although the reproduction in her book was crude to begin with and had faded over time, those stars and stripes were still unmistakably waving on the red, white and blue banner hanging from one of the largest buildings in the Margeel neighborhood. She had put on her burgundy dress, hoping it might convey respectability, and approached the door hugging the flat children's book.

Although she had already crossed so many lines, Kathmiya still had to steel herself before knocking on the front door. A broad-shouldered man older than her father opened it and boomed mysterious words she guessed were English. Her large eyes widened as she wondered: *Is he the one, the one who gave this to my mother so many years before, who she said loved me?*

Kathmiya smiled and held up the book. The man didn't bother to speak even a greeting in Arabic, just harassed her in his language with gestures anyone would understand to mean "get lost." Pointing to the book's inscription made no difference; he wouldn't even acknowledge it with a tilt of his head, instead saying a few more foreign words before turning away.

In desperation, she pulled out the U.S. *dinar*, hoping to buy some attention. The older, foreign man took the bill and folded it before tucking it back in Kathmiya's pocket.

The *jinn*! She ran off with a queasy guilt that it was her fault he had violated her with that frightful touch.

Not the kind man who had helped her mother years before; he couldn't be.

And then Kathmiya realized all too clearly that she would never find that person now.

She walked along the streets where she once enjoyed some solitude feeling nothing but emptiness. *What next?*

Her pocket money was running out but if she dipped into the vase, she would be violating her pact with Allah. She should have handed it over to Fatimah when she had the chance.

Worse, no one—not a soul in the world—knew where she was.

The only place for a lone Marsh Arab girl at that hour was the market, and Kathmiya doubled back to the busy street near the diplomatic neighborhood where there were three kinds of yoghurt and four kinds of feta cheese and more camel-themed trinkets than any real Iraqi would ever need. She was no longer stunned, as she had been when she first arrived in Basra so many years before, by the ostentatious variety of the displays, just relieved that amid all the bustle, she could blend in.

But even on the busiest, most cosmopolitan street in Basra, Kathmiya stood out, her unusually large eyes even more stunning against the dark wine dress that she had cut to fit her petite frame. And then there was the vivid emotion etched on her young face, that hurt imbuing her with vulnerable beauty, like an actress whose star shines brighter after she's lived through real drama in life.

Sitting next to a carpet salesman with her book in her lap, Kathmiya soon felt the strangers watching her, most of them white-skinned like the broad-shouldered man. These were the same looks she had received all of her life: some pitying, some judgmental, but none respectful, none that regarded her as a person. In that moment, as a parade of people looked at the forlorn but pretty *Midaan* girl sitting near a pile of freshly combed carpets with an incongruous English children's book at her feet, Kathmiya remembered Shafiq. Only he—he and her mother, but that was different—ever seemed to really see her.

People began offering to buy her book, but Kathmiya just pointed to the inscription and asked, "*Wain?*"—where?—in response. Where was this benefactor from so long ago?

Finally, one of the women came over with a servant. Kathmiya explained in Arabic that she was not selling the book but looking for the people who had given it to her. The servant then translated to the freckled white woman, who responded in English.

"She asks about your ring," said the servant in a disinterested tone, glad to lord it over someone even lower on the social ladder.

Kathmiya instinctively touched the stone and shook her head. "Please," she asked again in Arabic, "can you just show her this?"

When the servant held the book up for the freckled woman to read, Kathmiya covered the ring with her other hand. Everyday sapphires, she had learned from Shafiq, were blue—the most feared color in the marshes, filled with bad luck. But this one was special because it was pink.

The freckled woman had called over a friend, short and round, who read the inscription and then spoke to Kathmiya in crude but serviceable Arabic.

"These people lived here, but they're long gone."

Kathmiya remembered nothing of the couple, and knew only the barest facts about their time in Basra, but the grief she felt was overwhelming.

"Where are they now?" she managed to ask.

"*Amrika,*" came the response.

Of course. America. Just like Shafiq—lost to America. Kathmiya closed the book and was ready to go who-knew-where, when the round woman spoke. "I can show you their home," she offered kindly.

The house was modest—smaller than Leah and Salim's—but there, in the doorway, were the two signs Kathmiya had been searching for: the flag and the cross.

A mother, also American, greeted them holding a writhing baby while trying to calm a wailing toddler. She smiled when she saw the book and, using her friend as an interpreter, invited Kathmiya in, telling her the people who had given her the keepsake had been missionaries in Iraq years before.

"Missionaries?" Kathmiya remembered Jamila using that strange word.

"Here to spread the Word of our God. That's what I'm doing too."

The baby started to fuss, and Kathmiya, with absolutely no plan for her distant future, knew exactly what to do in that instant. Leaning in to take the child from the exhausted mother, she placed it on her hip and began fluffing pillows while soothing the baby.

Soon the two American women were drinking sweetened black tea that Kathmiya had brewed. They were chattering in English while she lulled the baby to sleep, bathed the toddler, and polished the silverware. And before the plump woman departed without her, Kathmiya was hired.

Leah and Salim's house had never felt so much like a home to Kathmiya as it did in the two weeks since she had left there for this stone-quiet existence. The new family was unnaturally small, with no relatives and few visitors, but worse than that, their language was so different she was shut out of all conversation. Even her primitive reading skills were useless in a home literate only in English.

But the isolation had its benefits; here she could forget the past. It was as though there were no girl called Kathmiya Mahmoud, with such a complicated history or even a burgundy dress; there was just an anonymous Marsh Arab maid, known only to the two little children who would leave soon and never remember her after. As startling as it was to have lost all of the features of her previous life, she also left behind the parts that shamed her most.

But then the smells became unbearable.

And she felt perpetually sick.

And she realized the bleeding would never come back.

And she remembered Leah's conversation with Reema and knew, just knew, that one encounter, one terrible mistake, one impossible dream had engendered a human life.

The American missionaries she worked for paid three times as much as Leah and Salim, but they had never even learned Kathmiya's name, and she left without a look back.

Kathmiya had for too, too long been struggling by herself, and although her throat felt thick as she headed out to see her mother, she also couldn't wait to confess so that it might finally unblock and let her breathe again.

Jamila, who didn't even know her daughter had changed jobs, smiled when she saw Kathmiya. "You look well." After a pause, she asked, "Is there good news?"

Kathmiya thought for a moment. Against her better judgment, she had enjoyed an unfamiliar but unmistakable sense of peace since discovering she was pregnant. It was a muffled happiness but it was there all the same: a certain power.

"I think I'm having a baby."

The piercing pain was instant. Kathmiya looked down to see Jamila's nails digging into her wrist. Her mother's face was steaming with fury, and she drew blood as she pulled her daughter inside, her fingers cutting like stigmata.

Words were gasped out only once they were alone: "How could you have damaged our HONOR?"

Kathmiya had already felt weak from the pregnancy, and now she was stung to the core. There was nothing to say, nothing to do, no way to explain that it was only one lapse—a colossal one—but just one. Because that would not even be true. When did she begin to love Shafiq? As guilty as Kathmiya felt, she also knew that her life would have been different if . . .

"If only *Abuyah* would have let me marry," she protested through the pain.

Jamila's eyes flashed and she tightened her grip, so that the blood started to drip. The more Kathmiya tried to wrest free, the deeper her mother's nails dragged into her skin.

"So you tried to find someone yourself? You stupid donkey! You stupid ass of a girl!" She twisted the bleeding arm backward. Kathmiya swallowed her cries back into her packed throat.

"The boy," she croaked defiantly, "wanted to marry me, but I ran away."

Jamila laughed maniacally, pulling Kathmiya's arm at an even more unnatural angle so that the pain stretched from her bleeding wrist to her neck. "He wanted to marry the maid? Ha! And don't try to tell me you slept with a *Midaan*; it was someone in Basra. Because one of our tribe would not be good enough for you, would they?"

That pushed Kathmiya straight into the calm eye of the storm. "He would be good enough," she enunciated like a knife cutting through rope. "He WOULD!" The pain grew worse as her body tensed, sending stinging arrows through her shoulders and neck. But this was nothing compared to the blows her mother's words struck at her tender, battered heart. "HE WOULD BUT YOU NEVER FOUND ME A *MIDAAN*!"

Jamila let her nails out of Kathmiya's flesh but her eyes shot daggers as she spoke. "That. Does. Not. Give. You. Any. Right. To. Sin!"

It was true. And it broke Kathmiya. She finally let the tears out, but her head was bent so low they streamed into her hair. She was beaten, not playing dead to avoid more punishment, but really finished.

"Where is he?"

"In Basra," Kathmiya said, but through the cloud of her self-abrogation she realized she could be sentencing Shafiq to death if she confessed too much, so she added, "but not for long. He's going to America."

It was true, as far as she knew, but saying it to someone else made it real. Shafiq was abandoning her to travel across oceans and learn English and probably forget all of his Arabic and all about her and the baby he would never know.

Kathmiya was so blurred by sadness she didn't notice the shock on Jamila's face or the fact that her mother's questions had suddenly stopped.

The daze started to lift only moments later when she realized Jamila was asking in a foreign, gentle tone, "How far along are you?" When Kathmiya said just a few weeks, her mother nodded.

"Let's go," said Jamila, standing. "But no eating— you have to stay thin."

"Where are we . . . ?"

"To Salwa. Quickly."

"But . . . ?" Kathmiya held up her arm, where four red stripes trickled from the cuts.

"Cover them, but don't let them heal," Jamila advised sternly. "If we're lucky, you'll need a handy source of blood."

Both mother and daughter had no faith in legitimate marriage brokers, but this one, Salwa assured them, was as dishonest as could be. "Every match she gets a commission, and she doesn't try for much besides forming as many couples as she can before anyone can change their mind."

The place looked like a tent, sea-green fabrics from India hanging from the center of the ceiling and pinned to its walls. Kathmiya felt like she was in the folds of a belly dancer's skirt. There were even little bits of shining mirror on the fabric. The dark-purple floor rug was dotted with round yellow and turquoise pillows scattered around. The colors clashed and the overall effect was dizzying.

Salwa was in costume too. "Pay no attention to the maid," she said when they sat down across from the old woman with tarnished, twisted rings on every finger. "She helps me out since my husband died."

Jamila sat playing her familiar role: the lowly servant. An insult, but Kathmiya was past the point of pride.

"What a fine young girl!" the old lady said. Her eyes were cloudy with cataracts, almost blue in color, and she stretched out a lumpy finger to pull Kathmiya's hair off of her face. Used to being exhibited in her search for a husband, Kathmiya didn't flinch. She was like every camel in the market being judged on its hump.

"Cooks, cleans, sews—and of course she can read and write," Salwa said, the perfect proud mother.

When Kathmiya and Jamila had gone to Salwa to confess everything, except of course the identity of the lover, she had just listened, nodding with her chin on her fist. Finally she said, "If we have to lie, we will. There's a life at stake—no, two."

I'm two, Kathmiya had thought, more amazed than afraid.

Under the sweeping green canopy, she squeezed Salwa's hand with unaffected emotion that would have convinced anyone they were mother and daughter. But the broker wasn't paying attention. She was calculating on those misshapen, fat fingers. "I can think of a match immediately," she said, a small well of foam gathering in the corner of her mouth. "Well off, too—a military man from a good family."

"And his character?" Salwa asked, like any mother would.

"Oh, he's good-hearted, very kind, I assure you. Either way, your daughter will have it easy; she'll be his fourth wife. Three times less work, I always say."

The woman looked directly into Kathmiya's beautiful eyes and smiled. Like no marriage broker ever had before.

384 • JESSICA JIJI

Still, it could fall through at any second . . .

"He's been asking," said the matchmaker, "for an educated young girl, and he specifically said she must have large, dark eyes . . ."

They say the same about the camels, thought Kathmiya. In that moment, she couldn't help but think of Shafiq, who admired her beauty but also saw her intelligence, her spirit, her heart.

". . . and just look at your daughter! Perfect."

"I'm not sure that her father will approve," said Salwa with manufactured hesitation. Just like with the camels, just like with every transaction in this unregulated, price-free economy, the buyer pretended to be disgruntled. The matchmaker played her part, insisting that the man was rare and good. Salwa kept up the act until the old woman said, "We can set the wedding right away—this week if you like—provided her honor is intact."

In the split second that passed before anyone spoke, Kathmiya saw it all collapsing—again.

Her future shot—again.

Her hope completely lost—for good.

"Of course," replied Salwa, and the deal was struck.

It was the moment Kathmiya had been waiting for all of her rushed adult life. And now that it had finally arrived, she felt numb.

Chapter XLIV

Each day that passed dimmed the chances that Shafiq would ever see Kathmiya. Without talking to her or knowing where she was, there was nothing he could do but hide behind his books.

He chalked up perfect scores but this was like digging a hole that kept getting filled by a mudslide, since they would do nothing to overcome the odds against him.

Omar kept trying to pull him out now that they were old enough to go to clubs with belly dancers and Cokes from America, but Shafiq kept declining, not because he wouldn't have fun but because he was afraid he would, and that would somehow break the vigil he'd been holding for Kathmiya.

Finally one day, Omar didn't ask, just slipped a note into that old space in the wall that used to seem so enormous when they were kids, like they might have driven a train through, but now looked stuffed with just one thin piece of paper inside.

Stuffed with promise. For the first time in months, Shafiq smiled.

This is from the best chapter, called "Love."

Shafiq stared at the paper. *He knows. He knows me.* It didn't change anything and yet it meant everything.

> *. . . if you love and must needs have desires, let these be your desires:*
>   *To melt and be like a running brook that sings its melody to the night.*
>   *To know the pain of too much tenderness.*
>   *To be wounded by your own understanding of love;*
>   *And to bleed willingly and joyfully.*

Feeling released at once, Shafiq put his head into his hands and let the sadness wash over him.

When he saw Omar, he thanked him, but he didn't answer any questions. He didn't have to; Omar never asked, he just stayed by Shafiq's side, willing him, through sheer friendship, to go on.

It seemed unreal, the letter with his full name spelled out in English type, but there it was. *"Congratulations, you have been accepted . . ."* Invitation to a new life.

"It's good that you'll be leaving," said Ezra when he heard. "With some luck, we'll all get out of Iraq."

"That's crazy." Shafiq laughed. It was one thing for him to go off to college, but quite another to imagine his parents, his cousins, and the whole stable tribe leaving en masse.

"The United Nations set up a committee in New York," Ezra explained. "On Palestine."

A heavy subject, but Shafiq still took it lightly. The Jews he knew were aware of the troubles but were still planning a future in Iraq. Not that Shafiq was tempted, but more and more of his Jewish friends at school were secretly embracing Communism in the hopes that it would lead to equality for all peoples.

A trip abroad, yes. An exodus? Never.

"How about tonight?" Omar asked.

Shafiq felt spent from studying for tests whose scores would mean nothing, like a calligrapher who wrote other peoples' names on diplomas he would never earn. But he couldn't let his friends down, so he put on his best suit to go out with Omar, Iskender and Yunis for a night on the town.

It was a scene shimmering with possibility, and Shafiq let himself relax into the moment. For too long he had been burdened by a terrible sense of foreboding, but now he just posed for pictures with his friends in front of a patched-up box camera, trying to pretend life was as normal as it seemed. The guilt over Kathmiya, the dissolute anger at the rules that tore them apart, and the agonizing uncertainty could start to fade. *I'm just a kid going off to college,* he told himself.

Shafiq's suit was white and he was careful not to muss it up. The sharp, cool evening skies at the outdoor club offered a respite from the heat of the sun, and the band played traditional *makaam* rhythms that lifted everyone's already festive mood.

With cold, hard, sweet Coca-Cola trickling down his throat, Shafiq thought about telling his friends he was leaving for America. But not yet—not until it was certain.

He listened as they toasted their accomplishments and boasted about prospects.

Yunis, especially, seemed destined for greatness. During a student-body-wide strike against the biology teacher in protest of his difficult exams, only Yunis had objected, sitting alone for the final while the rest of the seniors looked on, impressed and dumbfounded at once. He was polished, good-looking and extremely articulate. Shafiq could easily imagine him becoming a government minister someday.

Iskender, who planned to become an electrician, was always soldering wires to lights in his spare time. "I'll do your houses for free," he promised. "Outlets in every room, hide all the wires, you name it!"

Shafiq knew that Omar wanted to be a doctor. "When you become a surgeon, don't come near me with the knife," he joked.

"And you," Iskender nodded toward Shafiq, "speaking English all the time, are you leaving us for London or something?"

"Leaving you? You are all leaving me! I'll probably end up a waiter at one of these cafés!" Shafiq had been feeling obliged to stay in Basra as long as Kathmiya might be alive, but now that he was out on the town talking about the future with his friends, his sense of possibility returned. It was obvious he should grab the acceptance from Hope College and leave the whole mess behind. Probably, he told himself, this was the best way to help her in the long run.

A bejeweled belly dancer came out to entertain the crowd, her flawless flesh swaying in subtle jolts to the music. When she was through, the teens sat still, absorbing the memory of her kinetic curves. Iskender broke the awkwardness of the moment by gesturing at a nearby table toward a man with hairy ears and a large stomach hanging over his belt. "His wife sleeps around," Iskender said in a loud whisper. "I heard it—it's true."

The scandal! The danger! The hilarity! Shafiq felt completely released by the moment, giggles bubbling up like the frothy soda he had bought for fifty *fils* at the club.

None of them could stop laughing as the man turned around. They were too happy, too alive and knowledgeable and ready to inherit the mantle of adulthood and intoxicated by the promise of the future.

But when the burly man laid eyes on the group of laughing teens, he called them on the crime. "My honor," he screamed. "You defamed my honor!"

Only after one fat hand grabbed Iskender by the freshly cleaned collar and the other started pummeling him did their mirth die. Watching this buffoon hit Iskender in the name of honor undid all of the peace the evening had brought Shafiq. Unable and unwilling to control his fury, he leaned in and slammed the man as hard as he could. *Take that for your pathetic life*, he thought, stuffing his fists into the rubbery gut. After a shocked moment, the man landed a sweaty fist on Shafiq's temple. Pain shattered through his head but he continued striking out: *And take that for your insane pretense to dignity.* Shafiq could feel thick fingers poking his throat closed but he didn't care; he just took it. Another blow across his head, a sharp pain in his leg, he was down, he could feel a glass shattering against his ankle, but he took it.

Finally, his friends and some café workers got between Shafiq and the panting, insulted stranger.

But Shafiq struggled against their grip, sending two metal tables colliding into each other with a sibilant crash. The band had stopped playing and Shafiq could hear the sound of the man's feral breathing as he fought off the restraints of the others, still lunging for a punch.

Shafiq had never met this man, but he wanted to snap his head off of his neck. *Honor. Honor. Honor.* He had tried to live with honor and then had stolen it from the one he loved most. He had been ready to die for her and even then failed. But feeling the sting of sweat dripping into a cut the man's blow had left on his head, Shafiq knew he had finally achieved a solid measure of self-destruction.

The implosion was completed when the teens were forced to give up their names. Grinding his uneven teeth, their victim stormed out with a warning: "I will see you in court."

Later that night, parting at the wall where their houses met, Shafiq and Omar made a pact not to tell their families what had happened. This kind of disgrace shouldn't be mentioned to anyone.

"I'll take the blame," Shafiq insisted.

"Forget that," Omar said. Their code of honor was unbreakable.

He looked into Shafiq's eyes. "I understand you defending Iskender, but . . . why did you snap?"

Shafiq couldn't explain. The story was too long and he was too rattled. "I apologize," he said with feeling, sorry that he had lost control, that he couldn't say why, that his anger, sadness and suffering had finally hurt even his friends.

The following day, Shafiq went to the warehouse. He had been putting off speaking to his father about Hope until the right moment, but with trouble looming now it might be his last chance. *Maybe,* he thought with self-serving drama, *I will run away to America to avoid jail in Iraq.* The memory of Salim's descriptions—the stench of urine, the beatings, the endless nights—was haunting.

Roobain sat outside the warehouse in his usual spot, next to an empty chair. When he saw Shafiq approach, he smiled, eyes sparkling through the wrinkles hooding them.

Shafiq felt grounded in this familiar spot looking out at a very narrow, sloping lane crowded with shoppers. Strong Kurdish men carried heavy sacks on their backs, while others pushed two-wheel wooden carts filled with crates. Young boys delivering tea from the local café passed vendors selling cold yogurt drinks to passersby. Behind Shafiq was the large warehouse filled with boxes of redolent goods traded from India, Iran and beyond.

For so long, he had been resisting the idea of going to America because a trip there would foreclose the possibility that he might ever see Kathmiya again. But if he did go . . . Shafiq suddenly experienced a premonitory tug of nostalgia, thinking about all that he would leave behind should his father consent to his plan.

"I have been accepted to a college in America," he began, "and I'd like to attend."

Roobain nodded. "You raised so many pigeons, now it's your turn." He gestured toward the aqua sky overhead.

"I think it is the way to go, in case I don't get accepted here, but it will cost money." University in Iraq was free, while tuition in America was only the first of many expenses Shafiq would run up.

"I see," Roobain replied.

"Baba," Shafiq promised, "I'll do my best."

"I know," Roobain said. "Your cousin Yusef was the same, a model student, and look at him now," he added. "And you, you've always been a good son. I will support your education, whatever you need."

Each kind word only pressed on Shafiq's conscience, like another box stacked on the warehouse's massive balance.

Soon they were inside, swallowed by the bustle of people and scents of so many commodities under the light of the sun streaming in through handmade windows that had a soft buckle to them.

Rushing over to Sayed Barazani, Shafiq relayed his news. "I'm going to college in America!"

"Good for you!" his near-uncle replied. And then he called over to the other workers, making a great production over Shafiq. "Look at our young American," he told them.

"I'll send you things—boxes of treats, like you always gave me," Shafiq said, embracing Barazani warmly.

In the hundreds of times that Shafiq had gone to the warehouse he had always gotten something there—a stray handful of almonds, or a discarded strip of metal—but this was the only time he left with a bundle of *dinars*.

"For your future." Roobain smiled. "You'll be on your own soon enough."

Shafiq swallowed hard. He would be fine, but what about Kathmiya? She was just trying to survive—at least he hoped she still had that chance.

I have no future apart from Kathmiya, he realized, and then made a decision.

"Please, I need your help." He was facing Salwa in her familiar living room, which was like an echo of his own. "I have a friend, well, I don't know where she is . . ." He mumbled the gender, and Salwa didn't flinch, so he went on. ". . . And she's very religious, so I want to do *sadaka* in her name."

"There are many ways to do *sadaka,*" Salwa replied.

"I brought this," Shafiq said. It was a small envelope containing a portion of the money his father had given him for the trip to America. After deducting enough to survive for a week there, he pledged to find a job when he arrived and set aside the rest for the gift Kathmiya would have wanted most.

"Will you offer it to the mosque for me?" he asked. Shafiq knew that Salwa was a Sunni while Kathmiya a Shi'a, but he trusted that Allah was beneficent, and would understand.

"For you, yes." She smiled. "And for your friend, too."

———

Shafiq's passport application was with the government, and when an official-looking letter arrived in July, he hoped it was his way out. But inside, he found instead a court summons.

Salim had gone to prison for no crime at all, and Shafiq had assaulted a man in a frenzy of anger. Suffocating under a thick coating of shame, he went next door.

"Guess we're going to keep living side by side, but this time in cell blocks," Omar joked.

Shafiq couldn't laugh. "Don't—don't defend me if it gets you in trouble."

Omar gave Shafiq an exasperated look that said, *Of course I'll be defending you, dummy.*

The kindness drew Shafiq out. "What does the Poet say?"

"He says remorse is justice," Omar said. "Do you feel remorse?"

"If only you knew," Shafiq said quietly.

Omar asked, with no trace of judgment in his voice, "You okay?"

And with those two simple, compassionate words, he freed Shafiq to pour out his trapped secrets.

"That is unbelievable," said Omar when Shafiq was through.

"But it's true."

"No, what I mean is, I can't believe you just told me that, because I've heard this story before."

"I don't know where she is. She might never see me. She might be in really grave danger, or worse—"

For once, Omar did not finish Shafiq's sentence; he started an entirely new one. "My mother told me about this girl," he began.

"You don't understand," Shafiq interrupted.

"Listen!" Omar said. "My mother told me about a girl, a girl from the marshes. The girl's mother . . . well, it is such a long story, but I think I might be able to find her . . ."

Shafiq focused now. He listened. "Don't joke around," he said flatly.

"Would I joke about this?"

Omar wouldn't, Shafiq knew. "She's alive, then? You're sure?"

"Alive, and I think . . ." Omar hesitated, then added, "married."

Shafiq never knew he could be so heartbroken, but for a long minute, he actually wished she were dead instead of with someone else.

"Find her if you can, please," he asked, suddenly wanting to see her more than he ever had, to sweep her off her feet, to win her back.

Chapter XLV

Without Ali's support, Kathmiya had no one to present her to her new husband.

Until Uncle Haider rushed down to Basra. "Thank you," she breathed, profoundly grateful not only because he had come to help—though she needed that, for sure— but because he was living proof that she could feel some natural affection for a family member other than Jamila.

Haider, tall and tanned with gray streaking the front of his black hair, seemed to sweep in from the marshes still carrying the pride of their fierce people, that superiority that no one in the city ever recognized but that every *Midaan* claimed. As much as Kathmiya wanted to resent him for not arranging a match with his son, she couldn't help but be grateful that he was helping this time around.

"How's my father?" she asked.

"Good," he replied in a tight voice.

Wearing Western clothes borrowed from the late Hajji Abdullah and pretending Salwa was his wife, Uncle Haider could almost manage to fit in, if not for his heavy accent.

"Try not to say much," Kathmiya cautioned, not wanting to upset him.

As they rode the taxi to meet the groom, she felt her body sway with sickness. It wouldn't be long before she would show, and then her luck would be over—no chance to escape destitution, if not death.

She kept her veiled head down as they approached the home that might become hers. The door opened but all she really saw was the clean brick floor. When she heard his voice, though, she had to look up.

Older—maybe forty-five—with his hair thinning from the top back, hazel eyes and a small moustache. Haider's age, really. Like a father, or an uncle, a man who could take her in. She blushed when he looked at her, but held his gaze. "She must have large, dark eyes," the matchmaker had said. Kathmiya blinked hers. He nodded. She was confident she had passed the test, until he spoke.

"This girl looks nothing like either of you," the man said to Kathmiya's "parents," Uncle Haider, who was partly responsible for her being in this mess, and guardian Salwa, who was doing everything possible to get her out of it. "How do you explain that?"

"God is great," shrugged Salwa. Haider smiled. And the man bought it.

Kathmiya had her own Night of Henna, surrounded by strange women who painted brick-red designs on her hands while drummers and dancers performed. The air was thick with smoke from hand-rolled cigarettes and the burned sweetness of ashy incense. It was dizzying and exhausting and overwhelming, but Kathmiya rode a wave of euphoria. Two of the other wives looked nearly as young as she felt, and the third was free with advice. "He likes us to smile when he comes home from work." Kathmiya nodded as the soles of her feet were tickled by the tattoo artist's brush. "Never speak when he reads the newspaper," she went on, and Kathmiya smiled an *of course not.* "And don't let your hands get rough," the wife insisted. "That's for maids."

Kathmiya's fingers curled under her palms. But the only lighting was from candles stuck in little mounds of henna paste, and soon one of the servants was sprinkling her with fragrant rosewater, and she knew her skin was getting softer by the minute.

The next day, Kathmiya cleansed herself at the Turkish baths. She took off her clothes as though she was used to having other people pick them up and then went through a series of small pools, each in a room deeper and deeper down the noisy building's long hallway. The water got warmer and warmer, and by the time she emerged from the loofah scrub, she was so content she could barely remember how to clean up after others, and she was on her way to forgetting how long she had done it to survive.

All the boisterousness and noise and energy of the Night of Henna fell silent by the time the mullah arrived for the wedding ceremony. Kathmiya was alone with Salwa, sitting behind a curtain with an open Koran in her lap and a candle flickering in her hand.

"Any violation of this contract would be a sin," the mullah warned. And then he read the terms. She knew she would be companionable, but she hadn't been chaste. Still, when he called for her to procreate and raise children, Kathmiya was glad for the curtain concealing her secret smile.

"Does she agree?"

Salwa was supposed to answer, but she stayed quiet.

"I said, does she agree?"

It would have been suspicious for a mother to assent too quickly. So Salwa held quiet still, while Kathmiya held her breath. *Nearly there,* she thought.

"Agreed, or not?" the mullah asked.

Salwa spoke so softly even Kathmiya couldn't hear.

"Louder!" the mullah commanded, and even then, Salwa's voice was just above a whisper.

"Louder!"

"I said yes," she said, still faintly. Kathmiya wanted to accept herself, but after ten entreaties, Salwa was shouting, the mullah was satisfied, and the maid who a minute before had no certain future was finally married.

In the wedding suite that night, her new husband was too busy looking into her eyes to see her hands scraping the scabs on her wrist to bloody the sheets.

In her four-floor, nineteen-room home on the banks of the *Shat Al-Arab*, Kathmiya felt like the star of one of those movies that set everyone in Basra talking. She had never seen the films but read the titles in the newspaper: *A Wife by Proxy*, was one; and another seemed even more made for her: *His Highness Wishes to Marry.*

She acted the part of an educated, well-bred woman, navigating the household politics by charming each one of her husband's nine children. To all of the wives, separately, she praised their sons and their beauty over the others, and this easy pandering won her their affection.

The only time her real identity almost came to light was when her mother-in-law introduced Kathmiya to a pale girl in ragged clothes who looked no more than eleven years old. "This is your new maid."

Kathmiya felt like a hook had caught her and she was being reeled back in time to when she was first introduced to Salim's mother. She recognized the fright that darted through the girl as she tried to overcome the shock of her new surroundings.

"Welcome. What is your name?" Kathmiya asked.

The mother-in-law looked skeptical. "Better to tell her to do something!"

The girl just looked down.

"I'm Kathmiya." The new wife leaned down to eye level with the girl, who was so young the traces of her baby face still showed through. "We'll be together a lot, but there's nothing to worry about. And I'm just wondering, what do they call you?"

The sound was almost inaudible, but Kathmiya was listening closely. "Latifa. What a beautiful name. Welcome."

404 · JESSICA JIJI

When Kathmiya's pregnancy became apparent, her husband beamed with pride. She had spent many nights watching the side of his face and squirming under his weight, and now he had no doubt the baby was his.

She felt so lucky to be alive, safe, home, that she didn't think too much about what she was missing. Just as she had always anticipated, the simple act of finding a husband and a household had solved all of her problems and resolved all of her concerns.

The only tiny source of irritation for the proud wife was the fact that she had not been able to return triumphantly to the marshes. But Kathmiya still dreamed that someday, somehow, she would.

Silk dresses, sumptuous meals of juicy meats, flavored rice and tangy vegetables, even the bit of money Kathmiya had to spend—none of it was more strange than having leisure time.

With all the governesses and nannies and maids around, she could play with children only when she wanted to, and hand them to someone else as soon as they were fussy or she was bored. Then, she might stroll through the many rooms in the house, mussing up the bedding without bothering to remake it, or

scattering pillows, which would be collected by someone else, or leaving her teacups on any one of the polished side tables that flanked the upholstered chairs in
the cool, curtained front room.

The marshes were supposed to be a fading memory,
but the more Kathmiya tried to fill her mind with the
many distractions her new life afforded, the more her
old came rushing to the forefront of her thoughts.

Her husband's total lack of interest in her family
worked in Kathmiya's favor; for once, going unnoticed
was a blessing.

Kathmiya's kindness toward Latifa paid off as she
kept quiet when she accompanied her matron, now
and then, to meet with a strange *Midaan* woman at the
port.

Happiness was like the clear water of the marshes and
life a vessel to catch it. After her wedding, Kathmiya
felt filled to the brim, but it slowly seeped out through
the holes in her story. Too many unfilled gaps blocked
satisfaction from welling up.

The baby was kicking now, offering a steady reassurance that no matter what, she would never be alone.
But there was a thrumming fear nagging at Kathmiya.
She had never known affection from her father, and she
worried it would be the same with her child.

———

At the port on a bright day in late August, Kathmiya asked the young maid Latifa to wait in the distance and went to meet her mother.

"Ali is dead," Jamila said softly. Almost apologetically. But not quite sadly.

Kathmiya froze for a moment, then collapsed to the ground.

Latifa rushed over but Kathmiya was too encased in shock to wave her away. *He's not gone. He cannot be dead. Please he's alive, he's just so so sick but he's okay he'll be okay I'll see him again, I need to see him again, I need to tell him how sorry I am that I was not there to wipe his brow and soothe his pain and make him happy I never made him happy I just caused trouble Abuyah I am sorry for all my mistakes please Allah will I ever see him again? Will I ever see my father?*

If Ali had cherished her in life, the sadness would have been vivid, and it would have found a permanent home in her heart. Since he had not, and now she would never have a chance to make it right, the pain was dull and surrounded her like a mesh net she was powerless to escape.

And then she remembered her way out. "I have money—he can be buried at Najaf."

"Too late," said Jamila, and the desperation became permanent.

Chapter XLVI

The court was pungent with people. There were obviously criminal elements among the crowds waiting for a hearing. One man had a scruffy beard and holes in his clothes. Another had a visible scar across his chest and scabs on his arms. A prostitute with red-painted cheeks leaned against a greasy-looking pimp, who took the seat nearest to the fan and splayed his legs wide.

Now that Shafiq knew he might find Kathmiya, a harsh sentence would be all the more ruinous.

"Look at this mess." Iskender tried to be disgusted but he was really just terrified.

"We're here to meet justice," Yunis replied in the authoritative voice that matched his natural stature.

"The guy started it," Iskender said. That was their entire defense.

Three sweaty hours later, when the friends finally stood before the judge, the sputtering attacker railed about the injury to his honor and his right to defend it.

The judge cast his eyes across the boys. "Look around you," he instructed. "Petty thieves, violent criminals—I've even had murderers. Now," continued the judge, "here I have four clean-cut young men." He read their names out loud and it was obvious that each came from a different background. "What do you have in common?" he asked.

Yunis answered. "We are all basically good, and one stupid bar fight should not destroy our futures."

"Is that so?" asked the judge from his lofty bench.

"I hope to go into politics," Yunis said with the even tone of a future leader.

"I'm planning to be a doctor," Omar chirped.

"Electrical engineering," Iskender put in.

All eyes were now on Shafiq.

He knew he was supposed to pretend to have a future, to hide the fact that he was torn between leaving the country and staying to find the girl he loved. His friends needed him to rescue them. And he needed to keep them all out of that long brick building with a cave for an entrance and a special latrine for beating prisoners.

I plan . . . I intend . . .

But Shafiq couldn't lie. He would never be a doctor or a lawyer.

"He's a very serious young man," said Omar, prompting him.

"And I want, with all my heart, to serve the great nation of Iraq," Shafiq declared. It had the virtue of being true, if impossible.

"Decent young men, as I suspected," said the judge. "Dismissed."

Salwa refused to say who Kathmiya had married, but she gave Omar enough clues to investigate, and now it was time.

Every detail was in place. The plan. The house. The widow.

When Omar and Shafiq got there, they caught sight of the old lady leaving, as if Allah were guiding them, as if kismet were on their side, as though Kathmiya herself might answer the door and run off with Shafiq to some future that was as black as night and just as dream-filled.

A girl answered, too young to be Kathmiya's mother.

"Is Jamila there?" Omar asked, flashing his winning smile. The girl looked so genuinely confused it was clear she had no idea who he meant.

"She works for Nafisa?"

"I'm the only one working here," the girl said, and closed the door.

"Wait!" Shafiq tried, but it was no use. Jamila must have left, fading back into the deep pool of nameless *Midaan*, and no doubt her employer had never bothered to learn where she lived, let alone where she worked now.

The two teens walked away quietly under the shade of second-floor balconies hanging over the attached houses that lined the streets.

"We'll keep looking," Omar said comfortingly. Then he added, in a voice that barely rose above the sounds of city, "Shafiq? I always knew."

"You what?"

"The few times I saw you together, the way your eyes lit up—both of you—I saw it right away. I didn't know you . . ." he stopped himself rather than describe what Shafiq had done. "But I always knew it was her."

Kismet was beautiful and magnificent and crushing.

Shafiq had only one plan left, but it was already summer and unless the government sent his passport soon, he'd miss school in America. The looming partition of Palestine provoked so much anger against the Jews it was not only ruining his chances of leaving Iraq, it was also complicating his efforts to stay.

The interviewers at Baghdad University did their part.

"So is your father's name Abraham or what?" one taunted.

And then, in rapid, impossible succession, "What are the ingredients in nylon?"

"Using English words, name all of the bones in the foot."

"On what fundamental principle is atomic explosion based?"

Shafiq didn't know any of the answers, which was perfect, because the panel was trying to fail him.

It seemed the only fact left in his head was one Salim had taught him years before: Iraq's national currency was established thanks in part to the efforts of a patriotic Jew named Abraham al-Kabir.

Back in Basra, the light September air, usually so welcome after the incessant heat of summer, was just a reminder that Hope College had started without Shafiq, that Omar had left for Baghdad to study, and that Kathmiya would never be found.

But then it came.

When he entered the government office in Ashar, Shafiq still could not believe any plan in his life would ever come to fruition. But when he walked out, he was holding a small red book with his photo inside and the Iraqi national emblem on its hard cover. Thick ticket to a glorious future.

Walking home near the same path he had followed after discovering Sayed Mustapha's disappearance, Shafiq felt none of the sweet fondness for his country that had clung to him then. Instead, he was buoyantly comparing the mediocre life he led in this quiet corner of the Middle East with the star-spangled future that awaited in the capital of the world. America! Land of the free, winner of all wars, maker of stars, she could anoint the weak and slay the powerful.

Passing a hunched old woman wrapped in black, Shafiq imagined his future surrounded on every street corner by skyscrapers and starlets dressed in sleeveless shirts and cute culottes. As he walked by the sleepy cafés in Basra where men smoked long-stemmed water pipes, he pictured the bustling restaurants of Chicago crowded with mobsters more powerful than kings. Shafiq tried to conceive of Broadway, the great road he heard ran across the entire United States and was so wide you needed a bus just to cross it. Imagine that, compared to the short paths of this little town! Schools in Michigan were so large they had their own highways. Shafiq's had nothing but a dusty soccer field.

When a driver honked at Shafiq as he bounded toward the Corniche, he thought: *In America people are civilized, they don't honk, lose their tempers, get angry, feel pain or otherwise suffer any malady.* How could they? They are in the U-S-A.

America. Not caring whether anyone was looking he peeked at his passport, which was tucked in the inside pocket of his jacket, and then kissed the little official booklet.

What were "for spacious skies"? Shafiq had read the lyric in a magazine once. He imagined heavens broader and grander than any over Iraq. Whatever they were, he would soon find out.

November of 1947 was half over. Classes at Hope had begun, but Shafiq planned to catch up as soon as he got there. All that remained, besides the airline ticket, were his visa and his exit permit.

"This letter offers you admission in September," said the Iraqi staff member working at the U.S. consulate in Basra when Shafiq asked for a visa. "You're two months late."

Staring at the wooden counter, scratched from years of paperwork, Shafiq knew his plan was doomed.

What a terrible bureaucratic hell to be damned in; he was delayed because of the massive red tape involved in securing his documents, and now that they were in hand, it was too late. "Isn't there anything I can do?"

"If you receive another letter offering admission for the next semester, well, I suppose you could go then."

The clerk might as well have suggested that Shafiq row to America in a homemade tin canoe. The time it had taken just to apply to Hope, the slowness of the mail across continents, the transcripts and letters to be gathered—how could he do it all over again?

When Shafiq returned home, he collapsed on the couch facedown, refusing to even look at his parents.

It was over. The dream, the future, the "for spacious skies." The only reason to stay in Iraq was Kathmiya, but she was like the candlelit kite: spectacular but fleeting.

Roobain shook Shafiq from his stupor with this suggestion: "We have to go see Yusef." His cousin, the one with savvy.

"Could we send a telegram?" Shafiq asked when they arrived at Yusef's office, where he worked as the chief secretary to one of the most prominent members of the community, a successful businessman who did not only imports and exports but also had the only car dealership in all of Basra.

"Don't just send it," Yusef counseled. "Prepay the return postage for them."

"But will they care enough to answer quickly?" Shafiq worried. "And what if the telegram isn't delivered?"

"You think this is Iraq we are dealing with, but don't forget, the college is in America."

America the beautiful.

URGENTLY NEEDED SPRING TERM ADMISSION FOR VISA. SEND BY PREPAID TELEGRAM.

Eleven words to a new future.

The yellow envelope arrived two days later. And Shafiq understood the meaning of "for spacious skies."

Chapter XLVII

Kathmiya went into labor slowly, contractions coming randomly and infrequently but often enough to summon the midwives. As the hours passed, they took turns leaving the room for air and refreshments while she endured the waves of pain that never gathered in pace or intensity, just wore away at her like water against sand.

Kathmiya's life did not pass before her eyes in an instant, but through the agonizing day that turned to night and back to day again. She wished her father hadn't died so that he could meet her child, but knew that even if Ali were alive, he would not receive them. And she wished her mother could be by her side but knew that forever forward she would have to sneak visits to Jamila, whom the baby would never know as his grandmother. And she longed, above all, for the warm look that Shafiq used to give her so freely and unselfconsciously, but as another stab of pain sent her abdomen throbbing, she knew that only their separation had kept them and their child alive this long.

Kathmiya was slipping into an unconsciousness mired in defeat. She was not pushing, not even moving, so the midwives stood her up to let gravity do the work. But the sudden change in position sapped her spent reserves of strength, and she fell into a final, cold sweat.

Still, life persisted. The child crowned, but Kathmiya could barely hear the bustle that trembled through the room, the midwives screaming "Push!" or even the hearts that beat inside of her. Even if she lived, what was left?

Ali: dead.

Jamila: all but erased.

Shafiq: gone forever.

It was the end, the very end, until a rough hand rubbed a towel across her brow. Then she heard, like a song, the gentle voice of the maid Latifa encouraging her, "Your beautiful baby is almost here. Come on, just a little more. Just stay with us. Stay with us please. Your baby is coming."

Suddenly, Kathmiya was energized by an overpowering love for her child. For nine months, facing tribulations she had never thought she could survive, Kathmiya had silently communicated with the life in her body, wrenching her thoughts from depression for him and thanks to him and their life together. And she could not leave now.

Reviving from a near state of shock, she could feel again as the baby twisted out of her. She collapsed back on the bed and they placed the crying, wet infant boy on her chest. The pain was now unbearable, the contractions still pounding through her body, the gash he had left stinging like the cut from a serrated knife. But when Kathmiya looked at her son, her eyes filled with tears.

"Ali," she breathed, naming him.

Later, when they were alone at the end of the most interminable day of her life, Kathmiya was able to look into his eyes. The resemblance was faint but unmistakable: that familiar warmth and love. Yes, the separation from Shafiq had kept them all alive so far, but now she was strong enough to see him. And he deserved to know. Everything.

"Listen to this," Ezra told Shafiq, reading from a newspaper. "They're gathering in New York. Countries. Meeting at the United Nations to vote on the partition of Palestine."

For years, it seemed, Ezra had been able to invest just about every pronouncement with an ominous tone, and Shafiq had learned to stay calm. But this time, his own plans were at stake and he worried.

"Oh," Ezra added as an afterthought. "This came for you."

When Shafiq saw the envelope, his fears and dreams flared like an oil fire.

Dear Shafiq,

When I left you, I was pregnant. I got married and now I have a son named Ali. He is ours. He is beautiful.

My mother knows but she will never let me see you, and I will never disobey her. But if you receive this note, leave a small paper in the wall where you used to write to Omar and I will get it. Do not write anything about love, though. And do not try to find me or approach me. If you do, it will endanger both me and our son.

I am trusting you because Ali has your kind eyes. Destroy this letter now.

Kathmiya

Stunned, confused and euphoric, Shafiq ran up to the roof. He had a son, a beautiful son, with Kathmiya. All the sadness he had felt on first learning she was married evaporated. Even the stain of dishonor was washed away by a flood of shining pride. "Ali has your kind eyes." Kathmiya loved their son and she loved Shafiq, who loved her too, but she would not see him and he was leaving for America and—

Could he still leave for America? The letter foreclosed the possibility that they would ever be together again, but she had invited Shafiq to write. Without being able to tell her that he loved her, he could never win her back.

And yet. There was an implicit challenge in her message. If he could find a way through this very narrow opening, he might still be able to see her. And he knew he had to try—to see Kathmiya and his son.

Shafiq stayed on the roof through the night, unable to sleep. It was cold in the evening, but he covered himself with a scratchy rug and stared up at the night sky that had offered him so much comfort as a child, the coda to his magical days. Now, as then, he let his thoughts unravel as he watched the stars sparkling above.

He tried to imagine Kathmiya in a new household, and the life his child was having. What a contrast to how she had grown up; when they'd met, she had never seen a sink, or worn shoes, or eaten at a table.

But that had seemed so odd then. With her out-standing beauty and natural sophistication, Kathmiya had always appeared destined for a life beyond the marshes.

Thinking back on his trip there, Shafiq remem-bered the faces in the reed hut—the woman who had Kathmiya's same unruly hair, her ugly daughter and the father, bloated from drink. As though back there in the marshes, he returned to the scene and watched their sleeping faces again: the mother, her daughter, the father. This time he did not flinch.

This time, he saw.

Kathmiya was of their world, but also she was not. The same was true of baby Ali. Kismet was suddenly more awesome and mysterious than ever, but the pieces of this story now fit.

Dear Kathmiya,

Thank you for your letter. You are right to trust me; I will never go against your wishes. I am plan-ning to go to America but I want to keep in contact. I understand why your mother will not let you see me but I also know this is not just. If you ask her why she kept that strange dinar for so many years, you will learn why.

Shafiq

After curling up the message and placing it in the special channel where his family had first bored a hole to share their water with Omar's, he departed for Baghdad, still trying to secure his exit permit.

Walking through Baghdad's bustling Jewish neighborhood on the way to his cousin's home, Shafiq registered a tense excitement in the air.

"That's it!" Someone ran out of the small Hebrew school.

"That's it!" Another person emerged from the corner butcher shop.

"It's done!" A passing man in a wrinkled suit shouted.

Shafiq had been so absorbed by his own inner tumult, it took him several moments to understand: the United Nations had approved a plan for the partition of Palestine. Jews around the world were rejoicing, but Shafiq had a bleak sense of foreboding.

The next day, he walked to the government office surrounded by protestors marching down the main street, called *Shaara Al-Rasheed.*

"LONG LIVE PALESTINE!"

"DOWN WITH THE JEWS!"

"NO TO ZIONISM!"

The crowds were orderly. There was no mob menace. There was no immediate threat to Shafiq.

There was only the seismic shift in the dynamics of the Middle East that would forever alter the region, and the world.

Shafiq was dressed in his best clothes, but he did not stand tall. He slouched from one government building to another, trying to secure his exit permit, the chanting of the masses echoing in the air.

"DOWN WITH THE JEWS!"

"LONG LIVE PALESTINE!"

"NO TO ZIONISM!"

He remembered being among the demonstrators when King Ghazi had been killed. *I'm just like you,* he'd felt then and wanted to explain now. *I'm going to America, not illegally emigrating to the new Jewish state in Palestine.* But of course saying this out loud would only make the situation worse.

Shafiq returned to his cousin's house that evening empty-handed. At night he wondered whether it was not all part of a grand plan to keep him in Iraq with Kathmiya and their son. At the same time, he knew that while the outcry against Zionism might prevent him from leaving the country, it would make it even more impossible for them to have a life together if he stayed.

Stuck in Baghdad, trying to extract help from a government that had suddenly turned more hostile than ever, Shafiq had nowhere left to turn.

424 • JESSICA JIJI

"We are alone but for the people we trust most," his father had said.

Two. Seven. One.

"Why didn't you tell us you were coming to Baghdad?" Anwar asked when Shafiq arrived at the brother's apartment after calling in search of his best friend. "We always have room for you."

"Thanks . . . I just . . . Omar!"

Ten minutes later, the two old friends were at the Baghdad Equestrian Club, which was filled with men in fedoras lighting individual cigarettes instead of sucking their tobacco smoke through communal pipes. Omar was trying to fit in with his own second-hand version of the jaunty hat. It covered his head but nothing could cast a shadow on that wide smile. "So which do you like?" he asked.

Shafiq looked at the thoroughbreds being led to the starting line at the far end of the chalked-up open field. "It's fixed, don't you know?"

"Sure!" Omar laughed. "The trick is not to look for the fastest horse, but the best-connected owner."

Then he threw an arm around Shafiq and their bodies were close.

Nothing could overpower their solidarity, which had even freed Salim from jail.

Shafiq hadn't said a word about the exit visa, but thanks to Omar, his head cleared enough to realize what to do.

The old fire was detectable again in Salim's voice. "Partition will be the ruin of us all," he said through the staticky post-office phone. "But what about you? The papers for America?"

Shafiq explained the problem.

"I have a friend," Salim said. "Hussein al-Nakeeb."

The attorney's name was written on a sign adorning the door of his second-floor office on the *Shaara Al-Rasheed*. Inside, a crimson-and-vermillion carpet added grandeur to the already large space, which overlooked the busy street. Shafiq sat down in one of two polished wooden chairs surrounding a matching coffee table.

Hussein was as casual as Salim and obviously so fond of Shafiq's brother-in-law that he immediately conversed openly.

"America, huh? Lots of ideals but a long way to go before they're realized."

"I plan to study very, very hard," Shafiq said, trying to be worthy of support. On the wide avenue below, hundreds of men, young and old, continued their march.

"Will you go to the library a lot then?" Hussein asked.

Shafiq had heard of libraries but there was none in all of Ashar or Basra, much less at any of the schools he'd attended. "Yes, I'll keep my head in my books." After a moment, he added, "So far, Khalil Gibran is my favorite writer."

Hussein nodded, then placed a call to the Ministry of External Affairs. "My nephew needs some help," he told the person on the other end.

Before long, the two were walking down the *Shaara Al-Rasheed*. Around them, the orderly but passionate chants of the demonstrators rang out in opposition to Zionism and the Jews.

Hussein guided him through the crowded, two-story ministry building. It seemed so formal and formidable, but Shafiq left there with an exit permit.

On the street, still surrounded by protestors denouncing the Jews, Shafiq embraced Hussein, thinking, *he really did treat me like his nephew.*

"Study hard in America."

"I will," Shafiq said. "And if you ever want to visit," he promised, "I'll make sure you get your visa."

Shafiq was determined to keep his word, but he doubted he'd ever have the chance. A successful man like Hussein al-Nakeeb was safe and sound in Iraq.

Chapter XLVIII

They met at a new café in Ashar that was just for women, where Kathmiya sat with baby Ali nursing under her shirt.

"What a blessed child," Jamila cooed.

"That's what you always said about me." The U.S. *dinar* burned in Kathmiya's pocket, but she was still not sure whether she would heed Shafiq's request. When she looked at baby Ali, she couldn't help but want them to see each other. But her place in society had been stitched together through a fragile net of lies that threatened to unravel if she were not extremely careful.

"Well, you are blessed," Jamila insisted.

"But I wasn't always."

"No," Jamila disagreed. "You always were."

Kathmiya felt her throat constrict. She could not mention her dead father, but the painful memory of him lodged in her chest. The marshes were lost to her forever, she barely had her mother's company, and she had only narrowly escaped death. "How can you say that?" she said, struggling to keep her voice down. Even at the all-female café, a woman of society had no reason to talk to a *Midaan*.

"You have a much better life than any of us," clucked Jamila.

Kathmiya felt her cheeks grow hotter than the tea she was sipping. "Me? I was sent to work as a maid while Fatimah got married and had children. I was alone in this city for years, waiting and hoping you would find me a husband."

"I tried—"

"Taking care of a baby and thinking I would never have one of my own. Do you know, I used to avoid going out at lunch hour because schoolchildren would be everywhere, and I just knew none of them were coming home to hug me—I was invisible, alone."

"You weren't alone. I did all I could—"

"I must have been cursed then, because everywhere we went they sent us away like we were criminals."

"You sinned," Jamila whispered harshly.

Anger rushed to Kathmiya's temples, but then she felt the baby's wet mouth release her breast as he sank back into sleep. Whatever sin had occurred, she had been blessed with a beautiful son. She had survived so much to have him, and she could endure anything for him to have a better life.

Not for Shafiq, or even for herself, but for her son's future happiness, she spoke up. "My baby's real father wants to see me again."

"Never," Jamila said flatly. She was poorer than Kathmiya, more anonymous and more outcast, but she would always be the mother.

Kathmiya drew the strange *dinar* from her pocket gently, careful not to wake her sleeping infant. Jamila's eyes widened. "Where did that come from?" she asked.

"Please," Kathmiya begged. "Please tell me."

"**He stormed** out after our first and only fight," Jamila began, and Kathmiya imagined she was talking about Ali.

". . . but I still had to buy his cigarettes at the American market, and when he got back I threw the change at him but he said to keep it. They call this a dollar. That's all."

That's all? "Who is 'he'?"

Jamila looked around the café nervously, as though she had something to hide. "Do I have to tell you this now?"

Kathmiya stared hard until her mother started speaking again. "After Fatimah was born, Ali and I burned our outdoor bed for firewood. We were just so sure we'd build another one when it was warm enough to sleep outside again."

This had nothing to do with Americans, dollars or cigarettes, but Kathmiya waited.

"It was the year of the Great Floods. Some said they were so destructive because of the winter rains or the snowmelt from Iran, but really we all knew it was the *jinn* on a mass scale. The waters swept everything away. We couldn't even tell where our home used to be. Ali was a good builder, and people needed that more than ever, but there were no materials. No work meant no food. Everything was gone.

"Of course we couldn't rebuild our bed—we couldn't even feed our baby more than a bit of rice gruel. I had no choice. I had to go to Basra to sell baskets."

Kathmiya had long known about the floods that had sent Jamila to work, but when she studied her mother she saw now a distant look in her eyes, heard the tinge of nostalgia in her voice, noticed a long-stored after-glow lighting her cheeks.

"I had nothing to eat on the trip down the river. By the time I reached the market I was starving. Everyone around me had food and money and things—so many things I'd never seen before. I could smell the white beans with onions simmering in oil. And I missed my baby so much, my little Fatimah, just a year old."

Kathmiya cocked her head back. She knew she should feel sorry for her mother, but something in Jamila's tone did not invite pity, only fascination. Or maybe even excitement.

"A couple came over. I didn't know they were Americans—I had no idea what Americans were! But they were obviously foreign, the woman trying to blend in by wearing a veil, her face so white and thin she looked old, even though she was young."

"They were the missionaries?" Kathmiya guessed with rapt interest. "Who gave me the book?"

"No." Jamila shook her head and took a sip of her lukewarm tea. "I mean yes, they were missionaries, but they never met you."

"So . . . ?" Kathmiya wanted an answer; the slow introduction was killing her.

"I always wanted to tell you. When I said you are blessed I meant it. I just never told you how I knew."

Kathmiya tried waiting for more but her mother looked stuck. "Tell me now," she prompted.

Jamila shook her head, but then slowly picked up her story. "I went to work for the Americans the day I got to Basra."

"And?"

"Kathmiya, you cannot imagine how desperate I was. No one was going to buy my sad little baskets and even if they did I would never earn enough for the family."

"So you got a job," Kathmiya said. "What's wrong with that?"

"The woman didn't want to hire me, so I turned right to him. The American. I looked straight into his blue eyes. I should have been frightened because they were so unlucky—blue! But he looked at me warmly. And I wasn't scared; I was encouraged."

"No *jinn*?" Kathmiya asked.

"I should have feared the *jinn* but I was too busy fighting to survive. I said, 'Take my best basket for your wife.' When he accepted, I knew I was hired."

"What was his name?" Kathmiya wondered.

Jamila shrugged. "I don't even know. I mean, he had a name but I couldn't pronounce it. To me he was always just 'the American.' Living in Iraq to spread the Word, or so he always said."

"You are telling me all about a mysterious man whose name you never even knew," Kathmiya pointed out, struggling to make sense of her mother's garbled confession.

"I didn't know his name, but I knew more about him than anyone else," Jamila said. When Kathmiya stared in puzzlement, her mother said quietly, "I knew how to make him smile. I knew his laugh. I learned things I never should have."

In that instant, showered by a hot mix of anger, embarrassment and shame, Kathmiya suddenly understood.

Anger at Jamila for being so righteous when she had sinned.

Embarrassment at learning that her mother had those feelings.

And shame that she herself understood them so well.

"You?" Kathmiya said incredulously, accusingly.

Jamila spoke so quietly it was almost impossible to hear her over the café conversations except that Kathmiya was tuned in only to her mother's words. "I cannot apologize. You should know why. You know what it is like to be the *Midaan* maid. I wish you had no idea what I mean. Because I never wanted you to experience this, even though it was the best experience of my life and it gave me you."

"What do you mean, 'it gave me you'?" Kathmiya asked slowly. She felt her head fill with space, and

felt the space fill her ears, and wished she wouldn't
hear the answer—but on a deeper level, she already
knew it.

"The American is your father."

"Ali is my father!" Kathmiya nearly screamed. It
was too much to tolerate. That her mother had sinned,
Kathmiya could barely understand. But that her whole
life had been based on a lie—it felt like she would crack
apart trying to assimilate this impossible news. To hear
that Ali was not her father was like learning that the
earth was not under the sky.

Overcome by a tangled confusion, she stood abruptly,
deciding she must clear her head, walk outside, gather
her strength . . .

But her sudden movement startled baby Ali, and he
started to wail. Before Kathmiya could go anywhere,
she had to take care of him. She held him over her
shoulder and started bouncing lightly on her feet. "It's
okay, my son. It's okay, sweet Ali. Shhh . . . that's right,
just sleep . . ." she coaxed.

As she rocked Ali, Kathmiya started to cry. Here,
in her arms, was the greatest blessing she had ever experienced. The blessing of love had given her a beautiful child, and, she believed, allowed them to survive in
a world where her sin should have been punished by
murder.

"I was stupid," Jamila confessed simply. "I thought if I had his baby, he would leave his wife and stay with me. I don't know how I thought we would survive, or what would happen to Fatimah, least of all Ali—I just didn't think."

The baby was wailing with all his might, which was still not much, but enough to keep Kathmiya from thinking only about this father who had left before she ever met him.

"When I realized I was pregnant, it was like dreaming with a fever, with the worst malaria, just dreaming and nearly dying but losing touch with everything that is real in life," Jamila said.

"But even in my delusion I knew I could be killed. I was terrified that the baby would have blue eyes. Unlucky blue, but also blue that would reveal the sin. I would be dead and so would my child. So would you."

Kathmiya knew that terror. Worse than the most searing labor pain.

"When I had to leave their home and go back to the marshes for the birth, the wife presented me with that strange glass bottle, said it was to feed you. I felt the *jinn* as soon as I touched it, like a cold sweat drenching my skin. I hated it. What could I do though? I put it in my pocket and right away I felt the bad spirits clinging tighter. That's when I started to really feel scared."

The sound of the glass bottle crashing on the rocks rang in Kathmiya's ears. But it was not loud enough to block out the rest of the story.

"When I got home it was like the fever broke. It was Ali, and it was Fatimah, and it was our world. I felt terrified of the curse. The pains were so hard and fast. I couldn't face Ali, but there was Haider, your uncle. I told him they would know by the eyes. I was scared of the blue eyes."

"You told Uncle Haider?" Kathmiya was stunned. How could he have cared for her all these years knowing the truth?

"His duty was to protect our honor by ending my life. And I was ready to die. But he didn't kill me. He just said, 'Shh, Jamila, please breathe. Just breathe.' That's all I did. I kept breathing. And when you were born with the blackest, most beautiful eyes in all of Iraq, I knew you were blessed."

"But what about Ali?" The man was dead. And Kathmiya had never thanked him for tolerating her, the living proof of her mother's sin.

"Ali was not there," Jamila said curtly. "He was already filled with hate, for me and for himself."

Kathmiya felt like she was lost in the desert under a blinding sun. There was too much shimmering light to see through, too much illumination of the past to be able to distinguish right from wrong. "Ali," she said slowly, "deserved to hate you."

Jamila looked sad. "Did I kill him?" she wondered.

"No!" Kathmiya replied, deeply startled. If Jamila had killed Ali by having a baby outside of marriage, then Kathmiya would be widowed before long.

Jamila responded to this unspoken worry. "I thought about it. But you are different. You left him. I went back."

"You what? Where is he?" Was there was a possibility that Kathmiya might find her father? Ali was suddenly completely obscured by the American with blue eyes.

"Don't hope like that," Jamila said quickly. "It leads nowhere."

Suddenly, instead of her mother's voice, Kathmiya could hear only the sounds of the café: the cackling women trading stories and secrets, the clink of cups and silverware, the scuffle of feet on the wooden floor. All that ordinary life, none of it hers. She strained to listen.

"When I brought you back to Basra, he was gone. I stood there with you in my arms and I knew I had been completely crazy to think he ever loved me. I started crying. That's when the new missionaries took us in."

More missionaries . . . but these Kathmiya knew.
"They gave me the book," she said.

"More than that, they gave you love. But I had to
take you far away from them. My greatest fear was that
you would grow up around foreigners and suffer my
fate."

Mother and daugther, in that noisy café surrounded
by chattering women, stared at each other. Kismet was
too strict and too forbidding to escape.

Kathmiya thought about Ali, his face always crimson with anger and drink, and wished she could miss
him. But instead she was longing to meet someone she
had never laid eyes on, and never would. A sob escaped
her throat.

She couldn't tell how long she cried, but slowly, her
tear-soaked melancholy was replaced by a soothing
relief. Because a lifetime of wondering why she was different, judged and shunned was over, and her greatest
fear about the future was gone. *It will not repeat,* she
realized. *I am not like my father, incapable of loving a
child, because my father is not Ali.*

The baby had fallen asleep. Kathmiya felt an unfamiliar sense of self-confidence.

"What kind of person leaves their child behind?"
Jamila asked for the first time aloud if the millionth
in her head.

My father does, Kathmiya thought bitterly. But then she remembered that Shafiq wanted to see Ali. The past had repeated, but not exactly. "I want to see him—at least once."

"I told you, the American is gone," Jamila said.

"Shafiq," Kathmiya corrected. "He is still Iraqi, still here."

And there was still time.

Chapter XLIX

"Please," Shafiq said, kissing Jamila's hand and then lowering himself to kiss her feet. "Please. I know it was wrong. But it was not—" here Shafiq began to cry, dry but still real sobs, "it was not out of disrespect. It was only because, she, well . . ." He didn't dare say he loved her, but he had to say something. "Kathmiya is a blessing, a blessing in my life."

Jamila listened.

"I want to see her and meet my son."

"Aren't you going to America?"

"Not if she'll let me be in their life. If you'll let me. Or if you want," he began promising wildly, "I'll disappear forever if I can just meet them once."

As soon as he said it, he knew this was too much. It would probably ruin his chances, but he had to backtrack. He stood up.

"No." He looked into Kathmiya's mother's probing eyes. "I may travel to America but I could never forget her or our son. I won't disrupt her life but I will always be there, I will try to help her in any way I can. Say I was her teacher, say I was her employer, say whatever you want but let me stay connected to Kathmiya and our son. Please."

Shafiq was putting everything on the line, from his true feelings to his future to the expectations of his deeply traditional family, but he had to insist on this point. "I was thinking of going to America, but I will always be Iraqi. Always."

"You are a man," Jamila said slowly, as though deciding as she formed the words, "of honor."

Honor. What they had all lived through in its name, what they had all nearly lost. Kathmiya's mother was praising him, but Shafiq couldn't relax yet. "Please," he asked, falling down in front of her again.

"You can see her—but just to say good-bye," Jamila ruled. "Kathmiya is finally safe and I cannot let her run off with you into danger. But I remember. I understand."

"So I can see them?" Shafiq looked up.

"Once."

"I— What do you mean?"

"Once before you go to America," Jamila instructed. "After that, you can write letters, maybe we will have visits, and no matter what, we will keep contact."

The meeting was set. Kathmiya and America.

Shafiq packed quickly: cotton shirts and one good suit and underclothes and pants and pajamas and his fringed prayer shawl, along with a folder full of his college documents, all in the heavy leather suitcase that his father had bought from an Indian import dealer.

Then he carefully wrapped a dozen black-and-white photographs, some posed at the photographer's studio with a Persian rug hanging in the background, others more spontaneous: Ezra and Naji on the roof; Reema sticking dough to the blistering sides of the rooftop oven; he and Omar on their street; Aziza being held by Kathmiya, the sparkle in her eyes now shining in Shafiq's own.

Jamila stood guard at a distance while Shafiq walked with Kathmiya and Ali in a neighborhood alley.

"I love you. I have always loved you," he said, straining against the impulse to embrace her. "And I love him now too. He's beautiful." Shafiq was filled with a sweet happiness he could not imagine walking away from.

Kathmiya beamed, ever more stunning in the glow of new motherhood. "Just like you, just like I wrote," she said, her own large eyes moist with tears.

"Ali, my son." He stared at the boy. What did it mean that the child would never learn to do *Kaddish*? Surely blood ties were transcendent even without religion. "I did *sadaka* for you," Shafiq said. Kathmiya smiled.

Ten paces away, Jamila shuffled her feet. It was understood their few moments together would soon be over.

"Kathmiya, I wish I could stay to be with you and to see Ali grow up, to maybe—one day—"

But she cut him off. She had made her peace with Jamila's decision. The promise of knowing she might see Shafiq again salved the wound of their separation. *It may only be temporary*, she reassured herself. Jamila had already said Shafiq was a man of honor, not like Kathmiya's father.

There was a chance that her husband would outlive her, a chance that she would never leave Iraq, and even a chance that Shafiq might never come back, but Kathmiya was certain he would remain true.

"Shafiq, you are always in my heart."

"Yes, and now I'm here with you," he said, stroking his son's small cheek while trying to memorize every aspect of the tiny, miraculous being. "I am not here to say good-bye to you. I am not leaving Iraq forever. I am going to America, yes, because I want to be a better man. But—" he was aware of Jamila hovering nearer.

Shafiq knew what he was about to say might sound hopelessly idealistic, but he trusted Kathmiya to understand. "There will be a different future for you, for me, for our son. The war is over now. The world is changing. Someday all of us can live in peace, and I can come back to Iraq, to rejoin my family and return to you. We can be together again."

Jamila started walking over. Kathmiya reached into her dress pocket and handed Shafiq the pink sapphire ring. Brimming with feeling, he slipped it on her right ring finger, then leaned down and brushed his lips against the sleeping boy.

"You are always in my heart," he said, as Jamila positioned herself between them.

"Always."

Shafiq's entire family and Salwa were on hand to wave him off at the Margeel station.

Reema wept. "You are so strong," she said. "Leaving my house. Leaving my country." Tears flowed like Iraq's twin rivers down her still-youthful face.

"My son," Salwa said, holding Shafiq tight.

Everyone swarmed the America-bound teen for hugs. Marcelle even offered a warm farewell. Ezra was grinning. But none of their good wishes or affection or love could outweigh the terrible absence of Naji. *My favorite brother. How will he find me?* His name had not been mentioned for a long time, but Shafiq had to break the silence. "Naji," he said to the group. "When he comes back, I'll be here. Or I'll take him to America. Or something. But please, please, let me know when you hear from Naji." He looked quickly away so they wouldn't see the emotion on his face.

The ache of parting pressed down on his chest. Shafiq thought of Kathmiya again and closed his eyes briefly in order to remember hers.

Kathmiya had been conceived in love. This was an understanding Shafiq and Jamila shared. And Ali, too, was similarly blessed.

He hugged Reema, who kissed him through tears. Then Roobain leaned over and whispered, "I want to see you again, but don't come back."

Shafiq kissed his father's hand, the ultimate gesture of respect, love and appreciation. But he knew in his heart that no matter how bad the situation got, he would someday return to see Kathmiya and Ali again.

At the travel agent's office in Baghdad the following day, Shafiq obtained a KLM ticket: Baghdad-Rome-Amsterdam-Glasgow-Newfoundland-New York.

With a few hours left in Iraq, Shafiq went to see his Uncle Dahood. By then in his seventies, the old bachelor owned the house where he lived and rented rooms to different tenants, including women who did the cooking and cleaning that a wife would. The modest, low structure stood in a dusty neighborhood and featured a large interior courtyard alive with a small tree, one old donkey, and two dirty goats.

Uncle Dahood, wearing an old-fashioned robe-like *zboon*, was sitting on the floor of his unfurnished room, scraping the cement off of a pile of bricks so he could use them again.

He remained seated on the bare floor as Shafiq approached, thinking about how his uncle had taught him to raise pigeons. Back in those days, Shafiq's summers were spent largely in the house or at the neighbors', and the sight of the birds being released into the open skies overhead had satisfied some of his longing to be free.

"Uncle Dahood, I came to say good-bye," Shafiq said, feeling still like a boy. Although headed to what he thought of as the most modern place on earth, he remained in awe of his uncle's quiet, determined strength. "I'm going to study in America."

"Is it far?" Uncle Dahood asked, separating the crumbling cement from the sun-weathered yellow bricks.

"Very far."

"Will I see you again?"

"*In-shall-lah*," Shafiq replied using the Jewish pronunciation to say God willing.

Shafiq was leaving his uncle behind, but he would never forget all that he had gained since receiving a special gift of two perforated boxes containing his first birds. Surprised by a sudden rush of emotion, he kissed his uncle's rough hand with silent but strong appreciation for the life lessons it had so naturally imparted.

"*Allah wi-yaak*," Uncle Dahood replied. May Allah be with you.

The crowd that accompanied Shafiq to the Baghdad airport was more like an entourage surrounding a star. The fact that someone they knew was going to America was enough of a rarity for cousins and in-laws and associates alike to interrupt whatever it was they were doing that weekday and make their way to the airport.

The group gathered on a veranda overlooking the runways, where a few planes were parked.

They were treating him like a diplomat, like he represented all of their aspirations and potentials. But Shafiq did not want to bathe in any adulation. He wanted to play stickball with Omar. But there was no time for that. Only for a tight hug.

"My brother," Omar said, "this is from my family to you."

"My brother." Shafiq accepted the package. "Do I open it now?"

"On the plane," Omar said. "Think of me."

"Omar, I will always think of you." Shafiq held the gift gently to his chest and bowed toward it reverently. Even America could not compete for this affection.

Inside the plane, Shafiq felt a terrific buzzing in his heart. As other passengers settled into their seats, he wanted to jump out of his own. Where was he going? What would it be like? As mystified as he was at that moment, setting out on the forty-five-hour journey to America, he knew he would soon be enlightened to life there. He would gain the power to decode the unfathomable.

With a few minutes to go before takeoff, Shafiq carefully opened the small package Omar had given him.

A book. The book. *The Prophet.*

Hajji Abdullah's prized possession, and Omar's only family heirloom except for its companion volume, *A*

Tear and a Smile. Shafiq experienced both when he realized Omar had broken up the pair of books in order to ensure that each boy got half of the whole, just as they always felt they were.

Inside, a photo marked a page. Shafiq had seen the image in Omar's house and cherished it. He and Omar, just about ten years old, were pretending to fence with sticks. Looking at the scene, he could almost feel the bark rubbing on his palms, taste the salty summer day, hear the laughter ring.

After absorbing the image on the photo, Shafiq carefully returned it to the place it had been holding in the book of poetry.

> *And a youth said, "Speak to us of Friendship."*
> *Your friend is your needs answered.*
> *He is your field which you sow with love and*
> *reap with thanksgiving.*
> *And he is your board and your fireside.*
> *For you come to him with your hunger,*
> *and you seek him for peace.*
> *When your friend speaks his mind you fear*
> *not the "nay" in your own mind, nor do you*
> *withhold the "ay."*
> *And when he is silent your heart ceases*
> *not to listen to his heart;*

For without words, in friendship, all thoughts,
all desires, all expectations are born and shared,
with joy that is unacclaimed.

Shafiq felt a pang spreading from the center of his head toward its crown as he realized he was really leaving Iraq, his family, Omar, Kathmiya and Ali. The ache gripped him until he read the next verse:

When you part from your friend, you grieve not;
For that which you love most in him may be
clearer in his absence, as the mountain to the
climber is clearer from the plain.

Suddenly he felt released. Out the window, the runway appeared to be moving away from him.

As the plane took off, Shafiq thought of how he and Kathmiya used to watch his birds flying through the sky. She is with me now, he thought, preparing to soar.

Acknowledgments

This book would not have been possible without the love, help, support and constant encouragement of my father, Latif, the world's best.

My mother, Vera, also number one on the planet, inspired me with her awesome example.

My brother, Brian, donated his best skills with characteristic generosity and enthusiasm, and my sister Elissa cheerfully helped me more times than most people would have patience for.

I am deeply grateful to my agent, Jennifer Lyons, for believing in me from the day we met; my editor, Lyssa Keusch, who always challenged me to do better and then showed me how; and her assistant, Wendy Lee, who provided indispensable help along the way.

I thank Paul Grossman for teaching me so much about writing, and for all the fun we had in the process.

My dear friend Beth rescued me from giving up before I began, and my dearest Lydia guided me through to the end.

Finally, to my husband, Jeff, who I love more than I could ever say, thank you for this great life we share.

THE NEW LUXURY IN READING

We hope you enjoyed reading
our new, comfortable print size and found it
an experience you would like to repeat.

Well – you're in luck!

HarperLuxe offers the finest in fiction and
nonfiction books in this same larger print size and
paperback format. Light and easy to read, HarperLuxe
paperbacks are for book lovers who want to see
what they are reading without the strain.

For a full listing of titles and
new releases to come, please visit our website:
www.HarperLuxe.com

SEEING IS BELIEVING!